NOR'WESTER

NOR'WESTER

CJ BLACK

DEAD SOUTH BOOK CO.

admin@deadsouthbookco.co.nz

Hardback ISBN 978 1 7386082 0 1
Trade Paperback ISBN 978 1 7386082 1 8
eBook ISBN 978 1 7386082 2 5
Dead South Book Co.
Invercargill, Southland
New Zealand
admin@deadsouthbookco.co.nz

First Printing, 2023

Thank you for nurturing and supporting my love of reading.
Your gift has enriched my life beyond expectation.
I love you, Mom xoxo.

To my boys. Love you to bits.

PROLOGUE

She had trouble seeing. Gale force wind whipped her long, dark hair into a frenzy. It covered her face like octopus tentacles, squeezing the life out of her. The grumble of nature's orchestra in the dead of the night made her body tremble, the sound of a hundred invisible freight trains barreling toward her. Canterbury's Nor'wester wind was on full display.

A hot, dry, gale-force wind barreled through the Okuku riverbed at 140 kilometers an hour. The surrounding trees bent their branches violently toward the water, the spray plastering her thin nightgown to her body. She realized she wasn't alone.

A rush of dry vegetation and sand burned her eyes as a massive gust nearly knocked her off her feet. She used the ax she brought for protection as support. The moonlight highlighted her wild eyes as she looked around to see how close they were. She could hear them. They were calling her, taunting her.

They'd come to fetch her son in the middle of the night to take him away. They surrounded him, these figures hiding their faces, levitating his sleeping body to bring him to the river to claim him as their own. Panicked, she ran to wake her husband, but the bed was empty. He was gone. Her screams went unheard as they transported her unresponsive son to the bank of the Okuku River. She followed, armed with an ax. She wouldn't let them have her son.

Her son struggled to make friends when they moved to the area. They lived so far away from town on Harper's Road that he couldn't hang out with his schoolmates. He spent most of his time in the plantation, watching TV alone in his room at night.

She was initially happy when a young man came around. He was older than her son. She thought he was a neighboring kid he'd met at school. It didn't take long for her to change her mind.

He hung out her son's window, dressed in a hoodie and jeans, his hood hiding his face. She saw him often while he sat watching TV in his room and asked him why he wouldn't bring him in, why he stood there looking at him, hiding his face. Her son looked at her like she was mad, claiming no one was outside in that typical 'leave me alone, you don't know anything' teenager tone.

She should have done something then; she should have stopped him. She didn't think he was a threat until he brought the others. It was too late now.

Her tongue licked her beloved son's blood on her lips. She'd claimed his body, throwing herself on him while they tried to feed from his soul. The wind blew them away, but only for a moment.

She paused as a horrid revolt grew deep inside her belly. They surrounded her now, their faceless bodies circling her, spinning faster and faster. Her eyes looked down at the braided river's black water. Half-submerged, a body lay at her feet, her son's body.

A groan escaped his face, barely discernible within the chaos of the Nor'wester wind pounding the Canterbury landscape. She could feel the entities becoming part of the surrounding wind, suffocating her. Her boot-clad foot lifted momentarily and pressed down firmly where her son lay, driving his head into the dark water of the Okuku riverbed. She felt a faint gurgle, followed by stillness as the wind spirits danced around her.

Her burden lifted; she raised her eyes toward the heavens. She'd won; they couldn't claim him. Moving at record speeds, the clouds created an eerie calico pattern as they played games with the moon. She felt a hand grab her shoulder.

A wave of terror tore through her. She turned to see her son dripping wet, his eyes black holes in his pale, waxen face.

She stepped back in horror, tripping then falling, her flimsy cotton nightgown clinging to her wet body. She looked up, his shadow darkening the moon's light. He stood on top of her now, faces with black eyes floating in the wind behind him.

His lips became a grin as he lifted the ax high above her head and paused. A barely audible cackle spewed from her, tears flowing from her eyes. She raised her hand toward her son, silently begging for mercy.

Moonlight caught the blade and glinted as it made its descent. She gazed at her son adoringly as he forced the ax edge into her forehead.

PART 1

| 1 |

The Move

September 2009

Excitement washed over her as she studied her son's face. Jimmy looked out the window, viewing the country they were about to settle in for the first time. He squirmed in his seat.

She grabbed his hand and squeezed it. "We're almost there."

The mountain ranges revealed themselves through the clouds, their snow-capped peaks so different from the rust-red dirt she'd grown accustomed to. Kate Neilson begged for a change of scenery after spending the last few years in Australia.

The Australian travel brochures she perused for years had promised heaven on earth. The country hadn't delivered those dreams. She found herself lost in the foreign world of Western Australia, missing the rugged nature of her Canadian homeland.

"Mom, we're here. Look, Mom, mountains!"

He bounced in his seat, unable to contain himself. Jimmy's smile filled her heart with joy.

Her son's enthusiasm momentarily buried the memories of what her life had been like in Australia. She'd tried her best but never fit in. She struggled to make friends, left alone by her husband continually.

She wrung her hands unconsciously, thinking of the loneliness, despair heavy enough to drown her. The crackling on the loudspeaker refocused her thoughts.

"This is your pilot speaking. We've started our descent to Christchurch airport. The weather is clear, with a temperature of eighteen degrees. It's another beautiful spring day in Canterbury."

She smiled. The weather here sounded better than the scorching heat they had endured in Australia.

Jimmy kept moving in his seat. The energy her twelve-year-old generated was palpable. Through the plane window, they could see a sea of green pastures, braided rivers, and the city of Christchurch.

***

"Welcome to New Zealand." A smiling customs agent delivered the reality they had a new home by stamping both their passports.

The automatic doors opened to the lobby. Kate scanned the room apprehensively for her husband, hoping he would be there.

They waited eight hours in the Perth airport for him to arrive after three days of traveling from Canada to Australia. She remembered how panic and doubt had made those hours feel like days.

Nick worked as a fly-in, fly-out mine worker in the underbelly of the outback and needed to wait for the first available flight out of his mine site to meet them. He hadn't meant to leave her hanging, but it started things off on a sour note.

Her heart jumped with relief seeing him in the lounge.

This place would be different. A new start. A fabulous new world. Kate was confident this would be a different experience than what she'd dealt with in Australia.

Her son left her side to embrace Nick. He was not Jimmy's biological father, but they'd forged a strong friendship.

"Welcome home, Kate," Nick said as they embraced.

She hoped he meant his home as well. He was a restless soul, needing a high level of excitement in his life, often shifting from one job to another, from one country to another. This time, things would be different. They leased a lifestyle block out of Rangiora in Okuku, and

Nick cemented a hazard training job with a local company in Christchurch. The job was well suited for him; frequent travel throughout New Zealand to train workers on-site shouldn't bore him. She hoped it was enough to satisfy his wandering spirit.

The sun's brightness made her squint before she stepped out of the airport doors. She closed her eyes and lifted her head to take a deep breath of sweet-smelling air. They followed Nick into the depths of the parking garage. Kate was impressed at the vehicle his work gave him. She helped pile their luggage in the back of the Holden Colorado.

"You guys hungry?" Nick asked.

They already knew Jimmy's answer.

"Yeah, is there a McDonald's here in New Zealand?" he asked, his face plastered to the backseat window.

"Of course there is," Nick said, amused.

Traffic was lighter than she expected. She was used to the bustling city center of Perth. Christchurch was a bit more laid back and much less crowded. The sun shone through the passenger window, casting rays of warmth as they proceeded through the drive-through. The familiar smell of McDonald's burgers and fries filled the work truck as they set out for Harper's Road.

They drove through the quaint town of Rangiora. Several heritage buildings graced the main street, contrasting the newer, modern structures. Nick explained there were no stores close to where they lived; the family would have to do their groceries and other essentials in Rangiora. Kate's mind wandered. How far would they be from town? She wished she could have inspected the rental they found online before they committed to the lease. A nervous pang hit her stomach. She snapped out of it as she looked at the snow-capped mountains filling the view from afar.

The road led to a sharp left turn, the landscape changing from residential to farmland. The land, spotted by lifestyle blocks and farms, seemed so foreign to her. They slowed down at a tiny community called Loburn. A small cluster of houses around the primary school looked like something out of a picture book.

"This is where you'll go to school, bud," Nick said to Jimmy.

Jimmy looked intrigued; he hadn't attended a small country school yet.

"Looks alright," he responded, content with the school's charming persona.

They sped up and left the village behind them.

They slowed their pace when they came across a braided river.

"There are exceptional fishing spots out here, guys," Nick said, eying out the banks.

Fishing was a favorite pastime of Kate's growing up in Canada. She looked forward to spending time on the shores of the surrounding rivers. They drove past creeks and farmland to a substantial pine plantation. It smelled so familiar. She hadn't experienced the smell of pine trees since they left Canada two years ago.

"We're here," Nick said, turning left to a single-lane dirt road.

Kate looked out at the mass expanse of mature pine plantation that was now her backyard. Could it be true? It looked like she was back in Canada. Joy overwhelmed her as they pulled into the drive. Her new home was a stately four-bedroom, slate gray weatherboard home surrounded by a vast yard with a pond and dug-in fire pit area.

She exited the vehicle and breathed a breath of fresh, sweet-smelling air. The lush pine plantation covered such a large area of their property that it shielded them from all signs of neighboring life. She felt like they were the only ones on the planet.

Jimmy dashed out of the truck, running toward their beloved dog, Chinook. Their 6-month-old brown-eyed husky flew in via pet carrier a few days before. Chinook leaped happily, climbing Jimmy to lick his face, his baseball cap blowing off, exposing his sandy-colored hair.

"Can I go play, Mom?" he asked. Not waiting for an answer, he ran behind the house, followed by Chinook. They wouldn't get bored soon with a large backyard and plantation to explore.

"This is pretty exceptional," Kate whispered while leaning on her husband. The gentle breeze comforted the warm day, and the trees sang their version of a melody.

"It certainly is!" Nick said as he looked over the beautiful house they now called home. "Let me give you a tour."

Nick flew in a week ago to start his new job and get everything sorted. He spent a few nights in the house and was familiar with the surroundings. As they walked along their long driveway, lined by native plantings and flowers, the property's vastness became clear. The entire parcel's footprint was nearly eight hectares. The house stood in the middle, surrounded by a three hundred sixty-degree pillow of scented pine plantation impenetrable by the eye.

"Is the container arriving on time?" Nick asked. Their furniture had been shipped via container ship six weeks ago and was due to arrive shortly.

"Three o'clock tomorrow," Kate said, grinning, seeing the relief in her husband's eyes. They'd done without furniture and belongings for long enough.

Nick opened the door to the attached garage to unpack the truck. A loud hum erupted around them, so loud it thickened the air, making breathing difficult.

Kate ran out of the garage, calling out to Jimmy. The loud, gut-penetrating hum from the forest competed with all other sounds. Nick headed for the area that Jimmy and Chinook ran off to.

"Quick, Kate, Chinook might get spooked and run away," Nick said, coming out of the covered fire pit.

"Nick, the noise sounds like it's coming from the ground in the forest."

She could feel the pulsating hum vibrate inside her, driven to higher levels with the mounting panic she sensed. The noise made her clench her teeth savagely. Nick turned to face her. His eyes widened. Something was behind her. She turned to face what disturbed her husband, tasting bile in her mouth.

Jimmy and Chinook were walking in the forest behind them, oblivious to their presence or the loud hum. Kate rushed to her son's side.

"Jimmy, are you okay?" she screamed as she grasped her son's shoulders to get his attention. Jimmy slowly moved his gaze from the ground to stare blankly at his mother.

"We found this."

She looked down to see a row of teeth, putrid flesh hanging from a decomposing jaw. Her horror propelled her backward. She stumbled, felt a sharp pain in her head, and fell into darkness.

| 2 |

Mike

"What the hell, Mike! I said you can stay here if I never have to see you," Mona said, her words like daggers, droplets of spit propelling out of her mouth.

Mike looked at his torn work boots. He was overdue for a new pair, but it wasn't in his budget. The large-framed farmer turned to face her with slumped shoulders.

"Mona, you wouldn't have seen me if you hadn't driven to my shed. I haven't come close to our house or the yard. I've been working out in the far paddocks drafting the ewes," Mike said, his voice calm, the pain in his eyes showing the extent of his emotions.

"It's not *our* house, Mike. It's mine, and Kevin's now. We agreed you could keep farming and live in the shed, but we don't want to see you around. Ever!" Mona's hands balled into fists.

"I only agreed you could stay in the house because I wanted the kids to keep their home. It's not fair to Jake and Kelly you've moved Kevin in. My name is on the title, Mona, and I am being more than generous. I shouldn't be giving you thirty-five percent of the stock profits on top of maintenance. This is my family's farm, not yours. You never lifted a finger to help, even to care for the kids when I worked." Mike said, struggling to keep his cool, his voice rising.

"You'll have to maximize your space because I'm here to tell you Kevin needs a place for his pigs. He wants the paddock to the left of the shed, so stay clear of it," she said, spitting at him, her diminutive body shaking.

She'd gotten thin since their separation, and Mike couldn't help but notice how unhealthy she looked. A vein throbbed at Mike's temple, and a slight change in his jaw indicated he was clenching his teeth.

"I need that paddock for the lambs, Mona. What the hell is he going to do with pigs? Kevin isn't a farmer. He owns a used car dealership, for God's sake. He doesn't know how to take care of stock."

Anger raged in his gut as he saw her smile.

She didn't care. Mona's defiant smile scared Mike more than anything he had encountered in his forty-two years. Married since they were twenty-two, he'd seen the vile, evil darkness living in his wife. It made his blood run cold, thinking of what she was capable of.

"He gets the paddock he wants, or... I'll burn your shed down," Mona said, her hands on her hips.

Mona's fiery stare foreshadowed what would happen if he crossed her. His shoulders slumped from the weight of the situation, Mike retreated and looked down.

She pivoted on her heels, headed back to her late-model Landcruiser, and sped down the drive.

Mike secured the farm gate and headed for his woodpile. He walked up to the farm shed, an armful of firewood in his grasp. The pieces of wood toppled out of the overfilled basket by the wood stove. It hadn't been cold enough to start a fire in at least a month, but he couldn't resist the habit.

The rudimentary shelter he built by segregating a third of the shed for his living area was nothing flashy. His bed lay in one corner, the wood stove in the other, a TV in another, and a small kitchen graced the other corner. A small table and a used sofa adorned the middle of the room. He grabbed a cold beer from the fridge.

Outside on the porch, sitting on an old bench covered in faded green cushions, he closed his eyes. The warming rays comforted him as the sun slowly set.

A low grumble of an approaching vehicle piqued his interest. His property stood at a crossroads. Large pine trees shielded oncoming traffic, and most of the time, the dust generated from the gravel road served as the only indicator of the vehicle's location. It was always a guess what road the car would eventually appear on. He spotted the plume and had a fair idea he knew the identity of the oncoming vehicle.

A well-worn, red Toyota flatbed truck appeared, being driven by his good mate, Matt Stewart. Mike stood up to greet him by waving his beer.

The car stopped in front of the shed. A tall, slim man exited the vehicle.

Matt stood next to his mate in height but not in build, Mike sporting a more muscular appearance than his friend. He grabbed the beer held out to him and nodded. Both took seats on the small porch.

"Good day, mate. What's new?" Matt asked, looking over the sun-drenched pastures. The ewes hobbled with bellies full of offspring. Mike's stock was in perfect condition, and it impressed Matt. His husbandry skills always stood well above the other farmers in the area.

"Mona came over. Kevin is taking one of my sheep grazing paddocks for his pigs." Mike pointed to the sizeable verdant patch behind them.

Matt looked at the spot he was pointing at, then shifted his gaze to his friend.

"Listen, mate, I know she's nuts, but you can't let her get away with this. He doesn't know what he's doing. You'll lose your prime paddock and have to feed those pigs yourself. The guy she's with is a lazy loser. It's a ridiculous idea. He doesn't understand the work involved," Matt said, trying to get his point across.

Mike stared at his friend, slumped his shoulders, and sighed.

"I don't know why you don't divorce her and take your farm back. She's playing you like a fool, and you let her step all over you. I don't get it, Mike. You used to have the strongest backbone of us all. It's like she's poisoned you."

Matt's words stung. Mike took a swig of beer and gazed over his paddocks.

"She's threatened to take the kids to Perth, Australia," he said, pausing to take another swig. "If I wasn't sure that she would do it and I would never see my kids again, I would divorce that monster in a second. Those kids mean the world to me. It's bad enough that she's put them into a boarding school to control my access. I can't take the chance, Matt. I've got to wait until they are of legal age and can make their own decisions before I get rid of Mona." Mike's eyes glimmered with emotion.

Matt nodded, turning his gaze to the dirt at their feet.

"New people moved into Paterson's old place. I saw them come in late this afternoon," Mike said, looking toward the block of pines on the opposite side of the road running by his property.

"Oh...No. Those poor people don't know what they've walked into," Matt said. Both men fell silent, staring toward Paterson's pine plantation.

| 3 |

The House

Kate awoke to the bright sun burning through her eyelids. She propped herself up with difficulty, her bones aching from her odd position. Where was she? Reality rushed back to her. She was sitting on the deck at their new house. The fog in her head lifting, she remembered the hum, her son, the teeth. Her head throbbed. A vicious pang of nausea hit her. Where were Nick and Jimmy?

Her husband emerged from the forest brandishing a shovel, her son and dog following close behind. She wondered why her husband hadn't stayed with her after she passed out. He must not have been worried. Her vision blurred as her world spun in front of her.

"Babe, you're finally awake. Are you okay? You took a nasty fall and knocked your head."

"What happened? What was that thing?" Her mouth was so dry that the words struggled to escape.

Her husband grinned. "I think the old occupants were hunters. I found a pile of fresh bones in the back block. Chinook must have discovered them and dug them up in the past few days."

A sense of relief and embarrassment flooded her. How could she overreact like that? She made a fool of herself and frightened her son. She looked at him, his face brimming with excitement, oblivious to her mortifying performance.

"Mom, this place is so cool! Chinook and I love the forest. It even has a graveyard," Jimmy said, sitting with her.

"It's not a graveyard, boy," Nick said, his hand out to stop him. "I can bet that the only thing buried in the forest are the bones of the animals they hunted or killed off the farm. Please stay away until I can properly bury them."

Jimmy nodded.

"What about that loud hum?" Kate asked, looking at her husband. Nick shook his head.

"I'm not sure, babe. It vanished when we carried you out of the forest. There must be something underground, pipes or irrigation pumps. I'll ask at work if anyone knows where it comes from." It was apparent he wasn't bothered.

"What noise, Mom? I haven't heard any strange noises." Jimmy looked perplexed. His eyes told the truth; he'd heard nothing unusual. Kate couldn't help but think of the blank gaze on his face when they found him with that jaw. A chill ran through her body.

"Now, Mrs. Neilson, shall I help you up so you can see the inside of our new home?" Nick asked as he took Kate's hand to help her to her feet. He opened the French doors of the dining area. She peered inside to see an airy, open-planned kitchen, dining room, and living room.

"There's enough room for all our furniture here, guys," Nick said as she entered.

Nearly every wall had old-fashioned, cased windows with another set of French doors leading out of the living room onto an additional deck. A massive wood-burning stove stood in the back corner of the lounge, the home's only heat source. Kate wondered if it would heat the big house, not knowing how cold their winters would be. A formal entry and a hallway were past the living room. She decided the first room down the hallway would make a perfect office.

A generous main bedroom, with an ensuite and a large walk-in closet, appeared at the end of the hallway to the right. The door to the family bathroom was next to it.

Kate loved the large, inviting bathtub nestled under a picture window. The lack of privacy would usually put her off, but no one could see because of the thick, coniferous jacket surrounding them. The door to the attached garage was on the left. An additional corridor led to another large bedroom to the right and one at the end of the wing.

"I want this one," Jimmy pleaded when they came to the furthest room in the house at the end of the corridor. Irrational fear filled Kate.

"It's far from everything else in this enormous house, Jimmy. What if you call and I can't hear you?" she asked as she ruffled his hair.

"Oh, come on, Mom!" Jimmy moaned, rolling his eyes.

"It might be better for him. He won't hear the TV late at night or our guests when we entertain." Nick said, taking Jimmy's side.

Jimmy claimed his room with no further argument from Kate.

Kate looked out of his room window, overlooking the driveway. She wondered if he might try to escape during the night when her eye caught movement to her right. She moved to the window on the right wall and searched the tree line.

"What are you looking at, babe?" Nick asked, curious.

"Nothing, sweetheart. I thought I saw something move in the forest. It was probably nothing." The words escaped her lips a millisecond before she saw the figure of a man dressed in a gray hoodie and dark jeans.

"Nick. Look. Can you see him? I can see a man in the woods," Kate said, whispering to her husband, afraid to scare Jimmy.

Nick surveyed the area that Kate pointed to. He shook his head.

"Kate, changing timezones and hitting your head has worn you out. I can't see anything. It must have been an optical illusion caused by shadows in the forest."

He stepped behind her and laid his chin on her shoulder. She accepted his explanation and shook off the urge to keep looking for the man in the shadows.

She knew someone had been there.

***

The sun slowly descended, engulfed by the tall pine trees surrounding the house. The air chilled as darkness crept in.

"I've got a few blankets we can scatter around the living room floor tonight," her husband said, carrying a pile of coverlets in his arms. "I picked up frozen pizzas and juice for Jimmy before picking you up from the airport. We don't have a TV, but we have a radio to keep us occupied. I picked up some beers as well," Nick said as he cracked open a bottle.

Kate looked for cutlery and dishes but found none. They rigged the frozen pizza boxes into crude plates and used Nick's pocketknife to cut the freshly baked pizzas. Thankful that her new oven was quick to warm and easy to use, Kate looked forward to cooking many meals in her new kitchen.

They sat together before the fire, its glow reflecting off their skin while they listened to The Rock radio.

"This is comfy. I'm so glad we decided on this place and not a unit in Christchurch. It's much better for Jimmy and Chinook." Kate said, her emotions bubbling close to the surface. She stopped talking before tears ran from her eyes.

The exhaustion from the long voyage and the day's events weighed on Kate's shoulders. Her head was pounding, and she couldn't relax.

"We'll hit the shops tomorrow and prepare for the furniture movers to arrive. Fancy getting up early for breakfast in Rangiora?" Nick asked.

Jimmy immediately responded. "Yeah, that would be great, Nick."

They could barely understand Jimmy with his mouth full of pizza.

"It's a plan." Kate grinned at the boys. They couldn't muster anything for breakfast until the furniture movers brought their kitchen essentials in anyway. She looked forward to exploring Rangiora.

They lounged comfortably in their improvised camping setup. Jimmy finished the pizza while Nick enjoyed another beer.

Jimmy was the first to fall asleep, and soon after, Kate found herself incapable of keeping her eyes open. She succumbed and slipped into a deep slumber.

| 4 |

Lorraine

"I swear, Dan, I heard something in the attic."

Lorraine's short frame was perched precariously on a wobbly bar stool, trying to get closer to the attic trapdoor. She stared at the sliding panel on the ceiling, knowing she wouldn't be brave enough to slide it open.

"Get down, Lorraine," Dan said, scolding his wife. "We live in the country now. There are mice and other rodents that make their way into attics. I'll check it out tomorrow. Get down before you kill yourself."

Dan's exacerbated look said it all. He was over his wife's charades.

They moved three years ago, but Lorraine still hadn't settled in. She kept comparing everything to their cottage in Buckinghamshire, England.

"I think it's back, Dan," she said, climbing down from the stool.

"We aren't starting that again, Lorraine. There is nothing here. There never was anything here. You knew the old man who lived here wanted to die at home when he became sick. His family made that happen for him. There is nothing sinister in that. You even got thosefreaks to cleanse the place," Dan said, frustration thick in his voice.

Lorraine went through every single nook and cranny of the house before they bought it. She loved everything about the place. The vendors were honest, forthcoming folks. They disclosed the past owner dying in the dwelling early in the discussions. Lorraine never questioned it, spoke of it, or acknowledged it until one day, four months after they moved in.

That day changed Lorraine. She became convinced that a man haunted the house. She saw things that made her think the old man's ghost had returned in its younger version.

Dan worried about her mental health, never having seen such behavior in his wife. He initially supported her theory but eventually lost faith in her claims after seeing nothing she described in the house or on the property. What she saw, what she heard, what she experienced, Dan couldn't understand. He lost interest in the continual conversations about the man that haunted the house. It was always on her mind, and she would talk about it incessantly.

A ring derailed his train of thought. He grabbed his mobile.

"Talbot here." He said, observing his wife looking up at the ceiling. He frowned and shook his head. "Yeah, no worries, I'll check it out."

Lorraine stared at him as he got up from the chair.

"Are you heading out?" she asked, her voice shaking.

He looked at his wife, panic ripe on her face like a deer, knowing it was about to be hit by a semi-truck. She looked petrified.

"I have to, Lorraine. They need me to check something out. Why are you like this? You've been a police officer's wife for over 15 years. You knew moving here that the force was small, and I would be on call most nights." He grabbed his police-issued jacket, shaking his head at the scene she was making.

"I'm scared, Dan." Lorraine cowered, close to tears. Her hands were clenched before her, the skin on her knuckles waxy from the strain.

"Come on, Lorraine, Jeffrey is in his room. Just watch TV with him while I'm gone." Dan put on his jacket and headed out the door.

***

Lorraine watched him leave, fear rendering her incapable of protesting further. She regained her composure and headed down the hallway toward her son's bedroom.

The door was slightly ajar. Lorraine could hear murmuring coming from behind it. She slowly pushed the door open and peered inside.

Jeffrey was sitting on the bed, slowly rocking back and forth, mumbling softly. He was staring at something in his lap. She stepped inside the room cautiously, concerned about her son's odd behavior. His head snapped up as he sensed her enter his room.

"Mom," Jeffrey exclaimed as he pushed up his glasses, the movement displaying the book on his lap. She smiled. He never lost the habit of reading aloud, still mumbling his words although quietly.

"What are you reading, sweetheart?" she asked, sitting beside him on the bed.

He positioned himself next to her. "An adventure book I got at school, Mommy," he replied, pushing up his thick glasses.

"That's good, Jeffrey. I like it when you read. Would you like to join me for some TV and hot cocoa?" she asked, squeezing his knee.

His face lit up instantly. He bounded off the bed and rushed to the kitchen. Lorraine followed him down the hallway, relieved she wasn't alone.

"Where's dad?" Jeffrey asked while sipping his hot cocoa.

"He got called out to look at something, hunny. He should be back shortly," Lorraine said, desperately hoping he would be.

| 5 |

The Night

Kate woke to an icy breeze on her cheek. She reluctantly rose from her slumber, taking in her surroundings. The faint glow from the outside light glazed the living room, where they slept peacefully on the floor.

Why was it so cold?

She looked at the living room windows to see if one was open. A frigid burst of air hit her face like someone had blown their icy breath on her. The current was so strong it moved the long strands of her black hair.

Startled, she stood up and looked at the French doors leading off the dining room to the deck.

They were open.

Impossible. Those doors were latched, top and bottom, and locked before bed.

The curtains the previous occupants left flapped gently in the wind, revealing glimpses of the deck she sat on that afternoon after her fall.

A sudden burst of wind exposed the area thoroughly.

A hooded man stood in the night. The one she saw in the forest that afternoon.

Kate screamed.

| 6 |

Shannon & Luke

"Talbot, to dispatch, I've arrived on site." Dan pressed the button of his radio and got out of his cruiser.

He'd driven to Dalton's property after being briefed at the station. Shannon and Luke were at it again.

Night after night, they moved vehicles into and out of their shed. Dan couldn't understand where the cars came from. They were all registered as being newly sold to Shannon and Luke. How could they afford to own so many vehicles? Where did they come from, and where were they going?

Luke built a massive shed with open walls that housed the cars. The shed was the finest thing on the parcel of land they occupied.

The Daltons lived with their two children in a small, run-down shack that didn't have running water or electricity. They'd driven the same white Ford Ranger for the past eight years. They were filthy, rude, and never mixed with the locals.

Dan had been scouting their place for three hours, all the while seeing nothing but darkness. He walked the barriers of the pine plantation to get a better view of the shed. Looking over to the barely discernible house in the distance, he took note to introduce himself to the new folks renting Paterson's place.

Shannon and Luke lived next door to the newcomers, hidden within their pine forest. He felt terrible for the new folks having the Daltons as neighbors. Thankfully, they didn't have power, so loud music wouldn't be an issue.

He'd been told that many came and went from Paterson's property before he moved his family to the area. The place had been vacant since he arrived.

The new owners bought the property, thinking it would make a perfect place to retire. They spent eight months building and refurbishing it but never spent a night in the house. They claimed a terrific opportunity to buy land and build in Christchurch City was the reason for the sudden change of plans. They put it up for rent, but tenants often broke the lease. The property stayed vacant most of the time. It might have been too far from town for most folks.

Dan considered packing it in when he finally heard the noise of vehicles approaching. Shannon and Luke had scored a big haul. Five sets of car lights advanced toward the shed. They had help this time, which surprised him. They usually worked alone.

He'd gone by the shed late that afternoon and spied inside. It was full of legally registered vehicles. Now, it was nearly empty, with more than half of them gone. The five cars followed each other into the front parking area of the property and moved toward the shed. Four vehicles parked close to other cars in the shed, making space for more to come. One of them looked like a getaway car, and they all gathered around it. From his vantage point, he could see three males and two females.

Dan whispered into his radio. "Talbot here. Back-up requested at the site. Five persons of interest."

He got confirmation they were sending a cruiser and crept in closer to them. They were oblivious to his presence in the dark. It worked to his advantage, but the minimal light made it difficult to make out facial features. Dan was close enough to make out Shannon's face and the woman standing...

A piercing, guttural scream shattered the night, chilling his blood. Dan snapped back, exposing his presence to the crew, who instantly got into the getaway car and sped off.

Backup should be on its way already. He grabbed his radio.

"Talbot here. Persons of interest on the move. The vehicle is a BMW registration K9R L6T headed northeast. I'm going to attend another event at Paterson's place."

Dispatch promptly responded with confirmation. They could only observe the Daltons tonight, not having found any reason to arrest them.

Yet.

| 7 |

The Man

Dan decided against walking to Paterson's place to investigate. It would look odd and make the new occupants nervous if he divulged why he was scouting the barrier of their property. He returned to his patrol car and made his way to their driveway.

The new occupants were awake, with all the lights blazing and the dog barking. As he disembarked the vehicle, a dark-haired man of about the same build and stature met him.

"Officer Talbot. I was patrolling the area when I heard a scream. Is everything alright?" Dan said, offering his hand to Nick.

"Nick Neilson, we just moved in from Australia. My wife, Kate, and our son, Jimmy, arrived yesterday afternoon. My wife thought she'd seen someone in the woods yesterday and awoke thinking he was on our dining room deck. I looked around the property but couldn't find any evidence of anyone having been here except for us," Nick said, concern evident in his voice. He wrapped his jacket tighter around him, not accustomed to the cooler weather.

"A man? Can you give me a description?" Dan asked, taking out his notepad.

Nick led Dan to the living room, where Kate was sitting on the floor shaking, Jimmy holding her close.

"Hi Kate, my name is Officer Dan Talbot. Your husband said you saw a man on your dining room deck tonight. I was wondering if you could describe him to me?" he asked, his tone deliberately soft.

Kate looked up at him, her eyes red from crying. She couldn't stop shaking.

"I woke up during the night because I was cold. The French doors out of the dining room were open. A man was standing on the deck. It was the same man I saw yesterday afternoon in the forest," Kate replied, her voice weak.

"You saw the same man this afternoon in the forest? What did he look like?" Dan asked, his pen waiting patiently to write her words.

"He was in his early twenties, tall with an average build. He was wearing dark jeans and a gray hoodie. The hood shaded his face."

"Hmm..." Dan thought out loud. "Doesn't give us much to go by. I know of at least twenty locals that would fit that description. Have you seen any vehicles parked close to your property since you moved in?"

"I haven't seen a single vehicle turn down Harper's Road since I got here a few days ago. Apart from the odd tractor, I can hear but not see because of the plantation; there's been no one," Nick said, looking around the dimly lit property, trying to find an answer to what scared his wife.

"Kate took a knock to the head this afternoon when Jimmy came upon what looked like a row of teeth with rotting flesh hanging off it. The previous occupants must have been hunters and buried their kills in the forest. Chinook must have dug up the bones. It shocked Kate so badly that she passed out and hit her head on a tree," Nick said.

Dan looked at Nick blankly. "Bones?"

"The previous owners weren't hunters or farmers. He worked at our local bank as the manager, and she was a receptionist at the medical clinic. Both were city folk and didn't own a firearm. They lived here a long time ago. There would be nothing left on the bones if they were responsible."

Dan could see concern building in Nick's eyes and reassuringly added.

"It might have been a local hunter that used your plantation to bury his kills. I'll have a look tomorrow in the daylight. I'll also ask if any locals were having parties tonight. A farmhand might have noticed the lights in the house and come over to investigate. This place has been vacant for a while."

Nick relaxed. "That would be great, Officer Talbot. It would be unpleasant for Chinook to dig up more rotting flesh and bring it home."

Dan warned Nick that Chinook needed to be kept on a lead to ensure he wouldn't hurt the surrounding stock.

"Consensus with the farmers here is to shoot to kill if they see a stray dog attacking their stock, and I wouldn't want your son to lose his best mate."

Nick nodded, understanding that their life in New Zealand would bring on specific changes. They walked the property boundary together, trying to find evidence of an intruder.

"I haven't seen anything to substantiate someone trying to break into your house. Do you think Kate might have hit her head hard enough to see things? Visual disturbances can occur after a head injury. She should get herself checked at the medical clinic in Rangiora tomorrow in case something is wrong, or it could be nothing." Dan said. He was confident her vision was simply a nightmare generated by a bruised and tired brain.

"Yeah, I think you are right, Officer Talbot. We need to head into Rangiora in the morning to stock up before the furniture movers arrive at three. We'll pop into the medical clinic while we're there,"

"Call me Dan, please. We're neighbors. My family lives in the closest house to your east, a few minutes away. If I don't get called out, I'll help you move your furniture," Dan said, happy to volunteer. Having found nothing to prove the man's presence, Dan was confident that her tired and probably bruised mind made up the apparition.

Nick nodded and shook Dan's hand again.

"Yeah, it most likely was a dream, but what gets me is the dining room's French doors were both fully open. I'm certain I bolted those doors shut and locked them," Nick said, looking at Dan questioningly.

Dan looked toward the plantation, worry etching his face.

| 8 |

Mona

Mona looked out the kitchen window and scanned the sweeping view of the Ashley River. She remembered when they first built the house, how they'd designed everything to ensure she captured the best panorama from every window.

Her mind darkened at the memory of when Mike brought her to the family farm to begin their new life together. She hated it from the start.

Born and bred in Christchurch, Mona did not intend to work on a farm or be surrounded by stinky animals. How did she get herself into this situation to start with?

Mike promised her a good life, but he'd not delivered. He came from a wealthy family; she had expected them to care for her financially if she married him. It was a farce. The family was asset-rich but wasn't rolling in cash unless they sold their land. They had to work to survive like most of the wealthy farmers around. She felt cheated.

Although he built her a new home and supported her financially, she'd grown tired of the rural farming life. She didn't get along with the local farmer's wives and found them too dull to entertain a relationship with them.

After years of feeling repressed, Mona needed to let her hair down. She would party it up at an old school friend's house in Christchurch most Fridays, only returning to the farm on Sunday evening after supper. That's how she met Kevin.

Kevin, a used car dealer in Rangiora, was a breath of fresh air for Mona. Always up for a party and closing the bars, Kevin dabbled in cocaine, which Mona happily imbibed in, furthering her rebellion. Mona had only visited Kevin at his apartment once but decided it wouldn't do. How could she live in a plain, two-bedroom upstairs flat in the city when she had a reputation to adhere to? She deserved the finest and wouldn't compromise.

It was best to get Mike to move out since he'd not kept up with his side of the bargain. She deserved luxurious holidays, designer clothes, and late-model prestige vehicles. He didn't like any of those things. Family outings at the lake were his idea of a holiday. His loss, she thought, feeling quite self-righteous.

Her mind meandered back to the view.

Wait, what did she see in the far corner to the right? Was that Mike?

A fresh wave of anger swelled inside her. She opened the back door to investigate and marched off, planning on telling Mike off for being too close. As she approached the far-right paddock, she could see the shape of a man standing in the field.

Propelled by her hatred, she barged toward the figure, thinking she should have brought an ax to clarify her point. A slight motion to her left caught her eye, and she hesitated.

Mike was working the paddocks close to the road. She watched him move stock with his motorbike. If that's where Mike was, then who was she walking to?

Her gaze shifted to where the man had been standing. As she searched for him, a powerful hum filled the air. Like high-voltage electricity, it crackled and instantly engulfed her. She retched from overwhelming nausea.

Mona refocused her gaze. The man was no longer there. She looked around, a strong sense of panic overtaking her. The humming felt like it was poisoning her.

Mike must have his mates over, and one wandered into the back paddocks. She decided this would be the most probable answer and knew who to blame: Mike.

Ready to tell Mike to keep himself and his mates away from her house, she turned to head back to pick up her car.

Standing there, barely ten meters away, was a man dressed in dark jeans and a gray hoodie. Terror rocked her, and the grating hum infusing the air made her panic. Mona screamed.

The fog of fear lifted lightly, her rage developing into an inferno as she saw Mike come to her rescue.

***

"Are you okay, Mona? I heard you scream. What happened?" Mike asked as he tried to steady Mona on her feet.

"Don't touch me, you piece of shit," she screamed at him, looking like a wild animal caught in a trap. She brushed her bleached blond hair from her face and lurched at Mike.

"How often have I told you. I don't want to see you. I've had enough of you and your mates coming here and taking over my place. Get that mate of yours off my property before I call the cops!" She spat at him, pulling away from his grasp.

"What mate, Mona? I'm alone here, working in the far paddocks. The ewes are lambing. I've been flat out. Did you see someone?"

Fully believing that Mike was gaslighting her, the hum still heavy in her head, she grabbed at her ears and screamed louder.

Mike, wide-eyed, looked on as if she was possessed.

"Stop that bloody noise, Mike! I know what you are trying to do, and I won't take it. You can't run me off my land. This place is mine now. I deserve it after all the years of being stuck here with you, having to live your pathetic farmer's lifestyle," she said, clutching her ears. She bent over, hoping for relief from the crushing noise.

Although bitten by the attack, Mike showed no sign of the sour taste left in his mouth.

"Mona, what noise? I can't hear anything," Mike said, shaking his head. He couldn't understand what she was talking about and couldn't hear any noise.

Mona swayed, her legs about to give way. He tried to hold her up. She lunged at his arm, trying to bite him.

Mike pulled back and watched her stumble back to the house. Mona slipped into the confines of the house's darkness, still holding her ears, the hum following her.

| 9 |

The Town

Nick got up earlier than Kate. He thought it best to let her sleep after her fright last night.

When Jimmy woke up, Nick coaxed him outside to give his mother a few more moments of precious rest.

The sun shone brightly, reflecting a shower of diamonds on the pond at the far corner of their property.

"Do you think it has fish in it?" Jimmy asked, his eyes glinting with wonderment at the possibilities hidden within the pond's depths.

"I don't think so, bud. I don't know how deep it is or if fish could live there. We can try to throw a line in and see if we catch something," Nick said playfully.

There wasn't any vegetation growing inside the water's boundary. It looked like the body of water was lined with black pond liner, making it dark and mysterious. Nick couldn't see how any fish could live in it without being fed. They hadn't received instructions on pond maintenance from the landlords. Apart from the solar water fountain, no other equipment was required to oxygenate it. The landlords hadn't left fish food either.

"Hey, Mom's up," Jimmy said before running to meet her.

"How are you feeling today, babe?" Nick asked when he caught up with them. She looked pale.

"Yeah, it was a rough day and night, but I'm willing to put it past me," Kate said, shrugging her shoulders. Her head still hurt, and her brain felt foggy.

"Officer Dan thinks you should get checked out at the medical clinic in Rangiora in case you might have hurt yourself when you fell. We'll be doing that." Nick said, his attention already back to the pond.

It was more an order than a request. Kate nodded reluctantly. They returned to the house to get ready for their trip to Rangiora.

* * *

"Good as gold," Kate said as she climbed into the truck. Her brief checkup at the medical clinic set her mind at ease. She'd suffered a concussion from her fall but was expected to fully recover.

"They think the humming noise I heard was caused by a change in inner ear pressure from yesterday's flight. Makes sense to me." Kate said as they drove away from the clinic.

That answer made sense to her, although Nick hadn't bought it. He'd flown more than anyone he knew and never had issues with his ears, but he'd also heard the humming. He decided it was best to drop the subject.

Nick drove to the grocery store to do their shopping. Jimmy was sleeping away his food coma in the backseat, having eaten his weight in pancakes at the restaurant.

"It's a shame to wake him," Kate said when they pulled into the grocery store car park. The sudden jolt when the vehicle stopped woke Jimmy. He burst into life.

"Yeah, grocery shopping. I'm hungry," Jimmy said gleefully.

Kate and Nick looked at each other and laughed. Jimmy had no limit when it came to food consumption, although his slim frame would make you think he barely ate.

They strode through the aisles and purchased every new food they could find, keen on tasting New Zealand cuisine.

Nick picked up a local newspaper as they were bagging their purchases. It was unusual for him to read the paper, but since only dial-up internet was available in the area, it was the best way to stay current.

The headline read *'Strong Nor'wester Forecast for this Monday'*.

They were heading home earlier than expected, having done their shopping in record time. They had two hours to wait before the moving truck arrived, so Nick stopped at Jimmy's new school to get acquainted before his first day on Monday. They disembarked the vehicle, heading straight for the administration office.

"Good day, everyone. How can I help?" a bubbly voice from a young, dark-haired administration assistant welcomed them. "My name is Nicole,"

Kate explained that Jimmy was starting school on Monday.

Nicole clicked and automatically referred to the admission forms she emailed a few weeks back.

"Yes, of course. Jimmy. Perfect! I think we have everything we need." She smiled at Jimmy and shook his hand.

"Welcome, Jimmy. We will get a tour sorted for you in a minute. I'll show you where your classes are and where your desk will be. Just need to get your new address, and we should be ready to go." Nicole's smile was brighter than ever, her bubbly enthusiasm rubbing off on them.

"Eighty Harper's Road," Kate responded cheerfully.

It had the same effect as throwing a glass of cold water at Nicole's face. Her smile soured.

"Oh, I see. How long will you be staying?" Nicole asked. Kate couldn't believe the sudden change in her demeanor. Why would she react like that?

"We are here for the long run. If we enjoy living there, we will look at buying the house," Nick replied, also wondering what brought the sudden change in Nicole. She somewhat faked a smile and waved at Jimmy to follow her. Kate and Nick looked at each other nervously.

"Welcome," a man exclaimed from behind their backs, his voice bowling over the concern they felt. They turned to greet a middle-aged bald man standing there with his arm out, ready to shake the hand of whichever of them was the quickest. Nick extended his hand in greeting.

"I'm Tane Moaraki, the principal," he said, his smile warm and welcoming. "I think Jimmy will like it here. We will closely monitor him to ensure he enjoys his new surroundings." He had such a reassuring nature Kate immediately warmed up to him.

"Thank you, Mr. Moaraki, that's appreciated. Jimmy has attended many schools in the past because of our travels. Changing schools was never a problem for him. I am sure it won't take him long to adjust," Kate said, shaking his hand. The man's handshake was gentle, but she sensed a strong presence. He was a man who automatically commanded respect.

"So, how are you finding it so far?" the principal asked.

Nick spoke, showing their appreciation and awe of the place. A worried look took over Kate's face, thinking of last night's incident, but she swiftly fought it off. Thankfully, Mr. Moaraki didn't notice.

"We read the headline in the local paper saying we have wind headed our way," Kate quipped to divert from her worry. It didn't help when she saw Mr. Moaraki's expression darken.

"Yes, the Nor'wester is coming, our legendary Canterbury wind. Make sure you secure your lawn furniture and batten down the hatches. The wind is strong, hot, and dry and can last for days. The one predicted will last at least four to five days," Mr. Moaraki explained calmly.

"Well, that's not too bad. It's only wind," Nick said, not taking the warning seriously. The principal's face darkened further.

"It's not a normal wind. It becomes relentless and tiring as the days roll on. If exposed for a long period, your skin feels like parchment paper. Normal farm chores become tedious and even dangerous. Suicides and domestic violence incidences rise during the Nor'wester. The constant assault from the wind wears even the strongest ones down. We sometimes keep the children inside when it blows."

Surely it can't be that bad, Kate thought to herself. They'd gone through freezing blizzards that would last for days and cut off entire towns in Canada. She assumed the locals reacted this way to the Nor'wester because it was the only severe weather event they faced.

"You don't need to worry about us. We'll batten down the hatches," Nick replied, somewhat amused.

Kate wasn't so sure it was a laughing matter.

| 10 |

The Talbots

Lorraine was still upset with Dan. His call-out had taken him away until the wee hours of the night, leaving her alone again. It never bothered her when he left for work in England. She understood her husband's job and was familiar with its demands. Things were different now. She felt alone and misunderstood.

He refused to tell her why he'd met the new occupants of Paterson's place during the middle of the night, which added to her anger. She knew they'd asked Dan to watch Shannon and Luke's activities. Paterson's place was their closest neighbor, but how did Dan end up there in the middle of the night? He mentioned that the moving truck arrived at three in the afternoon and planned to help if possible. Maybe she should also introduce herself to her new neighbors and help them settle in.

A loud sigh escaped her. She looked up from her paper. The Nor'wester was coming again, forecast for Monday in three days. She despised the ferocious warm wind, the way it howled during the night, never abating. It made her imagination go wild.

She headed to the laundry, leaving her tea and paper aside. Her washing needed doing before the wind stole it off the line.

***

It was three in the afternoon. Lorraine hadn't heard from Dan yet. She hemmed and hawed. Should she show up at Paterson's place without her husband? What would that look like? Would Dan get upset at her for inviting herself if he was there?

Desperately wanting to meet new friends and satisfy her curiosity, she fought her anxiety and decided to go.

Lorraine picked up a plate of freshly baked scones with clotted cream and jam and headed toward Paterson's place.

Her tummy grew nervous the closer she got to her neighbors. Lorraine considered turning back and waiting for Dan to come home. She relaxed when she saw Dan's cruiser parked beside the moving van.

She parked her car and took a moment to calm her jittery nerves. Picking up the scones and taking a deep breath, Lorraine set out to meet her new neighbors.

"Lorraine," Dan called out, waving to her.

"This is my beautiful wife," he indicated to her as she joined the group. Dan seemed happy to see her. Relief washed over her. Nick automatically extended his hand as she approached.

"Nice to meet you, Lorraine. I'm Nick, and this is my wife, Kate," Nick said as Kate extended her hand to shake Lorraine's and help her with the plate of scones, the large platter overpowering the woman's small frame.

"Come inside, Lorraine," Kate said, towering over her newfound acquaintance. Lorraine was a tiny little thing with mousy brown curly hair and alert, darting brown eyes. Jimmy was already taller than her. Lorraine followed close behind silently until they stepped inside the house. She was awed at the large sunlit lounge.

"Wow, I've never been inside before. It's gorgeous. I have heard a lot about this place but never had a chance to visit. You must be happy to have this beautiful house as your home." Kate nodded and warmed to Lorraine. She was a welcomed distraction from emptying the moving truck.

"Oh, you also have a son?" Lorraine asked as she saw Jimmy running with Chinook through the kitchen window. The way she asked, Kate knew they also had a son Jimmy's age.

"Yes, we do, Jimmy. He's twelve years old and will attend Loburn school on Monday," Kate said as she looked out the window, happy that Jimmy would have someone to play with. Lorraine smiled broadly.

"We have Jeffrey. He's ten and attends the same school. We must get them together sometime. The only other children around are Mike and Mona's, but they are in boarding school in Christchurch. The Daltons have two girls, but they don't associate with anyone. Once the Nor'wester passes, we should catch up for a cup of tea and a play date."

Once again, the Nor'wester. Obviously, in these parts, life stopped only to resume after the storm subsided. Hearing the men laugh in the backyard, Kate picked up a few beers and the plate of scones and headed off with Lorraine.

"How are we doing, gentlemen?" Kate asked, joining them at the fire pit. The pit's massive tarpaulin top shielded everything under its cover from the sun or rain. The men sat opposite each other on the outdoor sofas. Kate placed the scones on the coffee table and sat beside her husband. Lorraine followed suit.

"All good, now that we can finally have a cold beer," Nick replied cheekily. Kate realized Dan might still be on duty and hesitated when she handed him a beer, wondering if she should offer him something else. Dan smiled and grabbed the can of beer she was offering.

"I'm off duty. I worked late last night. My co-worker took the afternoon shift and callouts tonight. I can enjoy a cold beer without worry," he said reassuringly.

Lorraine dramatically sighed and placed her hand on her husband's leg. Everyone could sense her relief at her husband getting the night off. It perturbed Kate.

Was Dan so busy he was always away from home, or was something else going on? Regardless, the woman was immensely relieved.

"Thanks for coming over last night, Dan," Nick said, taking a swig of beer.

Dan tipped his head, smiling. "No problem, that's what we are here for. Did you have time to get checked over at the clinic, Kate?" Dan asked, looking directly into Kate's eyes. He'd been serious when he recommended she go to the clinic.

"What happened last night?" Lorraine asked nervously. Dan glared at her from the corner of his eyes. She knew better than to ask about his police business.

"Kate took a nasty fall in the woods during the day after a fright and knocked her head so badly she blacked out and thought she saw a man in the forest during the day and again on the front deck at night. Dan was working nearby when he heard her scream," Nick replied, his gaze shifting to the deck where Kate had seen the intruder.

"Oh, my… are you alright, Kate? Did they find something wrong at the clinic?" Lorraine asked, concerned.

"No damage done. I've been given the all-clear. The doctor thinks the humming I heard was middle ear pressure from the flights." Kate felt embarrassed about her fall and wished the incident wouldn't have happened. She didn't want to discuss it.

"You saw a man?" Lorraine asked, goosebumps raising on her arms.

"Yes, I am certain of it. The man was wearing dark navy jeans and a gray hoodie. The hood covers his head. I couldn't see his face."

Before she could go on, Lorraine gasped and looked directly into her husband's face.

"It's the same man, Dan!"

| 11 |

The Daltons

"Hurry, Luke," Shannon growled, pressing Luke to get on with the job. They stood alone in the darkness.

"I'm trying, Shannon. This one's a mess," Luke said as he ran his fingers through his hair.

The blue 1992 Corolla, hidden on the shores of the Okuku River, was filled with rubbish. Old fast-food wrappers, beer bottles, and empty cigarette packets littered every internal space in the dilapidated car.

"I don't think this one will be worth it," he sighed, pausing to complain.

"Shut up, Luke. You know what we've got to do. Once repainted and re-plated, we can get rid of it."

Shannon pressed on with impatience. "It's not about how much we get from Barry. We've already gotten the money we need from the owner of this piece of shit. The few hundred that Barry gives us is for clean-up."

"I know, Shannon," he said as he kept on with his job of purging any evidence of the previous owner's existence.

It was such a simple way to make money. Barry hacked into the transport authority website, providing them with a list of newly registered vehicles belonging to foreign travelers. New Zealand was a hot spot for young tourists, determined to spend a few months in paradise while they toured the South Island. Every year, they would buy make-shift campers and secondhand vehicles, intent on living the dream and driving from coast to coast.

The lack of cell phone service and internet in the area made their disappearance even easier to cover. It was always a few days after their last communication that their families overseas would start to worry and call law enforcement. When the local authorities began their search, they couldn't trace the disappearances back to them. Shannon and Luke Dalton were professional serial killers. They relied on their skill to survive for the past ten years.

"I picked up some groceries," Shannon said, giving him another garbage bag.

Luke knew she used the cash or bank cards stolen from the Corolla's owner. His wife was quite cunning, always buying essentials from the local grocery store in Rangiora to dissuade any suspicion. Her cold and unwelcoming personality discouraged conversation from the locals. She always tried to pay with cash.

When cash was in short supply because many tourists now kept cash or credit cards, she wandered far from home to get supplies. She kept the purchases small enough not to alert the cashier when signing the credit card receipt with the cardholder's name. Shannon was forgettable with her long, greasy brown hair and thin frame.

"Where are you going to put him?" Shannon asked casually, leaning on the Corolla's peeling bonnet.

"Same place as usual," Luke said, his head buried in the back seat, fishing out rubbish and filling his bag.

"I'm not certain that's safe, Luke? New people are renting Paterson's place. It's too close for comfort. I heard a dog barking the other day. It wouldn't take much for the dog to go digging." She took the last drag of her cigarette and flicked the butt away.

Luke looked at her. A glimmer of moonlight lit the worry on his face. Shannon was right.

"I'll bury him in the Crown land on the other side of their property. The bush is thicker there, and the dog shouldn't be a problem because it's fenced. I'll dig up the remains in the plantation and move them." He exited the confines of the car, relieved that he'd finished the job.

"We could always bury them in the cesspit. They wouldn't dare come close to that," Luke said.

Shannon shook her head, lighting another cigarette. They'd converted an old dry well to hold their sewage. She knew damn well that the system was illegal but also knew that no one would want to peer inside the depths of that hellhole. The stench was already bad enough. Adding dead bodies to the mix wouldn't help the stink any.

"Talbot's right on our asses. What the hell was he doing in the plantation last night? What was that screaming all about? I knew getting Barry's mates to help move the cars from the painters was going to be a problem. From now on, we need to work alone, and we need to get a new painter. He can't keep up and is asking too many questions. I'll get Barry to sort him out. Meanwhile, we need to lie low for a bit to keep the heat off," Shannon said as she changed the car's plates.

"Don't worry, babe," Luke said in a comforting voice. "The Nor'wester is coming, Talbot will be busy enough."

He chuckled to himself, knowing what was coming.

| 12 |

Settling In

The Talbots quickly got away once Lorraine became convinced that Kate saw the same man she thought haunted her house.

Dan was quick to stifle Lorraine's claims about the ghost. He dismissed it as a strange idea that she put in her head and blamed the isolation she endured in the country. It was impossible not to see the embarrassment in Dan's eyes.

Their departure was bittersweet. Kate wanted to know more. She wanted to know everything that Lorraine had to say about her ghost. Why did she think it was the same man? Kate blamed the apparition on exhaustion and knocking her head.

Although she took to Lorraine initially, she saw her facade crack when she erratically described odd events happening to her at her house.

The incidents were innocent. Lorraine was sure she left the sugar bowl on the table but found it on the counter. She recounted the story wide-eyed like the ghost moved it. Dan commented that she had probably forgotten she'd moved it, only to have Lorraine savagely lash back at him, saying she hadn't. The same happened with the laundry basket.

The interaction was over the top and inappropriate, especially for a first-time visit. Kate brushed it off. The monumental task of unpacking boxes soon made her forget Lorraine's strange behavior.

Kate and Nick were putting Jimmy's bed together when a phone rang, making them jump. Cell coverage was virtually non-existent at the house. This was the first noise any of their mobiles made since their arrival.

Nick grabbed his phone and moved outside to capture a stronger signal. Kate looked through the window, seeing him walk back and forth on the lawn, listening more than talking. He nodded and hung up. Her stomach churned anxiously, awaiting the news.

"That was work. They want me to do a confined space course in Nelson on Monday. I need to fly out Sunday night, babe. Sorry."

Kate's shoulders dropped, and her eyes watered at her disappointment. Nervously twisting the bed bolts in her hand, she tried to think of a way to make him stay.

"There's nothing I can do about it, Kate. You guys will be fine," he said, aggravated by her reaction.

She felt she should say something, bring up the reason they were in New Zealand, remind him he promised to stay with her, but she remained silent, reason winning over emotion. What would it look like if he refused his first assignment? She was sure his boss wouldn't be impressed.

"That's ok, Nick, we will be all right," she said, her words not matching her body language.

"They need the work truck while I'm gone. We need to make sure that you have adequate supplies for the week. I'll look for a second-hand car for you when I come back. I know it's bad timing, babe. No car, phone, or internet, but at least you know where to go if you need help. Officer Talbot is only a few kilometers away. I'll ask him to check up on you while I'm gone. I should be back on Thursday at the latest, promise," Nick said as he packed his bag.

Kate nodded, worry gnawing at her stomach. "Can't anyone else take that course over? We just got here," she asked, pleading.

Nick stood up and heaved his shoulders. There was no way out. The company was short-staffed. Kate's mind reeled, dread filling her. The sun set without them noticing as they unpacked in silence.

| 13 |

Chinook

Kate slept better than she had in months.

Finally reunited with their bed, they fell asleep instantly, following the exhaustion of the day's unpacking. She woke to the glorious sunlight flooding through the cracks in the curtains. A single ray of light fell over her husband's body. She became momentarily transfixed as it danced on his chest, moving up and down lightly with each breath. They so rarely shared a bed it seemed foreign to her.

She got up, making sure not to disturb him, threw on her baby blue silk bathrobe, and tip-toed down the hallway to check on her son Jimmy. Still sleeping soundly, Jimmy purred softly.

She left the door ajar and made her way to the kitchen. The open-light-filled area acted like a shot of caffeine, instantly shaking off any residual sleepiness she felt.

In the yard, Chinook patrolled the area his long lead afforded him. Kate put the jug on and prepared her coffee as the water boiled.

Cup in hand, she opened the French doors and let herself out to the warm, sunny Saturday morning. Chinook let out a short yip, excited to see her. He ran to her to cuddle her legs. She promised him they would go for a walk after she finished her coffee.

Kate felt at home, strolling to the pond, its water sparkling in the sunlight. The pine trees perfumed the air. She sipped her coffee, loving her new home.

***

The house was still silent when Kate set out on her exploratory walk with Chinook. She hoped the excited dog wouldn't bark and wake Jimmy as they strolled down the driveway.

They turned left onto Harper's Road, a single-lane dirt road that followed the pine plantation to meet with the paved main thoroughfare.

Kate hurriedly crossed the vacant road and made her way east. She studied the area on Google Maps and made notes of their surroundings before leaving Perth. They lived in a triangle, with the only close neighbors directly behind them shrouded in their dense forest.

She tried to look through the impenetrable plantation to see if she could see their house but couldn't. Although the plantation floor was free of any shrubs or greenery, the scale and the sheer number of trees made seeing past the first few rows impossible.

The sound of a motorbike to her distant right grabbed her interest. She saw a farmer tending to his flock of sheep riding up and down his paddocks. The farmer noticed her and drove to the edge of his property. She nervously met him by the electric fence.

"Good day!" the farmer chirped. "Are you the new people renting the Paterson place?" He adjusted his baseball cap to keep the sun from his eyes.

"We sure are," Kate responded, putting her hand out. He wiped his hand on his jersey and shook her hand. He was much gentler than expected.

"My name is Kate Neilson, and this is our dog, Chinook. My husband, Nick, and son, Jimmy, are at home sleeping. We've had a long day unpacking and settling in," Kate explained, already warming to the gentle nature this substantial man displayed in his body language.

"Welcome to Okuku, I'm Mike McEwan. Born and bred here on this farm." He waved at the expanse of green in front of her.

"If you need to know something about the place, I'm the guy to ask," he said, winking.

The lush emerald carpet, speckled with white balls of fluff, looked like a postcard to her. Kate couldn't tear her eyes off the newborn lambs, never having seen them before. Canada's wild North didn't allow outdoor stock; the wolves and coyotes made it nearly impossible.

"Wow!" she said, fighting to hide her excitement but failing miserably. "How old are they?" She asked, sounding like a child full of wonderment.

Mike burst out laughing at her enthusiasm. "Is this the first time you see sheep up close? You aren't from around here, are you? With a dog like that and your accent, I'm betting you are from Canada or the US."

He had a way of squinting when he talked. She found it endearing.

"Northern Canada," Kate responded, blushing slightly.

"These little ones were born yesterday, and these wee ones were born about an hour ago." He pointed to a set of twins first, then triplets.

"I'm thrilled with them. The ewes have never been healthier, and the weather's provided ample tucker. Only another 220 ewes to lamb, and that should be it with lambing for this year." Mike said, pride evident in his voice and how he slightly pushed out his chest.

"That is so cool, Mike. I'm happy I wandered off this morning to walk Chinook. What a treat seeing this for the first time," Kate said, smiling broadly, squinting as the sun scolded her eyes.

Mike looked down at the dog that was sitting by her feet.

"We rarely see this breed of dog in this part of the country. Many farmers consider them too wild, making them dangerous to keep next to stock. Make sure he always stays on a leash. Don't let the neighboring farmers catch him in their paddocks." Mike said, delivering the message softly, ensuring the warning was clear.

Kate recoiled at the thought but understood it was her responsibility to ensure that Chinook was always under their control. Mike was right; his prey drive was fierce, and he couldn't stop himself given an opportunity. Both looked at the dog sitting at her feet, oblivious to the stock before him. It was hard to imagine that he could be a killer.

"I'll make sure of that, Mike. I would hate to see these gorgeous lambs harmed by anything," she said confidently, her eyes meeting his to reassure him.

"Chinook, that's a unique name for a dog. What does it mean?" he asked, repositioning himself again to avoid the sun's caustic rays.

"Where I'm from, the west of the country gets Chinooks. It's a weather occurrence that brings strong, warm winds. It warms the winters and eats the snow. Just like a warm wind is welcome, it was a perfect name for this little one as he has a strong, warm heart," Kate said, smiling as she looked at Mike, expecting the same expression. She was shocked to see fear.

"We have something similar, but we don't welcome it here. It has tortured this land and its people since the first inhabitants, a relentless, gale-force wind that can drive you mad. Many grow so tired of its endless assault that they keep their curtains closed, trying to banish its howling. You'll soon see." He quickly went from serious to smiling, realizing he was scaring her.

Mike winked playfully. "We have one coming Monday."

Kate frowned and shook her head. She was scared. Nick would be away, and this Nor'wester made her uneasy now.

He noticed the change in her immediately.

"Hey, don't worry, you're going to be okay," Mike laughed. "I'm sure your husband can take care of any issues on the property." He tried to comfort her with a soothing voice.

Kate met his eyes.

"My husband is leaving to work in Nelson on Sunday. I don't have a car yet. My cell phone barely works, and we have the worst internet I've ever seen," she said, her fear becoming undeniable.

"You can always come over if you need anything. I live in the shed up there," Mike said, pointing toward a barn, hoping it would relieve her.

She bit her lip nervously. She wasn't ready to be on her own yet, this wind thing was freaking her out.

"Are you free for dinner tonight? I would love for you to meet my husband before he leaves. We'll spark up the barbecue and have a few beers." She pleaded with her eyes, hoping that he would accept the offer.

He hesitated for a moment, then realized it made him look rude. He piped up immediately.

"I'm honored, Mrs. Neilson," he said, tipping his cap.

Relief washed over her. An enormous smile bloomed on her face.

"Perfect! We will see you at five for a few beers before dinner," she said, bouncing slightly. Chinook sensed it and popped up attentively.

"In this neck of the woods, dinner is called tea." He said, winking again.

She heard a faint call in the background and realized that Jimmy was calling Chinook. "I need to go. Jimmy is looking for his dog," she said with urgency.

He nodded, adjusting his cap as she turned to walk away.

When she was across the road, he exhaled heavily. Paterson's Place. A troubled look crossed his face. He was going to old man Paterson's place.

| 14 |

Dan

"Lorraine, what were you thinking yesterday at the Neilson's? Good God, you probably scared her to death with your ghost story," Dan said, reprimanding Lorraine at the breakfast table.

Lorraine averted his gaze while she poured cereal into her bowl and added milk, still livid at her husband for his disapproval of her sharing their house's secret with Kate. It was insulting; it made her feel like a child. She said her polite goodbyes and left in her car, horribly embarrassed. Dan followed not far behind in the cruiser.

***

Dan's fury at his wife's indiscretion made the veins at his temples throb. He drove home, his knuckles white on the steering wheel, wanting to hash this out once and for all when they arrived home.

He took a few minutes to compose himself before he entered the house. Lorraine had already locked herself in the spare bedroom.

In the morning, he turned in bed to see if Lorraine had joined him during the night. He stared at the empty spot on the bed next to him and shook his head. The bloody house and her baffling ideas were going to break them apart.

***

She looked from her cereal bowl to him, her eyes cold and dispassionate.

54

"Kate saw the same thing I saw, the ghost of the man that died here, his younger self." She stared at him, trying to convey her certainty.

Dan had enough. Frustrated, he pounded his fist on the table, looking outside to see if Jeffrey heard him. Jeffrey, unconcerned, played in the sandbox with his toy trucks.

Lorraine's stare didn't waver.

"Okay, listen, Lorraine, I'll contact the family and ask them for a picture of their father when he was younger. I'm certain you'll realize it's not what you think it is," he said, his hands in the air.

Lorraine, still staring at him, was indifferent to his plan. She got up and left the breakfast table, her cereal untouched.

Dan cleared the table and headed outside to the sandbox. Ignorant of the tension between his parents, Jeffrey played in the sandbox with his toys, his blue sun hat shading his little round face.

"Hey buddy, what are you building there?" Dan asked his son.

Jeffrey looked up and readjusted his glasses. He sat upright.

"It's a town, Dad. Here's our house, the grocery store, and the school," he said proudly, looking up, grinning.

Dan could see his plan; the young boy's imagination amazed him.

"That's outstanding, buddy. Do you want to ride in the cruiser with Dad for a bit?"

The little boy pushed up his glasses again, smiled, and nodded. "Yeah! Dad, can I put the lights on?"

Dan laughed and shook his head, imagining how the locals would worry if he were to zoom down the street with his lights on.

"Probably best we don't do that, bud," he said, laughing out loud at the visuals in his head. He grabbed his son's jacket and strapped him into the cruiser.

"Ready to go?" he asked before reversing the car down the driveway.

Jeffrey nodded.

"What about mom?" he asked, looking over at the house.

"She's tired, Jeff. She decided to lie down for a bit."

Jeffrey's gaze stayed steady on the house until they turned onto the main road.

The sun shone brightly; it made the green grass shine with a silver lining. Dan noticed the ever-increasing number of lambs being born at Mike McEwan's place. He slowed the car for Jeffrey to enjoy the show the lambs were putting on, bouncing and running about carefree.

Mike, as usual, was hard at work on his land, making sure the pastures were at their best. He held the reputation for having the best-looking and healthiest stock around. He sure worked for it, Dan thought.

"Hey bud, a new family moved close to us, and they have a twelve-year-old son who will go to your school on Monday. Do you want to stop by and meet him?" Dan asked Jeffrey.

The young boy nervously bit his lip.

"Okay, Dad," he replied apprehensively. "Do you think he will like me?" His small voice quivered.

Dan's caring eyes responded without words needing to be said. He put his hand on his son's head to reassure him.

| 15 |

The Kids

Dan pulled up the drive and spotted Jimmy playing with Chinook in the long grass of the front paddock. Jimmy noticed the cruiser and approached the driveway, Chinook following closely. Jeffrey bounced with excitement in his seat.

"Dad, he has a husky! Can I go play?" His hand was already on the door handle, wanting out of the car.

"Go ahead, bud, but stay close. We won't be staying for long," Dan instructed but knew it was falling on deaf ears. Jeffrey was too excited to listen. He watched the boys join up in the paddock. Their body language spoke volumes; both were happy to make friends.

Chinook danced around Jeffrey, trying to get his attention. The attention delighted the young boy since huskies were his favorite dog breed. His son's laughter filled him with joy.

Dan had dreamed this for them when they moved from England. Finally, things were falling into place.

Hearing the cruiser drive up, Kate and Nick exited the house and approached them smiling.

"Good day, mate," Nick greeted Dan jovially. "Up for a cup of coffee?"

"That would be damn fine," Dan responded enthusiastically. All three returned to the house, watching the boys playing close to the pond.

"This is good for Jeffrey. I apologize for Lorraine's behavior yester-day; she's been unwell lately. I don't think she's coping with the move." His sad eyes looked deep into his coffee cup. Nick was quick to comfort his newfound mate.

"I fully understand, Dan. Moving to another country and getting acquainted with your new surroundings is always difficult. I'm sure she'll come around soon. How long has it been since you moved to New Zealand?" Nick asked.

Dan looked up in despair and answered three years.

Both Kate and Nick glanced at each other with a look of surprise. Lorraine should be letting go of her past life and embracing her new one.

Kate said they asked Mike McEwan for a barbecue, hoping to lighten the mood. Grateful for the change of conversation, Dan's face lit up.

"He's a good bloke, old Mike. Where did you meet him?" Dan asked, sipping his coffee.

"I was walking the dog this morning, and he was tending to his flock. We yarned on the side of the road for a bit." Kate made sure that she used the local word for having a chat. She was trying her best to fit in.

"Nick must fly to Nelson tomorrow evening for a week. I don't have a car yet or any way of communicating with the outside world. Mike offered his help should I need it with this big wind coming. I thought it best that they meet before Nick left. I'm a bit apprehensive about this Nor'wester wind. Everyone we've met has been talking about it since we got here. It made the front-page news," Kate added, her eyes wide.

Dan looked over at Nick and spoke. "Mike McEwan is a good man, Nick. I wouldn't hesitate to trust him with my family's safety. He's been in these parts since he was born and is a well-respected man. Unfortunately, he picked Mona as his wife. Off the record, she is one insane bitch."

Kate's face dropped. She never expected Dan to describe anyone like that.

"I'm sorry, Kate," Dan said sheepishly. "The woman has done nothing but disrespect her husband since she arrived in these parts. She comes from a pretentious family. Her sisters are renowned for finding rich husbands and taking what they can from them when they leave.

"She's with this loser named Kevin. He's really bad news. He makes me cringe, always flaunting his fake wealth. Everyone knows he's in debt but depends on his phony persona to make an impression on the vulnerable people who buy his dodgy used cars.

"Mike and Mona have two children, Jake and Kelly. They go to boarding school in Christchurch, and we rarely see them. Mona enrolled them there to control how often Mike sees them, and she and Kevin have them out of their hair. She lost the respect of everyone around her when she forced Mike to live in the shed while she took over the house he'd built. I feel gutted for the guy. He doesn't deserve it."

Kate couldn't help but be sad about Mike's circumstances. She'd not seen any sadness in Mike's kind eyes this morning and wondered how deep in his enormous chest he'd driven his emotions down. A loud scuffle erupted as the boys made their way inside.

"Mom, I'm hungry. Can I have a snack?" Jimmy asked, already looking in the pantry for something to eat, Jeffrey standing silently next to him.

"Now that's something you can always depend on," Nick said. "Jimmy being hungry." The men laughed as she got up from her chair to tend to the boys.

"I have sausage rolls. Would you like some, Jeffrey?"

She immediately recognized that he was a shy child by how he looked at her from over his glasses. He nodded a hesitant yes. Kate prepared sausage rolls for the boys and gave them both a plate with tomato sauce.

She returned to the table and put down the residual for the men to feed on. The men were enthralled into a conversation.

"Kate, Dan will pop in daily to see if everything is okay with the house and check if you need anything picked up in town. Dan and I think it's a good idea to call Mike if you need anything urgent. He's our closest neighbor," Nick said, sounding official. It unnerved her.

"Well… closest, good neighbor. I see you haven't made it to the boundary to spy on your other neighbor's big open-sided shed full of cars. I wouldn't try to be friendly; they're not the type. They don't mingle with any of the locals and can be downright rude. The good news is you won't hear or see much of them as they live in a tiny shack without services. Their two young children take the school bus in the morning, keep to themselves during the day, and disappear once the school bus drops them off.

"I heard your scream, Kate, because headquarters asked me to scout their place. Cars keep on coming in and out of that big shed. We've found nothing to charge them with; they own those cars legally. Everyone at the force reckons that they are up to something big, but we haven't been able to pin anything on them apart from occasional jaywalking. My advice is to stay away," Dan said, his mouth stern.

Kate nodded, taking his warning seriously. She stood up nervously. The place was souring on her, first the wind, then this. She didn't like it.

"We can't win them all, babe." Nick looked up at her. "At least you came across the best neighbor first," he said, trying to jest.

Dan got up and put on his jacket, indicating to Jeffrey that they were leaving. His son's small hands clenched his sleeve.

"Can Jimmy come over to our house and play for a bit? I want to show him my sandbox and books."

It was nice to see Jeffrey's shyness wearing off. Dan ruffled his hair.

"We can do that if it's okay with his parents," Dan said to Jeffrey with admiration. His son was finally coming out of his shell.

"I can drop Jimmy off later this afternoon if that suits you," Dan asked, already knowing it would be fine by them. The kids were jumping around the yard excitedly.

"Sounds like a plan, boys," Nick said as they approached the cruiser.

"Can we put the lights on?" Jimmy pleaded.

Dan rolled his eyes and laughed.

| 16 |

Tea

The sun glowed bright orange in the late afternoon when she set things up for the barbecue. She basked in its warm rays as it covered the yard in a sparkling blanket. Kate wasn't sure if the intense greenery caused the effect or if the sun was a different color in New Zealand, but it reminded her of a butter commercial on TV.

Nick and Mike hit it off instantly. They were walking the yard's perimeter, beer in hand, looking like they'd been mates since primary school. Nick had that gift with everyone.

She arranged the potato salad, fresh-cut green salad, and this new dish she found at the deli called curried egg salad. The steaks and sausages were ready for the boys to barbecue undercover in the shade of the fire pit.

She hadn't expected to meet any locals for a few weeks after their arrival, knowing that rural living meant neighbors were sparse. She relished the opportunity to entertain their newfound friend. A sense of satisfaction and ownership filled her.

***

"Well, Mrs. Neilson, you certainly know how to put on some good Kiwi tucker. Everything was delicious." Mike said, wiping the sides of his mouth with his napkin. He'd grown accustomed to preparing his own meals and appreciated the company as well as the food they offered.

"Thanks, Mike, we might strike up an arrangement; your help should I ever need it in return for regular meals," Kate teased, but Mike's face said it all; he would do anything to help, and the meals would delight him.

"When are you back, Nick?" Mike asked, finishing his beer.

"I fly out tomorrow and fly back on Thursday. Kate's used to being alone. I've always worked away from home, although I'm uncomfortable leaving her alone without a car with a storm coming. Should we expect damage to the property? Has there been any damage to the property from the previous Nor'westers?" Nick looked at Mike with concern on his face.

Mike's usually stoic face turned dark, and his eyes fell to the ground. "Damage to the house and trees has been minimal in the past. Unfortunately, something happened with the past tenants during a Nor'wester that blew its fury for five straight days a few years ago." Mike's voice lowered.

A chill ran through Kate.

"What happened?" Kate asked, uncertain she wanted to know the answer, her instincts telling her that whatever Mike was about to say wouldn't be easy for her to forget.

"The husband worked at the district bank in Rangiora, and she was a secretary at the medical clinic. Their teenage son attended Rangiora High School. They kept to themselves, mostly having come from the North Island. They had no friends or relatives living close by.

"After three days of continual wind ranging from 120 to 140 kilometers an hour, he started acting strangely at work. They found him talking to himself in his office, repeating the words '*I saw them*' while scribbling faces with black eyes in his dairy.

"His co-workers thought he was burning out and told him to go home early.

"The next day, he didn't show up to work, she was missing from the clinic, and the son wasn't at school. It wasn't long before people started worrying about the new residents.

"The bank called to make sure everything was alright. The bank manager answered the phone and said they had food poisoning and would return to their duties the following day.

"That night, the wind reached its climax. It battered the land with such force that you could have sworn it was trying to peel the grass and roll it up."

Kate and Nick listened as Mike relived the memory.

"The next day, when they didn't show up as expected, the bank called again. No one answered. They reported it to the local police, but the house was vacant when they came to check. There wasn't any reason to think that something had gone awry.

"When the wind finally released its hold on us, the police launched a missing persons investigation. They found the teenage boy drowned in the Okuku River. His mother's body lay beside him, an obvious victim of murder. She had an ax sticking out of her head. They never found her husband." Mike said, his voice tapering off at the unfortunate ending.

Kate sat there wide-eyed, shivering nervously.

"Wow, how long ago was this, Mike?" Nick asked, his face grim.

"They couldn't find anyone to rent the place for over three years. You are the first ones to rent it since it happened."

Nick stood up abruptly, something in his mind clearly disturbing him.

"We found a pile of old rotting carcasses on the far corner of the plantation. We assumed that the prior tenants disposed of their hunting carcasses there."

Mike understood and lifted his hand in a calming manner. "There's a big possibility that someone local used the plantation to dispose of their carcasses because the place has been vacant for quite a while. There are pig hunters in the area, and they wouldn't want to keep bones around their dogs. I can come over on Monday and take care of it properly."

Both Nick and Kate found relief in his offer. Mike quickly changed the subject, noticing Kate's unease.

They continued with their evening, enjoying a few more beers.

Kate couldn't let go of the horrible sensation in her gut. She should have done more research. They found the place advertised for rent on a local classified site when they were still in Australia and had no idea of their new home's history. She downed her beer and tried to focus on the men's conversation.

***

Mike walked down Harper's Road, heading back to his shed. His reservations about joining the Neilsons for tea at Paterson's place were unfounded. He had a great time. Thinking of her new neighbor's situation, he felt for Kate. She was a strong woman. Few could move to a foreign country and be left isolated with a child on their third night.

A gust of wind ruffled his hair, the gravel crunching under his work boots; he walked blindly down the road.

A noise stopped him. He turned to face the direction it came from. He caught sight of a ray of light coming from the Crown Forest, lining the far side of the Paterson place. He strained his eyes to see if he could catch another glimpse of what he saw. He hadn't drunk many beers, but those few beers hit harder than usual. It had been a long time since he let his hair down.

His eyes searched the darkness but found nothing. Mike turned around and continued on his way. When he came to the paved road, he didn't hesitate to cross. There weren't many cars on the main road at night.

A few meters behind him, in the middle of Harper's Road, the shadow of a man stood in the night's gloom.

| 17 |

The Dig

Luke pushed the shovel's blade into the rocky dirt. The digging was hard in the Crown Land compared to the softer soil in the plantation. He had no choice. Now that someone was living at Paterson's place, he couldn't risk them discovering their little secret.

That evening, he spied on them, having a barbecue with that farmer, Mike. His blood boiled seeing them enjoy themselves.

He'd benefited from the locals' spreading rumors about the Paterson place. No one wanted to rent the home after the incident. The bank manager was still missing after all those years. They presumed he killed his wife and son and disappeared to avoid getting caught.

Luke knew better. The bank manager had never left Paterson's place.

Speaking gibberish, the man had ventured outside on that blustery night into the Daltons' yard. Delirious, the man said he could see them, spirits coming out of the ground trying to feed on him. Shannon told Luke to chase the man away. Luke grabbed his shotgun and ran after the man. The bank manager fell into the pond. Luke made sure he never came out.

A slight giggle escaped his lips as he struck the ground with his shovel, overturning large river rocks under the surface. He perceived a presence to his right and straightened himself to face his wife, Shannon.

"This is going to take forever." She rustled the river rocks Luke dug up with her foot. "Dig two holes, Luke. We must move what's buried in the plantation before that worthless cop or dumb farmer meddles to impress the new neighbors. I overheard them talking about what their dog found the other day. It's just a matter of time before those dumbasses go investigating," Shannon said, looking around to make sure they were alone.

"Listen, Shannon, I'll be here for a week trying to dig a hole deep enough, never mind two," Luke said, knowing his whining would be ineffective.

"Shh," she hushedhim. "Keep on going. I'll return to the shed and start cutting the body into smaller pieces; the mess will be easier to bury. I'll bring the wheelbarrow to the fence boundary and dump the pieces there. Grab the wheelbarrow and dump him into the hole. When you finish, take the wheelbarrow to the plantation and shovel the pile. Most of it should fall to bits anyway; it's been there for so long. The moon's covered in clouds; it's a perfect night to do the job. No one will disturb us tonight." She had it all planned out.

Luke swallowed hard. His wife was one brutally powerful woman capable of anything. He knew that if he ever crossed her, he might end up in a hole himself. He nodded and kept on digging.

***

He wiped the sweat from his forehead. Luke shoveled two holes deep enough to cover the body pieces and transfer the old dig spot in the plantation to the Crown Forest. He heard a slight shuffling to his left. Shannon came to the fence with the wheelbarrow filled with several pieces of the Corolla's owner's body.

Shannon dumped the carnage on the other side of the fence, unable to proceed further because of the stock barrier. She jumped over, picking up what looked like a lower leg and a foot, and headed toward Luke.

"Jesus, Shannon, that must have made a hell of a mess! What about all the blood? How are you going to clean that up?"

He trusted her but couldn't afford to let her make a mistake.

"Don't worry about it. I cut the guy up on top of the cesspit. It will be easy to hide, Luke."

Shannon had an answer for everything, Luke thought as he watched her throw the body pieces into the hole and return to pick up more. He followed his wife, picking up the head and an arm and heading back to the hallow.

| 18 |

Alone

She grinned, looking over the macaroni and cheese piled high on her son's plate. She often wondered how all that food could fit inside his little body.

They'd gone to pick up supplies they would need for the week before Nick packed his bag and headed to Christchurch to drop off the truck and fly to Nelson. Alone in the house now with Jimmy, she was determined to try to forget the strange tale Mike told them about the past tenants.

On their way back from town, the clouds spilled over the nearby mountaintops, cascading like a gentle waterfall. There was a warm breeze but nothing more to show that a strong Nor'wester was imminent.

She locked all the doors per her usual routine when Nick was away. This time, she ensured all the pins were secured on the French doors and all the latches on the cased windows were locked. As the sun set, she closed all the curtains, not wanting to face the growing darkness outside.

"Can Chinook sleep inside with me tonight?" Jimmy asked, giving her his puppy-dog gaze that always won his case. She thought about it for a moment. He was already a big dog and would grow substantially bigger. She didn't want to start the habit of having him sleep inside, but her son's bedroom was so far away from hers and the principal part of the house. A ripple of fear ran through her, and before realizing it, she shook her head in agreement with Jimmy.

They walked through the garage to access Chinook's enclosure. He bounced up on his back paws, excited to see them. He calmed down when he was inside, fully understanding he was in for a treat and shouldn't do anything to mess it up. Kate heard a car pull up in the driveway. She peered through her son's bedroom curtains and recognized Dan's cruiser.

"Stay here with Chinook, hunny. I'll talk with Jeffrey's dad." She unlocked the front door. Dan was already at the steps.

"Good evening, Mrs. Neilson." He smiled. "Just calling in to make sure that you have everything you require and that anything that could fly away when the wind comes tomorrow is secured," Dan said, making himself sound authoritarian as Kate gestured for him to enter the house.

"Cup of tea or coffee, Dan?" She was grateful for his visit and wanted him to stay for a bit.

"Nah, I popped in to check on you guys. You might want to move your picnic table, though. It could go airborne in the next few days."

Kate gasped. He must be kidding. "No way, that thing weighs a ton; surely it won't fly away."

Dan laughed and looked at her from the side of his eyes. "Well, the Ngāi Tahu have referred to the Nor'wester as Te Hau Kai Tangata, meaning the wind that devours humankind."

"What's the Ngāi Tahu?" Kate asked curiously.

Dan explained they are the principal Māori iwi tribe of the South Island and had been on the land way longer than the European settlers.

Kate agreed to move the picnic table and followed Dan to the back of the house. They could see lights and hear engine sounds coming from Dalton's place.

"They're moving vehicles again. I can't wait to figure out what they are up to," Dan said, looking toward the neighbor's place.

"They might be moving things to prepare for the wind," Kate responded while Dan picked up his side of the table.

"In the shed?" Dan asked, skeptical. Kate hunched her shoulders and grabbed her side of the table. Dan helped her carry it into its temporary home in the shed. Kate thanked Dan and promised if something went wrong, she would go see Mike.

Unbeknownst to Kate, Dan had spoken to Mike. They'd agreed to check in the new arrivals to ensure they remained safe.

"Hey, I usually run Jeffrey to school in the mornings because the bus picks up the children early. Poor kids must sit on the bus for an hour since they are the first to get picked up. I can bring Jimmy if he would like." Dan offered, and without even asking Jimmy, she agreed. She knew Jimmy would love to ride in a police cruiser to school. She thanked Dan and returned to the confines of the house, locking the door behind her and shutting out the darkness.

On the deck, behind the closed curtain, the shadow of a man stood facing the house, a few centimeters away from the glass of the dining room French doors.

| 19 |

It Arrives

Jimmy waved as he got into the cruiser the next morning. If he was nervous about his first day at his new school, he wasn't showing it.

Dan reassured her Jimmy would return no later than 3:30 p.m. that afternoon. If Dan could pick the kids up, he would; otherwise, they would get dropped off by the bus. She watched the car drive down the driveway and turned to walk back to the house.

The day dawned differently from what the doom and gloom warnings had promised. High-level clouds formed, and only a light breeze tickled the tops of the trees. Picking up Chinook's lead, she descended the dirt road to the paved one. Even if it was a main road, it sported a gravel shoulder suitable for walking. Once she reached the shoulder, she saw Mike across the street, kneeling beside his motorbike. She couldn't see what he was doing and feared he might be injured. She crossed the road and went to the boundary fence.

"Are you alright, Mike?" Kate called out.

Mike looked up and gestured for her to come over. "Hey Kate, come check this out. Just tie Chinook to the fence post and go through the gate."

Kate did as told, wonderment in her eyes as the lambs surrounded her. Her heart melted when she approached Mike. He held three tiny black lambs in his hands, keeping them warm and cleaning them up while the ewe recovered from giving birth. The little black lambs wriggled around, looking for their mother.

He explained that some farmers believe black sheep are a bad omen, but the health of his animals told him differently; each one was a blessing to him. Mike set them next to the ewe and encouraged them to feed. They took to her naturally. Mike stood up, a big smile on his dirt-smudged face.

"Join me for a cuppa?" he asked cheerfully, obviously having a great day.

"Sure. I'll walk Chinook to the shed and meet you there." She looked at the dirty motorbike and decided it would be tidier to walk instead of ride.

He drove off as she made her way toward the shed. She could hear the old kettle whistling as she tied Chinook next to Mike's truck. He greeted her on the porch.

"What do you have in your coffee, Kate?" He waved a jug of milk in the air with a quizzical look.

"Bit of milk and one sugar, please," she answered, examining his modest living quarters. She felt terrible for him. Mike was a good man, probably too nice for his own good. He let his ex-wife march all over him and couldn't stand up to her.

He had his muscular back to her while he prepared their coffees.

"I know it's not much of a place to live, but at least I can still farm my land." He turned to hand her a coffee cup. She noticed the sadness buried deep in his gray-blue eyes. His eyelashes acted like a dam, holding back the pain and embarrassment coursing through his heart.

Kate watched him cut up carrots, onions, and potatoes and add them to the slow cooker before adding beef chunks. She watched him prepare his dinner, his dark lashes contrasting heavily with his messy, light brown hair. Kate couldn't understand how his wife could be so nasty to him. She had no interest in meeting the evil woman.

She barely sipped her coffee when a stock truck turned off from the main road and headed for Mike's drive. His shoulders slumped like someone dropped tons of cement on them.

He mumbled, "Shit, Kevin's fucking pigs." He immediately looked at Kate and apologized for swearing, his head down like a beaten man.

"Who the fuck is Kevin?" Kate said innocently, although she knew who Kevin was from Dan's explanation of Mike's predicament.

Mike chuckled. He seemed relieved that he wasn't alone. She imagined the poor driver would have otherwise faced a more sour version of Mike.

"Have you ever seen a pig close up, Canuck?" he asked.

She shook her head no.

"Well, today's your lucky day. You get to meet the biggest pig in the world; you get to meet Kevin," he laughed. They headed outside.

Mike ensured Chinook had water and wiped down the motorbike with an old towel.

"Hop on," he said, smiling as she climbed behind him on the bike. She grew up riding motorbikes in Canada; this was her first opportunity to ride one since leaving her homeland. They zoomed through the farm to a lush paddock on the shed's left side to let the stock truck in.

A frail, cocky-looking man dressed in a bad suit stumbled down the paddock in gumboots that were too big for him.

"Jesus, he's wearing my boots now," Mike said, his voice showing how discouraged he was.

"He obviously can't fill your boots," Kate said as she winked at him. Mike chuckled.

"I've been stressing about this moment since Mona demanded I relinquish the paddock to Mike for his pigs. Your company is making things easier. Thanks for coming over, Kate." Mike said before they reached Kevin. She nodded, happy to be of help.

"Kev," Mike said, getting off the motorbike and approaching him.

Kate thought the man looked stupid, wearing a suit with gumboots in the middle of a paddock.

"Do you know how to take care of pigs, mate?" Mike asked Kevin as the stock truck unloaded a dozen large pigs into the pristine paddock.

Kevin's nasally voice replied. "Not much to know, mate, they eat anything. Easy as. No worries." He fidgeted with his nose nervously.

Kate thought he was trying to fake an Australian accent; he sounded like a cheap radio advert. She almost giggled but managed to stop herself.

"Kev, this is Kate," Mike said, introducing them to be polite but not explaining that Kate was the new neighbor. Kevin looked at her like he was trying to sum her up. Mike interrupted him.

"Listen, mate, you're the one responsible for these animals. Mona doesn't want me to interfere. Feed them right and make sure you care for them properly," Mike told Kevin as he closed and secured the gate to the pen.

"No worries, mate," Kevin said, replying in his annoying nasal tone.

Mike approached the bike, and Kate followed, his body language indicating he'd already reached his limit with Kevin and needed to leave before he punched his lights out. She hopped on and held on to him.

Once they were far from Kevin, he slowed down, looked at Kate, made a face, and blurted out, "He's such a fuckwit."

Kate laughed heartily as they drove back to the shed. Mike automatically chucked the cold brews and began making coffee again.

"Just a few things you must know when the wind comes this afternoon. As you would know, coming from Canada, high winds in a forest can be hazardous. Keep your eyes up and be wary of falling branches. Also, the rivers swell rapidly with the rain the mountains are getting. It's caught many people off guard, so stay away from the rivers until they subside." She nodded, thankful for getting the heads up.

"I'll get to your dead sheep hole and transfer any bones from there to my pit on the farm. Keep Chinook and Jimmy away; it's messy stuff."

She smiled and looked at him, her eyes showing gratitude without speaking. They sipped their coffee in comfortable silence, looking out at the army of lambs and their mothers.

| 20 |

Cold Shoulder

Kate left Mike's and headed down the road where her supposedly unfriendly neighbors lived. She could see parts of the shed roof poking out from the plantation. From the street fronting the property, she could see the fleet of random vehicles housed under its roof. A large flat area, heavily weeded and derelict looking, served as an improvised parking area near the shed. She kept walking, realizing she could see details of her house through the trees behind the shed. She shuddered, knowing that they could see everything in her yard.

The shed driveway finished at the primary access road, and another driveway disappeared into the thick woods in the other direction. Dan was right. Whatever abode they lived in must have been tiny compared to the hanger-sized shed; its footprint barely made a hole in the canopy of the dense trees.

A white Hilux came out from the driveway she was staring at, frightening her. She instinctively waved at the man and the woman in the truck. The woman sneered and looked the other way, pretending not to have seen her. The man stared at her strangely, a constant and vile stare that sent shivers down her spine. He continued staring until he got on the dirt road and sped away.

Wow! Kate thought to herself. Dan sure wasn't joking! She was glad he'd given her a heads-up. She kept on walking until she reached Harper's Road. The triangle they lived in was a perfect walking track.

| 21 |

Preparations

Lorraine woke early the following day and tip-toed out of the main bedroom, Dan still sleeping soundly. Still upset with him, her fear kept her from being defiant and sleeping in the spare bedroom. She made herself scarce until he left for work.

She had a lot to do after Jeffrey left for school with Dan. She had to install specially designed wind barriers over her roses, the lawn decorations and garden furniture had to go into the shed, and the driveway gates required to be tied open. Tying the gates would make it easier for them when the heavy winds came. Opening them in the wind was difficult, and no one enjoyed leaving the confines of the car in those conditions.

She brought in the last of the laundry and placed candles in every room; it was a frequent occurrence for the power to go out during the Nor'wester. Lorraine went to the kitchen for lunch before her afternoon routine of locking all the windows and doors, which she did twice daily unless Dan was home because he would criticize her.

She hated it when the wind came. She took a bite of her sandwich, contemplating what it would bring this time.

***

Jeffrey arrived before three-thirty that afternoon. The wind was howling its face off; the clouds were whipped by its cruel assault.

Lorraine wanted to go inside, but Jeffrey didn't mind the beginning of the Nor'wester before it got too intense. Since he would need to stay inside most of the week, she stayed with him while he played outside. The skies were mesmerizing to watch.

A glass of wine would be good, she thought to herself. It was past five, and Dan would be home soon. She promised herself she wouldn't bring up the ghost tonight to keep the peace.

The tall grass on the hilly vista in front of her displayed the wind's force as it bounced from one surface to another. She took another sip of wine and heard Dan's cruiser pull up.

***

Dan was in a good mood. Not only was he in a good mood, he was over the moon.

"I think I will join you, beautiful," Dan said, grabbing a beer and sitting beside her on the back porch. They sat in silence, both watching their son play in the sandbox. He remembered the last time the Nor'wester wind came, Lorraine lost the plot before it arrived. She'd duct-taped all the doors and windows shut, making the house a virtual death trap in the event of a fire. His wife raged when he took the tape off for their safety. Here she was tonight, still outside and sipping on her wine.

"Hey, Lorraine, the family that used to own the house gave me photographs of their father a short time before his death and when he was younger." He handed them over to her. She analyzed them intently.

"This is not the same man, Dan. That's not the man I've seen." She looked distraught.

He was hoping this wasn't going to set her off. Dan's mobile startled ringing. He grimaced. Sometimes, he hated the cell phone booster he'd gotten installed. The number on display caused him to worry; a look of concern and curiosity came over his face. Noticing her husband's distress, she turned her attention to him and took another sip of her wine.

"Mike?" Dan answered. Mike had a lot to say. Dan listened intently, his body stiffening. "Shit!" He exclaimed before pausing slightly. "I'll be right there."

Dan looked at his wife as he rose from his chair. "That was Mike. Something isn't right at Paterson's plantation. I need to go, Lorraine. I'm sorry." His tone showed disappointment at the change of plans.

"No, go, Dan. Those two are all alone out there; they need us to watch over them," she said, getting up and holding his jacket for him.

She would have flared into a rage if he'd left her during the Nor'wester, but knowing that Kate and Jimmy were alone, she wanted him to help.

Dan sped off toward Paterson's place.

| 22 |

Bones

Dan parked on the road behind Mike's Navara and met him at the edge of the plantation. The wind spun the tops of the pine trees, making it hard to hear without screaming. Mike was shaking and visually disturbed. Dan's hackles went up, seeing the usually composed man agitated.

"What have you got, Mike?" Dan asked nervously.

Mike unfolded a well-used rag to reveal a hand. It was impossible to decipher if it was a man's or a woman's because of the decomposition, but it couldn't be mistaken for anything else. Dan looked directly at Mike.

"Show me where you found this," Dan said, taking his notepad out.

Mike led him into the depths of the plantation. Near the hole, they could barely see their vehicles at the roadside and couldn't see Paterson's house.

His eyes on the treetops, Mike spoke. "I promised Kate I would dig out the bones and bring them to my dead sheep hole but found the pit already dug up. I moved things around and found a few small bones, and under that rock, the hand."

"Okay, Mike, we can't worry, Kate, about this. We need to keep it low-key for now, at least for tonight. I'll call the station and get a team in. In the meantime, can you help me secure the scene? It's going to be a late one."

Mike nodded in agreement.

"We should get a chainsaw and take down these problem branches before dark; otherwise, the team will be in danger tonight and tomorrow when the wind reaches its peak," Mike suggested.

Dan agreed and set out to complete the task at hand.

***

Both men worked tirelessly to ensure the site was safe for the forensic team. Thankfully, the wind carried the noise of the chainsaw away from Kate and Jimmy's location. They set up lights within a bivouac-style shelter, ensuring they were invisible from the house. The entire front block of the forestry near the road was cordoned off before night brought its darkness. They allocated parking for the team at the front of the plantation and on the shoulder of Mike's side. The sun dropped briskly, the pine trees consuming their rays hungrily. Mike and Dan took a break when the team arrived on site.

"Is she going to be okay out there alone? Do we have a killer on the loose, Dan?" Mike asked, troubled. He'd taken a shine to Kate after she'd made his morning tolerable during the pig drop-off. He wanted nothing more than for her and her family to be safe.

Dan shrugged. "I don't know what's going on, mate, but we will have cops crawling around the place with dogs tonight and tomorrow at least. I'm sorry she has to deal with this while her husband is away, but she is safe with all those blue shirts." Dan did his best to be reassuring.

It dawned on Mike. "She usually walks her dog in the morning right by here. She will wonder what all the hustle is about." Mike looked around helplessly, realizing Kate would find what they were trying to hide.

"Hmm, I will explain what's happened when I pick up Jimmy for school. Can you pop in to make sure she is doing alright tomorrow during the day? I'll talk to her tomorrow morning and bring Jimmy back after school to check in on her. I don't want to ask Lorraine to come over. She'll scare Kate with her ghost stories, especially with what's happened." Both men agreed in silence, looking toward Paterson's place.

***

The forensic team worked fervently under the canopy of dancing pines. They segregated the front of the plantation into sections and brought cadaver dogs to track human remains. One investigator approached the back end of the plantation block closest to the house. He could see light emanating from the property, which was odd since it was two in the morning. He brushed it off; it must be a motion sensor light activated by the wind. He stared at the deck intently. Illuminated by the light, he could see the figure of a man.

| 23 |

Panic

He looked at them, working their way through the plantation, the light from their flashlights bouncing off the tree trunks.

"We are screwed, Shannon!" Luke whispered his terror on full display. "They are going over the old pit. What if they find something? Those fucking neighbors. We should have killed them and made them disappear before they met any locals."

Unbothered by what was unfolding, Shannon took a drag from her smoke and responded.

"You cleaned that shit up Sunday night, Luke. They won't find anything. If they do, how will they trace it back to us? We must stick to our guns if they want to investigate our land. They can't come in without a warrant. In the meantime, spray all the cars and the insides with a strong-smelling disinfectant and soak the shovels in bleach to clean them. We've got to get ready in case they bring the dogs," Shannon instructed as she lounged on their used sofa, puffing on her cigarette.

"Shannon, it was dark. It was the middle of the night. I couldn't see anything. I might not have gotten all of it out; small bones might still be in there. Those guys know the difference between animal and human bones," Luke whimpered, replaying every moment of his gruesome shoveling mission. Had he left any evidence behind?

Shannon stood up and pounded her fist on the counter.

Luke jumped.

"Luke! Shut up and do what I told you to do; otherwise, you will be the next one to go missing."

Luke immediately complied and hurried off. He knew she was serious.

| **24** |

A Terrible Day

Kate woke to her cell phone ringing. How was that possible? Cell coverage was nearly non-existent and most likely nil during the Nor'wester. Staring at it in wonderment, she must have gotten lucky and captured a small wave of signal.

"Babe?" she answered, instantly happy to be talking to her husband.

"Yeah, babe, it's me. I got splendid news. The mine site I was on in Australia called yesterday and offered me a huge raise if I go back. They said they would help pay for my flights back to New Zealand." Nick's voice was booming with excitement while her heart slowly shattered, realizing what would transpire.

"When are you leaving?" she asked, knowing he'd already decided and wouldn't change his mind.

"I fly off this afternoon from Auckland." The excitement in his voice was palpable.

"What about your job here? You can't leave them in a lurch like that. What about us? You swore you wouldn't do this to us again. I've had enough of this circus; we haven't even been in New Zealand for a week, and you leave us high and dry once again." Kate couldn't hold back her disappointment.

"The job was going to be boring and shitty, constantly repeating the same information to different people daily. It's not worth my time!" he replied.

She started crying. She couldn't help it. "But we will be all alone out here." Her voice faltered. She knew she sounded weak but wanted him to realize she was counting on him to do the right thing this time.

"No, you won't, not for long. The mining company told me I could have a few weeks of leave in three or four months. We can plan a vacation and maybe go exploring our new country." His voice tried to be soothing, although his excitement ruined the effect.

"Three or four months! Are you serious, Nick?" She took a deep breath. "Nick, I don't have a car to get around in, and we are far from town." The entire gamut of what was occurring hit her, and she struggled to contain her sobs.

"Just ask Dan to bring you into town, take a grand from the savings account, and buy a used car. Come on, Kate, you know how to take care of yourself, and it's not the first time you've been alone. Listen, I need to go, Chuck's calling. He's picking me up from the airport to grab a beer before I leave for the mine site. Love you, babe. Talk soon."

The line went dead.

Her mouth was open, ready to argue and beg him to reconsider. She looked at her phone and realized that it was too late. She sat on the side of the bed, her face buried in her hands, and sobbed. He'd done this to her when she first got to Australia, and he was doing it again. A rash of worry spread through her brain, making her body shake.

The light of day creeping in did nothing to comfort her, the howling wind adding an ominous layer to the news she'd received. She got up, put on her dressing gown, and headed for the kitchen to plan her way out of her situation.

***

Dan's picking up Jimmy earlier than he did yesterday, she thought as she heard his cruiser come up the driveway. She immediately saw apprehension in his face and thought about her red, puffy eyes. He greeted Jimmy at the door, telling him to play with Jeffrey and that they would start school later today. Kate wondered what was happening, but before she could ask, Dan beat her to it and asked if she was okay. Trying to keep her composure, she explained her situation, tears uncontrollably flowing from her eyes. Dan's expression said it all; the lines on his face mirrored her disappointment.

"Oh, I'm so sorry, Kate. I'm sad for you. Don't worry. You have good people looking after you and Jimmy. Everything will be alright."

Kate accepted his hug. It made her feel better. "I need to find a car," she said sheepishly. "Nick thought I could buy a used one in Rangiora."

A look of alarm marked Dan's face. "Yeah! No! You are guaranteed to get ripped off at Kevin's car dealership. Let me work on it. I'll pick up the boys after school and bring them back. Something has happened that you need to know about. Mike set off to pick up the pile of bones that Chinook had dug up last night. He found the pile already removed but…." He looked down and swallowed. "He found a hand."

Kate's mind was spinning. She held her head in her hands. "What!" she yelled, panic and fear bubbling inside her. She fought back the vile image that came to her head.

"We know little yet and are working hard to figure out what's happened. The team is set up at the front of the plantation, scouring everything for clues. They might bring in the dogs to search the entire property. Listen, Kate, you are safe here. There are more than a dozen inspectors and officers working around you. You call out, and they will automatically come to help you."

Kate felt sick. She could no longer contain herself and sobbed uncontrollably. Dan put his hand on her shoulder and told her everything would be alright. She didn't believe him.

"You stay here today with Chinook while Jimmy is at school. I will do my best to keep the press away and keep this under wraps. The less the public knows, the better it is for us. We can't give whoever has done this notice that we've discovered their secret if we want to catch them.

Kate nodded and wiped away her tears. A flash of red and blue lights coming from the driveway startled her.

"Damn, the boys figured out how the lights work. You'd better go before they figure out how the siren works. I'll see you this afternoon." With that promise, he hurried back to his cruiser.

Kate did her best to keep calm. The wind's constant whistle was not something she'd seen before, and it amazed her how the clouds moved swiftly above her head. The warm, dry air felt like a blanket, comforting her from the loneliness surrounding her heart. She sat outside, her long black hair whipping around her face, dancing to the beat of the invisible force surrounding her.

| 25 |

Old Faithful

Mike pulled up Matt's drive, appreciating the lush paddocks his mate had worked so hard for. At one point, the land was sour and covered in weeds. Matt worked the reluctant land, coaxing it into submission and transforming it into high-quality feed. The cattle he grazed for his brother's neighboring dairy farm were in top form.

Melissa, his wife, exited the stalls where she was tending to her horses and waved.

"Good day, mate. What brings you to our neck of the woods?" She gave him a big hug when he exited his truck.

Melissa and Matt were childhood sweethearts. You couldn't imagine one without the other. He'd been the best man at their wedding and helped them build the house they were living in on the section of land they inherited when Matt's father passed away. Initially, he'd left the entire dairy farm to Matt and Eric, but Eric took control soon after his father's death and, with the help of lawyers, eventually took over the whole farm. Matt was close to his father and was heartbroken when he passed away. He couldn't find the capacity within himself to fight Eric in court. The brothers kept a cold distance since then, with Eric working the dairy farm and Matt grazing the cattle.

"Where's the old boy?" he asked Melissa as he scanned the land before them.

"Out by the effluent pond, I reckon. Matt mentioned there were issues with it and wanted to ensure it was compliant. It's technically Eric's problem, but it's sitting on our boundary. He doesn't want to be responsible for something Eric should have taken care of." Her shoulder-length blonde hair lashed her face as it danced with the wind.

"Righto! You take care, Melissa," Mike winked, tipping his cap. He got into his truck and drove down the dirt path to the pond. He was halfway there when he met Matt, returning to the sheds.

"Good day, mate, lovely breezy morning," Matt smiled broadly, seeing his mate. They often laughed off the Nor'wester at the start of its course. It was no longer a laughing matter after a few days of fighting with the wind, trying to bore through their souls. Matt noticed the worry in Mike's eyes.

"What's up, mate?" Matt asked.

"Do you still have my old Land Rover hunting truck stashed here? If it is and you aren't using it, I need to take it over for a few weeks." Mike caught his hat before it flew away in the rogue gust of wind.

"Yeah, mate, she's still sitting in the covered-in yards. Something wrong with the Navara?"

Mike explained what happened at Paterson's place. Dan popped in before driving the kids to school and told him how Kate had been left high and dry, alone in the middle of nowhere, having just arrived in the country.

"Damn!" Matt exclaimed sincerely. "That poor thing. I feel bad for her. I should get Melissa to take one of her horses out and call in to meet her."

Mike nodded as both men fell into a pensive silence, thinking of Kate's predicament.

***

Kate heard a car come up Harper's Road. Apprehension filled her.

What could it be now? she asked herself, her eyes rolling upwards as she shook her head.

It was Mike's pickup truck headed for the farmlands toward the hills. She relaxed slightly.

She tried her best to stay occupied that morning and take her mind off her husband. What a piece of work, abandoning her in such an unpleasant situation. She prepared herself a bowl of soup and a sandwich for lunch but had no appetite. To keep busy, she weeded the long expanse of plantings next to the driveway. Not knowing New Zealand's flora, she couldn't figure out what was a weed and what was a native plant; all the plants growing seemed too beautiful to be weeds.

She heard another vehicle coming, her body relaxing at the sight of Mike's truck. He pulled up and jumped out as she came to meet him.

"Good day, Kate," Mike said, tipping his old worn-out cap.

Kate, emotional, tried her best to keep the tears she walled up from spilling out. She bit her lip to control her emotions while she looked down, embarrassed. He felt her pain and instinctively wrapped his powerful arms around her. She melted in his grasp, sobbing quietly.

"It's going to be okay, Kate. Everything is going to be fine. You are not alone."

His words shocked her. She'd only met the man a few days ago but felt like he took responsibility for her care.

"Dan came by the farm this morning before he dropped off the kids at school and told me what's happened." He wrung his cap in his hands for fear of it flying away.

She shuffled her feet while looking down at the ground, embarrassed at her show of weakness but unable to muster any strength.

"What am I going to do, Mike? I need to buy a used car so I can get around. Nick doesn't think he will return for another three to four months. I only have supplies until the end of the week. I was hoping to look for a job to keep me occupied. What they discovered in the plantation is freaking me out." Suddenly realizing that Mike was the one to come across the gruesome finding, she put her hand on his arm.

"I'm sorry you found what you did, Mike. It makes my blood run cold thinking about it." Her voice cracked as the color ran out of her face.

"Hey, don't think about it. I am sure that Dan and his crew will find an explanation soon." He knew all too well that he didn't sound convincing.

"Anyway, I have something for you." He smiled and presented her with the keys to the Navara. Kate looked up at him, confused.

"You can borrow the Navara for as long as you need it," he proclaimed proudly.

"What! No, Mike, you need that truck. What will you drive?" Kate signaled with her head that she couldn't take him up on his offer.

"I have the old Land Rover hunting truck. It's a bitch to drive, constantly breaks down, and is about as dependable as Mona." He laughed, breaking the heavy moment.

"I think you should drive something safer and easier to handle. I've owned the old Land Rover since high school. She's like an old friend. I know her well, so it's easy for me to fix it," he said confidently.

Still incredulous at the offer, Kate couldn't find it in herself to accept the generous present.

"I can't, Mike. I would feel bad using it without paying, and I need a job before I can pay you. It's too big of a gift," she said, embarrassed.

Mike looked her over and came up with a solution. "I'll tell you what, Kate, I need help to feed a few miss-mothered lambs. If you come and help me, that will be payment enough."

She could see that he was serious. Excited at the prospect of being around the little bundles of joy, a smile erupted on her face. "Thanks, Mike, I would love that. I've never been around stock before, but I promise I'm a quick learner."

"Perfect," Mike said. "If you are not doing anything right now, how about you drive me home and meet your newly adopted woolly children?"

Kate smiled and looked up into Mike's eyes, enormous relief apparent in every fiber of her being. They jumped into the truck and drove silently past the installation the forensic team set up at the front of her property.

| 26 |

Insanity

Lorraine patiently waited for Dan to return from his callout at Paterson's place. As the wind picked up its pace and the last remnants of the sunlight lost their strength, her unease increased. Jeffrey had gone to bed after eating leftovers for dinner. She felt alone, jumping at every sound the wind made.

Sitting at the kitchen table, a slight movement in her peripheral vision made her look toward the dining room window. Standing there, a few centimeters from the glass, was the shadow of a man. Her hands flew to her mouth as she stifled her scream, not wanting to wake Jeffrey. Her heart beating erratically, she hid near the lounge door, struggling to keep herself sane. She peaked back at the dining-room window, hoping she'd imagined the man. There was no one there.

Moving quickly, she gathered all the foil and baking paper stored in the pantry and set out to cover each window so that no one could look in and she couldn't see out. Once she finished covering all the glass in the house, she triple-checked the locks on the doors and windows. She made sure all the lights were on, except for Jeffrey's room, and sat in the middle of the living room floor, holding the fireplace poker. She cracked open another bottle of wine.

The cacophony the wind performed as it hit the house and nearby trees was like a diabolical orchestra to her. She rocked nervously, gulping down her red wine as if it were a medicine that would cure her ailment. The lights flickered; it made her jump. Her heart raced to near-critical levels. She thought she could hear voices outside calling to her, taunting her. She grabbed at her ears desperately, pulling out clumps of her hair, the strands poking between her fingers. Her body rocked violently; she gulped the rest of the wine.

She thought she heard Jeffrey calling. Her heart begging that she wouldn't need to go through the house to his room, she winced as she looked up. The man stood a few centimeters away from her, his dark face shielded by his gray hoodie. Lorraine lost control of her faculties and passed out, soiling herself.

***

Dan arrived home at five thirty that morning. He had briefed the team and secured the area; he had done his job for now. He unlocked the front door and stood appalled at what he saw when he entered his home. Paper and foil covered the window like an insane person tried to gift wrap a gift they didn't care to give.

In the middle of the living room, passed out with a bottle of wine next to her, was Lorraine, sitting in a puddle of her urine. Dan's rage flared. What a mess she created. He tried to rouse her, but she was still obliviously drunk. He picked her up, noticed the clumps of hair between her fingers, and shivered. She's losing it, he thought as he brought her to their ensuite so she could clean herself up.

A dead weight, she didn't assist in his efforts.

Disgusted, he lay her at the foot of the shower in case she needed to vomit. He returned to the lounge and started taking down the foil and baking paper she used to cover the windows, the tape peeling off little flecks of paint where the adhesive bit down hard. He couldn't bear for Jeffrey to see the house like this and worked fastidiously to cover his wife's disturbing behavior.

He piled up all the paper and foil in a rubbish bag. Ironically, the bag reminded him of the wrapping paper they would end up with on Christmas day. He placed the bag in the garage, shaking his head. The puddle of urine in the middle of the lounge took longer to clean.

Satisfied he had done his best, Dan checked on Lorraine. She hadn't moved. He headed for the spare bedroom for an hour's worth of sleep before he needed to wake Jeffrey up. Dan felt like a broken man.

| 27 |

Shot Down

Kate followed Mike to a pen he'd prepared next to his shed for the miss-mothered lambs. Four innocent white faces beamed at her, their little tails whipping wildly.

"Unfortunately, these wee lambs born this morning got all muddled up because of the wind. The first one sometimes gets lost when the mother is busy giving birth to twins or triplets. With the wind howling, they cannot hear each other's cries, and often, the lamb gets cast aside by its mother. If we don't feed them, they won't survive," Mike explained, taking out the milk powder and mixing bowls.

He showed Kate how to prepare the milk supplement, check the condition of the lambs, and ensure proper suckling before introducing the bottle. She looked like a natural, the little lamb nestled close to Kate's chest, drinking the warm formula with vigor.

"They are insatiable and can often drink until their bellies are too full, causing gastrointestinal issues. They can also get milk in their lungs, so we must watch for that. If you think that is happening, take the bottle away and give them a minute or two before you give it back to them," Mike explained patiently.

Kate was in heaven. She forgot the drama and disappointment since she'd arrived and reveled in the loving look the sheep gave her when she fed it, protected in her warm arms.

"It's not fair, Mike. This isn't fair payment for the use of your truck. I feel like I should pay you for the opportunity to do this." She looked at him with admiration in her eyes.

"Well, here's the catch. We need to feed the lambs every two to three hours for the first few weeks, and the pen will fill up with the Nor'wester coming during lambing time. It's a big job." Kate was shocked that they needed feeding that often.

"Oh! It's a good thing you lent me your truck then, Mike," she teased.

He laughed wholeheartedly. Kate had yet to hear him laugh like that; it made her happy.

"I'll do nightly feedings, and you can take over day feedings. Deal?" He grabbed one lamb and looked it over while waiting for her answer.

"Deal," she responded enthusiastically.

"I can't pay you a lot, but I have a ton of vegetables in the garden, spare meat in the freezer, and catch enough fish from the rivers to help you with food," he said humbly.

"You don't need to pay me; using your truck is more than enough. I have savings from writing business plans, which should carry us over until I can write more." She was thankful for hiding her proceeds from Nick, as they would most likely have disappeared by now.

She looked down at the lamb about to fall asleep in her arms. "Thanks for doing this for us, Mike. I don't know what I would have done without you." She looked at him sincerely as he popped a Speights ball cap on her head.

"Sun's harsh here; you must wear a hat," he smiled brightly.

***

Three-thirty came in a flash. She was shocked to see Dan's cruiser coming up the paved road. Mike waved at him, and Dan pulled over to meet them at the edge of the boundary fence.

"Kate, Mike," Dan greeted them. "Get a vehicle sorted?"

"Yup," Mike responded, got Old Faithful from Matt's shed. Kate's going to take over the Navara for the time being. Old Faithful is, unfortunately, nothing like its namesake. Please look the other way until I can get it to the mechanic for a warrant in the next day or two. It's been sitting in the yards for a few years now, not needing registration."

Dan laughed and motioned his compliance with his head. "No worries, mate," he responded heartily.

Jimmy disembarked the cruiser struggling, holding on to the door to prevent it from bending back in the wind, and met Kate at the fence.

"Why don't you show Jimmy your new job, Kate? I think he'll be jealous," Mike chuckled.

The men watched Kate and Jimmy walk away toward the shed.

"That's bloody good of you, Mike, to help her like that. Poor thing. Imagine being in that predicament," Dan praised Mike.

The big man shook his head and answered. "I have her feeding the stay lambs. There are bound to be more coming because of this wind. What was he thinking, leaving her alone here? He should wind his neck in and be a real man." Catching himself becoming more upset than he should have, he changed subjects and asked if they'd found anything more in the plantation.

"Yeah, a few vertebrae and what they think is an ankle bone. They will need to scour the rest of the property with dogs tonight. Hopefully, we find nothing more; otherwise, the entire property will be a crime scene."

"At least she will be safe tonight with all those people around the house," Mike added, looking over at the vehicle coming up his drive to the shed. "Damn, it's Mona," he said, dejected. Dan picked up on the situation and quickly bid Mike his farewell.

***

Mona made it to the shed before him. He could hear her screaming, the disgust at her behavior burning at his temples.

"What the fuck are you doing on my property?" she yelled at Kate. "You have no right to be here interfering with my husband and my farm," she lashed out, towering over Kate, who was crouched down holding a lamb for Jimmy to feed. Kate was relieved to set eyes on Mike. She wanted out of the situation and pleaded wordlessly with him.

Mike's face was full of rage. He bellowed loudly. "Mona! Outside. Now!"

She stumbled backward, wide-eyed, like an invisible hand had slapped her across the face. Mike had never spoken to her in that way. She blinked and silently followed Mike outside the shed. Kate could still see them, the wind battling her bleached hair, making her look like a tacky Medusa statue.

Having no care that his hat had blown away, Mike waved his finger at her while his hair pulled back from the force of the wind.

"Don't you dare, Mona!" his voice thundered.

"What the fuck is she doing here, Mike? Who the fuck is she? This is bullshit, and you'll pay for this. How dare you cheat on me?" she spat at Mike.

He slowly wiped his wet cheek, trembling.

"It's over, Mona. Whatever you and I had was gone before you moved Kevin into our home. You have no business coming here or asking questions. It's none of your concern anymore. You don't want to see me around the house, fine, but guess what, Mona? I don't want you around my shed, either. Get back into your car, fuck off home, and don't come back!" His eyes were shooting as many bullets as his mouth was.

Stung and flabbergasted at his abrupt transformation, she once again was speechless. Stumbling, she walked back to her car, turning before she got in.

"You'll pay for this," she threatened as she sped up the drive, the wind twirling the dust she created into ghostly apparitions.

***

"I'm sorry. That was Mona, my ex-wife. She's nuts," Mike said, his head low, his boot kicking at the hard ground.

Kate lifted herself from kneeling next to the pen, put a hand on Mike's arm, and looked at him in the eyes. She didn't need to say anything. He could feel her support.

Jimmy was sitting in the pen, four little sheep climbing over him.

"Hey, do you guys want to grab some pizza at the Lodge tonight? I feel like celebrating, and I think you guys deserve a break. What do you think?" he ruffled Jimmy's hair.

Seeing that he had finally gotten something off his chest and wanted to enjoy his newfound confidence, Kate thought it was a brilliant idea.

"Sounds great, Mike. Where is the Lodge? How should I dress?" Kate asked nervously as she looked for confirmation from Jimmy.

He quickly nodded his agreement.

Mike realized that although so much had happened in a short time, Kate didn't know the lay of the land yet.

"Wear something nice, like country casual, and leave the rest to me. How about six o'clock?"

Jimmy looked up from his woolly paradise and smiled brightly.

"It's a plan," Kate smiled.

| 28 |

Paranoid

Luke was pacing back and forth in their little shack.

The kids had gone to school, and Shannon was out of town picking up groceries using a stolen credit card. It wouldn't have been worthwhile if they had to pay for diesel, but they easily siphoned any diesel they needed from their collected vehicles. He enjoyed dealing with the cars. He wished he could keep some of them, but Shannon said it would eventually blow their cover. They'd become skilled and no longer hesitated to kill the vehicle's occupants.

He remembered his first time and shook his head. He kept throwing up, and Shannon had to cut the guy up herself, barely sleeping for weeks until they did it again. In time, he became complacent to the vulgarities of the task.

The wind pounded the forested ceiling surrounding his cabin. Paterson's place was crawling with K9s. His gut churned as his complacency haunted him. He wanted to go out there and check, but Shannon told him to stay away. She wouldn't allow him to go into the car shed. Had he left anything behind that they could track back to him? What if they identified some remains and discovered he'd owned their car? Was it possible to know whose car it was after Barry did his thing? They couldn't track those cars back to those bodies, right? Luke was panicking.

He walked outside, making sure that he stayed close to the cabin. He could make out three cops with cadaver dogs brought in from Christchurch when he peered through the trees. They were grid-searching the entire property. One pair stopped at the corner of the road and the Crown Forest and motioned to the others that they found something. Luke looked on; a slight humming noise surrounded him, his blood pressure increasing as his heart beat faster.

"The dog found something. Fuck! Maybe I dropped something when I wheeled the corpses from the plantation pit to the Crown Forest in the wheelbarrow," he whispered.

Luke bit the side of his nail, tearing a piece of skin off. The hum increased steadily as he strained his eyes to see. From the commotion, his gut knew before his mind could admit it. They found a body part. Luke hurriedly returned to the confines of the shack, his head swimming in despair. He paced around the table before collapsing on an old chair, holding his head to steady the buzzing from the loud hum he was hearing.

"Arghh, stop it," he begged the invisible force torturing him. He clutched at his ears, violently tearing the skin that attached them to his skull, blood trickling down the side of his face.

He got up, walked to the kitchen, grabbed a ladle, and dunked it in the bucket of rainwater. The hum was so loud that it penetrated his brain like a hot poker. He poured the water on his head, hoping to resolve the pain. It made it worse. He impulsively turned to the doorway and hit his head on the frame, trying to knock the noise out. His breath coming in gasps, he struggled to breathe, the humming noise so abusive that he wondered if he was dying. He picked up the butcher's knife from the bench. The same knife he used to kill and dismember so many people in the past few years and aimed for his eye.

| **29** |

The Lodge

Kate and Jimmy arrived at the house to see a dozen or more people working on the grounds. What she saw at the boundary of the Crown Forest convinced her they'd found something else: a taped perimeter and a bivouac tent secured to survive a hurricane surrounded by a team in blue.

"Jimmy, do you know why the police are here working?" she probed, wondering how she would explain the situation to him.

"Yup, Officer Dan told us it's because they found something interesting, like on TV when they explored the pyramids. They don't know what it is yet, but he said it was like a boring piece of wood," he casually explained. "He came to school to explain why they were here, so kids don't mess with the dig site. No one at school cared about the old piece of wood they found anyway."

She sighed thankfully.

Upon entering the house, she recalled her conversation with Nick that morning and tried to call him before getting ready. The police installed a cell booster tower for their operations, giving her full coverage. She looked outside at the trees getting beaten by the wind's invisible fists while waiting for the line to connect. It rang once, and when the line picked up, she called his name only to hear a message.

"This cellular customer is not available. Please leave a message," the tone-deaf computer responded.

She would need to wait until he called her with his new Australian number.

Disappointment filled her heart. She knew she could never forgive Nick this time. She instructed Jimmy to wear a shirt and chinos and finish his homework before leaving for tea. Jimmy dashed for the confines of his bedroom, excited to go out for dinner.

She turned on the shower in the ensuite and got undressed. The warm water felt wonderful on her skin as it washed away the smell of the lambs. As the water cascaded down her dark hair to the curve in her back, she relived the drama from the past week. She finished washing, grateful for the blessings her newfound friends bestowed on her.

"Hmm... what to wear?" she said out loud, looking over her meager closet. She didn't enjoy shopping much, so she purchased her clothing with a classic style that would stand the test of time. Following fashion trends that changed seasonally meant too many shopping trips for her. As a single mother for years, she knew you could always pull off second-hand or older clothes if they were classics. She picked a cross-over black, small-print floral dress that reached over her knees at the front and extended slightly longer at the back. She thought the low-heeled black sandals would do the trick as she returned to the bathroom to dry her hair.

A sharp cry escaped her lips at what she saw in the mirror. A handprint, fingers wide open, cleared the mirror of its steam coating. She hurriedly investigated the bedroom, the walk-in closet, and again in the bathroom for anyone, but no one was there.

"Jimmy?" she called to her son, trying to keep her voice steady. "Did you come into Mom's bathroom?"

A little voice from the house's far reaches, drowned by the wind whistling outside, confirmed he hadn't. "No, Mom, finishing my homework."

She stepped back into the bathroom, incredulous at what she saw. A memory from her childhood came rushing back: shaving cream. They'd use it to prevent fog on mirrors. She thought it was a simple prank they set up when they cleaned the house before their arrival, wiping the mirror down with a towel.

She hastily tied a portion of her hair, leaving most of it to flow over her shoulders. She applied mascara to bring out her green eyes, raspberry lip stain to her plump lips, and a splash of her favorite fragrance. She noticed that the steam in the shower was still thick, filling the inside of the cubicle like smoke. She should treat it to shaving cream, she thought, as she crossed the door frame out of the bathroom into the hallway.

Immediately after her departure, a hand appeared on the shower glass door, leaving its mark on the fog.

***

"This truck is so cool, Mom," Jimmy said as they drove to Mike's.

Mike left the confines of the shed to greet them, looking different from what she expected. He swapped his dirty gumboots, short two-toned shorts, and a bush shirt for something more refined. His fitted dark jeans and light blue checked shirt suited him so perfectly that he could have been a spokesperson for the clothing company. She immediately thought of Mona and questioned her sanity, pushing this good man away.

"You are looking quite beautiful this evening, Mrs. Neilson," she heard him say as she held on to the truck door and the hem of her dress for fear of losing both to the wind. The comment made her smile. She looked at him, beaming.

"Shall we get going?" Mike asked, leading them to a shed that housed his motorbike and a smaller all-terrain vehicle. Mike cleaned his bike; it was spotless and looked new. The miniature bike took Jimmy's interest right away. He climbed on it without asking for permission, engrossed in the toy.

"Jimmy, ask first," Kate scolded, but Mike merely turned on the ignition, started the engine, and presented Jimmy with a helmet.

"You know how to drive one of these, boy?" Mike asked, looking directly at him to ascertain his skill level.

"Yeah, my granddad and uncle in Canada showed me how when I was a kid." Jimmy showed him he knew the basics of the bike.

Satisfied, Mike nodded.

"Hop on," he motioned to Kate with a smile. She sat sideways, folding her dress under her, and held on tight to Mike.

"Follow me," he said to Jimmy.

They exited the shed into the wind and headed for the side entrance of the property. Instead of getting on the road, Mike veered to follow it, driving between it and the shelter belt hedge bordering his land. Kate was now truly wondering what Mike was up to. Where were they going? He said pizza, right? She was at a loss. He slowed down to check on Jimmy and flashed her a big smile. His excitement transformed him. He seemed to have gotten younger since this afternoon.

After a short drive down the road next to his farmland, the road ended abruptly at two carved wooden gates. He motioned to Jimmy to park beside him and turned off his bike.

Kate was overtaken by what stood in front of her. A huge church transformed into a luxury lodge stood like a monument at the end of the road. Mike opened the gate and gestured them in. The wind died down inside the lodge's garden, the brunt of the fury absorbed by the heavy shrubs and trees surrounding them. The gardens were stunning. Rock walls held exotic-looking flowers upright, and an intricate waterfall feature emptied itself into a Koi Pond. He led them to the church's oversized wooden doors.

"Welcome to your local watering hole," Mike said, the pride at being the first to show her the fantastic place displayed on his face.

She looked around, awestruck. They'd converted a stunning church into a bar and restaurant. The craftsmanship of the church's wooden details was exceptional. It was hard to tear your eyes from the work of art they achieved on the ceiling. The publican at the bar interrupted her reverie.

"Mike! How are you, mate?" He was already pouring him a glass of beer. "Are you keeping out of the wind?"

"Mate, you know how impossible that is," Mike answered as he picked up his beer. "John, let me introduce to you Kate Neilson and her son, Jimmy. They are renting Paterson's old place." John quickly looked at him, but Mike pretended not to notice.

"Kate, this is John Wigmore, the owner of this fine establishment," Mike said, lifting his glass.

"Welcome, Kate, Jimmy," John smiled and nodded. "Pleasure meeting you. What can I get you, darling? It's on the house."

Being her first time at a bar in New Zealand and knowing little about the local beer, she didn't know what to order. She heard Mike mention Speight's, and he'd given her a ball cap with Speight's written on it. She gathered up her courage and spoke.

"A good old Speights mate... please," Kate asked in a distinctly Canadian accent. John burst out laughing as he poured her a beer.

"This one will fit right in, I reckon," John nodded approvingly to Mike.

She thought she could see a blush appear on Mike's face, but he hastily looked away.

They sat down at a table near the enormous stained-glass windows. Another couple with two children, a boy Jimmy's age and a younger girl, entered the bar. Jimmy recognized Callum, his schoolmate, and asked if he could play with him. Kate approved, and all three children went to play outside in the sheltered garden. Mike turned his attention to Kate.

"Didn't know, did you, that there was a pub and restaurant only a short walk from your place?" he teased, his eyes sparkling with glee.

"Certainly didn't," Kate replied and laughed at the wonderment of it all. They sat and chatted effortlessly. Mike asked her about her life in the frozen north of Canada, and she asked him about life in New Zealand.

Meanwhile, the forensic crew went through the new find in the Crown Land Forest.

| 30 |

It Ends

Kate took effortlessly to her new routine. In the mornings, Dan picked up Jimmy after she got him ready and packed hers and Mike's lunches. Once everything was locked and secured, she would head off to Mike's with Chinook tied to the back of the truck and tend to the group of miss-mothered lambs for their first feeding of the day.

Mike would always be there to greet her with coffee, no matter how early he started working on the farm, fencing and fixing gates.

Morning coffee with Mike was the best part of the day. It made for a good start as the blustery wind beat the land with its frenzy. She'd never lived with this type of phenomenon, and it awed her more than scared her. She often wondered why the locals made such a big deal out of the Nor'wester.

"It's supposed to die down this afternoon," Mike said as if tapping into her mind. "This wasn't a bad one. We got lucky."

A cloud of dust made them look toward the driveway's entrance. Mike followed Mona's Landcruiser with his eyes as it drove to his makeshift mailbox. She dropped something inside and sped away.

"Great, here we go again?" Mike's disdain was apparent in every word. "I'll be right back."

He got on the motorbike, held on to his hat, and drove away. Kate watched him head to the letterbox, the wind whipping the dust into creepy formations. He opened what looked like a letter and read it while holding on to it with both hands, trying to stop the paper from tearing or flying away. He stuffed the letter in the front pocket of his bush shirt and drove back to the shed with a wide grin.

"Whoo-hoo!" he hollered when he reached Kate. "The kids are coming this weekend for three days since it's Father's Day. Mona and Kevin will be in Queenstown. I get to see the kids for three days straight!" The news overjoyed him. "Hey, do you and Jimmy want to come for a barbecue tomorrow afternoon? The kids would love to meet Jimmy and ride the motorbikes with him," he said straight after.

It was hard to address that he might have been over-enthusiastic in inviting them.

She replied calmly. "Are you sure? Don't you want to spend the time alone with your kids since you haven't seen them in a long time?"

He replied without hesitation. "This will be good for the kids. They worry about me when it's lambing time, working the farm alone. They used to help before their mother sent them away to boarding school. Kelly and Jake took turns feeding the lambs since Mona refused to help. They will love meeting you and seeing me happy. It's been a long time since I have smiled, Kate. I want my kids to see me happy."

He looked directly into her eyes, embarrassment showing on his face. Or was it vulnerability? She knew he wasn't the type to speak of his feelings and left it at that.

"Sounds outstanding, Mike. We would love to come," she smiled back at him.

His eyes shone bright with joy and excitement.

"Well, I have a hungry tribe of wee lambs to feed Farmer Mike, and you are interfering with my work," she said as she placed her hands on her hips.

They both laughed and headed off to their duties.

***

Kate packed a pressed sandwich lunch for them, and Mike made a salad from the vegetable garden. They sat on his little porch for the first time since Monday, the wind having substantially lessened. They could finally bear to eat outside. The meteorologists predicted it would last five days, and they were correct. Friday afternoon finally gave them the respite they deserved.

The lambs were feeding well, and the ewes proved to be good mothers. As per habit, Kate started counting them to ensure none were missing. Her eyes shifted back to the road to see what she thought was Dan's cruiser, followed by two more police cruisers with their lights on. She held her breath as they headed for Shannon and Luke Dalton's place. Kate looked over at Mike in alarm. Wide-eyed, Mike looked back at her, shaking his head and showing he didn't know what was happening. The forensic team packed up and left this morning. Could this be related?

Kate and Mike sat eating quietly, looking forward to Dan dropping off Jimmy so he could report back.

| 31 |

Deception

When Shannon entered the shack that Tuesday, she saw Luke with a crazed look, about to plunge a knife into his head.

"Luke!" she shrieked. "What the fuck are you doing?"

Luke, wild-eyed, dropped the knife and faced Shannon. He grabbed at his ears like a wounded animal.

"The noise, Shannon, the loud humming noise, I can't breathe, it's killing me," he whined.

"The police found something. I might have dropped some bones when we moved everything to the other side. What if they come here and think I had something to do with it? What if they find the burial holes in the Crown Forest, Shannon? What if they find out what we've been doing?"

Frantic now, he paced around the table only to stop and hold on to it for support. He raised his head.

"We are fucked, Shannon." He looked at her in despair.

"Shut up, Luke." She approached him slowly. "We can't have them coming over here snooping. You've got to keep your cool; otherwise, you'll blow our cover. Show me where they found something."

He led her outside, still grasping at his ears. She followed him, realizing how much of a liability he was. He lifted his arm and pointed to the area cordoned off by the Crown Forest.

Shannon quickly swung the butcher knife she'd picked from the table and slashed Luke's exposed forearm. He recoiled wide-eyed immediately, looking at his wife in disbelief as the blood started pumping out from the gash in his forearm.

"What! Shannon! What are you doing?" he screeched, his voice nearly lost to the wind.

He swayed as he looked at the copious amount of blood pooling at his feet. Grabbing at his forearm, his efforts to stop the bleeding were futile. He dropped to his knees, near the point of fainting.

She took the opportunity to gash the inside of his other forearm.

"It's going to look like you've fucked yourself up on purpose, Lukee Boy!" she laughed.

Luke couldn't take any more: his eyes rolled back in his head, and he crumpled backward.

She looked down at him with disgust, spitting in his face. When his muscles stopped twitching, she dragged him to the cesspit and dropped him in, covering the pit with its heavy lid.

***

Shannon waited for days for the police to come and interview her about the gruesome findings at their neighbor's house. She'd conjured up a proper explanation. Luke went missing on Wednesday morning after everyone caught wind of what the police found at Paterson's place. She suspected his involvement. He must have left to avoid getting caught.

The wind helped move the smell coming from the cesspit. With the wind dying down, the stench of Shannon's husband's rotting corpse was unbearable. It would alarm the neighbors or any cops coming back to snoop around. She had to get rid of the situation fast. Shannon cracked open the cesspit lid enough for them to believe a man could fall in. She drove to the police station and requested they visit her house to investigate. Luke was missing, and there was an awful smell.

***

Talbot was first on the scene, noting that no cars were in the shed. Shannon ensured they disappeared during the week in the night's dark and howling wind. When they entered the shack, she had her two daughters sitting at the table, setting the scene she wanted.

He took out his notebook and interrogated her while looking around the filthy shack.

"When was the last time you saw Luke?" he asked her.

She said he acted erratically on Monday when the forensic team arrived at Paterson's. She said she wondered if he had anything to do with it because he was acting weird. He was worse on Tuesday and wasn't around by Wednesday morning.

Another investigating officer called out to Dan.

"We need to lift the lid," he stated, disgusted.

Dan couldn't believe that Shannon could stand having an effluent pit close to their home. As they lifted the lid off the hole, the smell of decay became intolerable. The officer peered in and confirmed their suspicions with a grimace.

"He's in there," he said, turning his head, retching.

Even where Dan was standing, the smell was overpowering. Shannon, doing her best to play the heartbroken wife, started weeping behind her hands.

"Okay, Shannon, we need you guys to leave while we investigate. It's unsafe for the girls, and you have been using an illegal septic system. There is more work for us to do here before you are allowed back," Officer Talbot declared, looking down at Shannon, sobbing.

"Where will I go? All my family is in Greymouth," she pleaded with her eyes, trying to see if the police would pay for a hotel room in town.

"It would be best for you to bring the girls to Greymouth until we can determine what happened to Luke and sort the situation out. Leave your contact details at the station before you head off; they will take your statement there. You need to call the funeral director to plan Luke's funeral," he advised. He saw her demeanor change instantly.

"His funeral isn't my problem."

Shannon left him after that statement to pack their meager possessions.

***

Talbot joined the other officers at the pit, where they'd fished out Luke's bloated, rotting corpse. The thick smell surrounding it would have made the most hardened officers queasy. As his body spun slowly, hanging from the hook, the cuts on his forearms, now bloated open, became apparent.

"Looks like suicide," another officer remarked, pointing to Luke's arms. "He might have been responsible for the body parts we found at the neighbors. Facing getting caught out, he ended it," he added, trying to sort things out.

Talbot nodded. The picture was coming together now.

| 32 |

Broken

Lorraine woke from that horrifying night, still lying in the ensuite shower, covered with her urine. Dan took down the foil and baking paper she put up to protect herself from the ghost. The house was empty; he took Jeffrey to school and went to work, leaving her alone in the house again. She hated the place and felt like she was going mad. Dan didn't understand or care. She needed to leave this horrible house and go home where it was safe.

As the wind battered the landscape, Lorraine arranged to return to the United Kingdom, taking Jeffrey with her. She called her travel agent and arranged her flights. Her plan was in motion. She would pick up Jeffrey on Friday from school and fly out of Christchurch airport, leaving this godforsaken country behind her. Her heart ached when she thought of leaving Dan. She loved him immensely, but he no longer believed her, and the disenchantment in his eyes broke her heart. She needed to go before this house killed her.

***

After Dan left with Jeffrey early Friday morning, she took out her suitcases and packed her and Jeffrey's belongings. She left a note on the table and prepared Dan's dinner, storing it in the fridge with instructions on how to reheat it. She did his laundry, put it out to dry, and prepared to pick up Jeffrey at lunchtime, telling the school he had a doctor's appointment in Christchurch.

Their plane left at three that afternoon.

| **33** |

Reality

When she heard Dan's car pull up, Kate was still in the shed, tending to the lambs. The wind had finally died to a delicate breeze, and you could make out the birds and lambs calling. She stepped outside to see Mike coming toward her with the motorbike. Jimmy bounced out of the cruiser and ran to them.

"Can I go play with the lambs?" he begged.

Mike nodded and smiled. He sped off toward the pen.

"Where's Jeffrey?" Kate asked. She'd enjoyed their daily chats when they would drop off Jimmy.

"School said that Lorraine picked him up for a doctor's appointment in Christchurch. He's been on the waiting list to go see an optometrist for a while; they must have gotten a cancellation," Dan responded, showing no concern. "Damn, cell phone coverage is so dodgy out here, and with what's happened this afternoon," his voice faded, realizing he had no choice but to explain the gruesome scene they'd witnessed.

"Yeah, we noticed a commotion at the Dalton's," Mike said. "Is everything okay?"

Dan's face said it all; he turned a pale, greenish hue. "Nah, mate, it's bad. Luke committed suicide and ended up in their illegal shit pit. He's been there for a few days, too, I reckon. Last seen around town on Tuesday, Shannon said Luke was acting erratic, nervous about the police presence at the Paterson place. When Wednesday rolled around, Luke was gone. She also mentioned that he'd been acting strangely and was paranoid about having the forensic team snooping around. She thought he might have been responsible for what they were finding. It's starting to make sense. We will be scouring that place for a while. She can't live there. She's taking the kids back to Greymouth."

Both Kate and Mike were speechless. Her mind tried to picture it all. Could Luke be the man she saw that night on the deck? The man in the forest might have been him as well. How close had they come to a killer? A violent shiver rocked her spine. Both Mike and Dan noticed.

"You alright, Kate?" Dan asked. "I know it's a lot to take in," he said, trying to be supportive. "That bloody Nor'wester always brings on death. This one might have been a blessing in disguise."

Mike nodded, still speechless that one of his neighbors harbored such a dark secret.

"I'm headed back to the station to do paperwork. Listen, Kate, we are bringing in spotlights to scour the Dalton property. Don't freak out if their forest looks like a spaceship has landed. Once again, the forensic team will do their thing at the Dalton's. You'll be safe tonight with the amount of people working around you." He turned to make his way out of the drive.

Kate and Mike looked at each other, astonished.

***

Dan returned to the station to file Shannon's statement. She'd packed the kids and a few possessions and left for Greymouth. He thought of the conditions they were living in, those poor girls, in that filth. The council and child protective services wouldn't allow them to live there again until they installed a proper sewage system. He shook his head. She would face a massive fine for having that cesspit on their property.

Who would ever want to live there again? He pondered, absorbing the likelihood that many people had died on that land. He got up, approached a sheet tacked onto the whiteboard, and marked it with a red tick. The Nor'Wester suicide list just claimed another member.

***

It was approximately six o'clock when he arrived home. He'd stopped at Dalton's place where the cadaver dogs were going wild, triggered by the victim's blood that seeped into the ground. The wind erased the tire tracks; there was nothing to indicate the shed had been full of cars recently. Even the yard was free of debris. Shannon had cleaned up the place well. It all was strange to him, considering he knew their activities well. They never had a clean yard, and Luke wasn't the type that would top himself. Was there more to it than a simple suicide?

He pulled into his driveway. No lights were visible when he got out of the cruiser. He thought that was odd, considering Lorraine always left the lights on. He investigated the shed where she usually parked her car. It wasn't there. Anxiety building in him, he tried to call her; it went straight to voicemail. Did they have an accident? Was Jeffrey sick? He rushed to the kitchen, hoping to find a clue as to their whereabouts. He saw the note she left him, sitting on the dining room table like a beacon in the gloom of the impending night.

| 34 |

Back to Normality

Kate was making potato salad and nibbles to bring to Mike's barbecue. So far, she'd spent nearly every day with him since moving to New Zealand. It shocked her. Was it because she was vulnerable here in this unknown land? Was she more trusting because of the things that were happening around her? Why was she so comfortable with someone she'd only known for such a short time? She hurried her thoughts to Nick. It soured her mood instantly.

Not one call, not one message, nothing at all. Nick didn't know about the bones in the pit, the forensic team setting up camp, and the suicidal serial killer neighbor. She was livid. No, he didn't know anything because he didn't care. He only cared for himself. She was seriously contemplating the future of their relationship when an odd noise made her jump.

"What the hell was that?" she said out loud, making her way out to the yard. A woman riding a beautiful horse was coming up the drive. She smiled as she saw Kate and called to her.

"Good day, Kate, I take it?" She made her way to Kate and shook her hand. "I'm Melissa. You're Mike's mate, aren't you? My husband, Matt, and I are good mates of Mike's. We live down the road that way," she pointed toward the northeast. Kate blushed at being called Mike's mate. Maybe it was normal here to make friends quickly and hang out with them constantly.

"I hope I'm not intruding." her voice fell in volume, apprehension kicking in.

Kate snapped out of her reverie.

"No, of course not, Melissa. Please come in for a hot drink. I was making snacks for Mike's barbecue," she said, waving her in enthusiastically, happy at the surprise visit.

Melissa sat on a stool on the kitchen bench and looked around in wonderment. "Wow, I haven't been here since they added the addition to the old house. This place is so big now."

Kate lifted an eye to look at her when pouring the tea. "Really, that's wild. What was it like?" she asked.

"Dirty, old, and creepy," Melissa blurted, barely holding back a shiver.

"A lot of pain happened at that house. Many people died there during the Spanish Flu. Probably best they gave it a new life." Her smile was so genuine it was magnetic. She could switch from sad to glad in an instant. She put her elbows on the counter, her hands holding her face, and stared at Kate with a smile.

"So, my husband Matt told me you have been left high and dry out here in our neck of the woods. You must be so mad at your husband," she blurted before realizing what she was saying; Melissa didn't have a verbal filter.

Kate burst out laughing. "You got that right, sister." She handed Melissa her tea. The women discussed the unbelievable events since Kate arrived in New Zealand. Melissa had an interesting way of always finding something to laugh about, making the conversation light and fun.

"Well, at least not everything turned out badly, at least not for Mike." She smiled broadly, watching Kate burst into a hot blush.

Kate spun her head to pick up a spoon from the opposite counter, shielding her embarrassment. For God's sake, she was married and had only met the man a short while ago. Still, there was no denying the chemistry between them. She chuckled as she turned back to face Melissa; she'd spent more time with Mike in a week than with her husband in over two months.

"You've been good for Mike. He was so beaten and battered after years of Mona's abuse that he became a shell of himself; the only thing he wanted to do was work and see his children. Matt told me he got his balls back and told Mona off." She had an incredulous look on her face.

"I know," Kate responded, curling her lips in a smirk. "I was there,"

Melissa couldn't hide her shock and surprise. She held her cup in mid-air, waiting for the story. Kate explained what happened to her in the shed, how Mona accused Mike of cheating, and how Mike told her where to go. Melissa sipped on her tea and looked directly into Kate's eyes.

"Kate, I've known Mike since I was a kid. He's finding himself again because something in you brings it out. You mean a lot to him already. There is no need to be nervous. There's no need to fear him. I saw it in his eyes; he has feelings for you, which makes you a well-protected woman. Let him have those feelings for a while longer if you can. We missed our old mate." Her eyes shined bright with emotion.

Kate realized how deep the wounds in Mike's heart were and how long they'd made their home there. Kate nodded a smile on her lips, telling Melissa with her eyes that she understood. Melissa placed her hand on Kate's and squeezed it.

***

They sat looking out at the stillness before them, the lambs restingin the sun's rays while their mothers grazed softly. Kate could hear them chew; the calmness was dreamlike. She and Mike took in the sun while the kids played in the shed.

She'd worn a blue gingham sundress instead of shorts over a white T-shirt and sandals. The day turned out to be a hot one. Even in her light attire, she was sticky and hot. Mike sat bare-chested, wearing tan board shorts. Kate envied him for having the option of taking his top off.

She heard Kelly laugh and looked over at her. The young woman stood like a mystical mare, her skin caramel glazed, her auburn hair shining. Kate was apprehensive about meeting them after the incident with their mother, but her doubts were unfounded. When introduced, Kelly hugged her, whispering "thank you" in her ear. Kate's heart melted at the sincere appreciation in both Kelly's and thirteen-year-old Jake's eyes. Jake, resembling his mother, was frailer in build than his sister. An old soul, he was a calm and level-headed young man. They got along with Jimmy like they'd known each other for years.

Kate told herself this is how life should be as she lay back in her chair, looking at Mike. She took in the tiny prisms of sweat gleaming on his hard stomach, running down past a gap in his board shorts. She glanced away, flushing, abating the physical desire growing in her. It must be the heat.

An oncoming thunder of feet announced the kid's arrival. They were over the heat and wanted to go swimming. Mike looked at Kate to get her approval. Kate didn't have a swimsuit with her, only planning on having a barbecue and not thinking she would be swimming. She told Mike she should probably get her togs from home.

Mike teased her. "Come on, Canuck, jump in with your skivvies. You're in New Zealand now."

She smirked.

No one bothered to bring anything but drinks on the trip to the river. The kids rode the motorbikes, Kelly with Jimmy in the back and Jake on the smaller bike. Mike explained they were taking the dirt track to the swimming hole and would follow by taking the road with the Navara. As Mike drove, Kate felt as carefree as a bird. New Zealand was glorious and full of happiness despite all the bad that had happened.

Mike pulled off the road onto the right and drove down a trail next to the river. Kate had never seen braided rivers and appreciated how the channels showed proof of their transformation when the mighty rain from the mountains came flowing.

Mike was so relaxed. The metamorphosis from the pained man she first met into a constantly grinning, happy-go-lucky man suited him. It made him seem younger. She remembered Melissa's request. It warmed her heart, knowing that she made him happy.

They came to a magical, tree-sheltered swimming hole that looked like it was part of a fairy tale. The kids also arrived. Jake went to the driver-side window of the Navara.

"Dad, that's your swimming hole. We want to go to the one with the slide. Can Jimmy, Kelly, and I go check it out?"

Mike considered it for a moment before saying yes. He explained to Kate that the kids used a shallow area a few minutes away with a tree trunk they used as a slide. The slimy layer of decomposition was enough to propel them into only enough water to get their butts wet. He rolled his eyes as he explained and shook his head. Kate giggled as she left the Navara and headed to check the swimming hole.

More than the forces of nature had transformed the pond. Someone had lined the hole with rocks, creating a tiled swimming pool effect; clear water shimmered where the trees allowed glimpses of light. Under the tree boughs, a rock ledge acted like a submerged seat. To the far right and left of the oblong pool, two channels kept the water flowing into and out of the pool.

"The sun should have warmed it up before the trees shaded it," Mike said, checking the water temperature with his hand. "Yup, perfect," he declared.

He took off his board shorts and jumped in, only wearing a pair of tight black underwear. The look on his face showed how refreshing the cool water was on his skin. Kate nervously shuffled her feet, embarrassed about taking her dress off.

"It's okay, Kate, I'll turn around. No need to be shy." He turned his back to her so she could undress.

She slipped off her sundress to reveal her tight white t-shirt and panties, keeping her bra on for modesty's sake, although the flimsy material didn't allow considerable coverage. She slipped into the water behind Mike.

Absolute bliss radiated from her pores; the cool water was delicious against her skin. Her dark hair floated around her shoulders, clinging to her near-transparent shirt, barely hiding her lace-covered breasts. She felt his eyes on her as she swam with her eyes closed. She felt him approach.

They drifted effortlessly into the cool, pristine water, facing each other, eyes locked in silence. Kate's heart galloped nervously. She approached him as she moved her arms to stay afloat. She could feel his body heat through the water only centimeters from touching his lips. His eyes burned with desire. He moved his hand to touch her waist and bring her close.

Loud oncoming motorbike noises snapped them out of their spell before Mike's hands could reach her. Both blushed and separated, embarrassed at how swept up they'd gotten. The kids arrived, dumped their bikes, and jumped into the pool with them. Mike and Kate looked at each other and broke out in giggles.

They frolicked in the swimming hole, soaking up the lazy afternoon until Jake and Jimmy complained of being hungry. Jimmy told Kelly and Jake about the pond in the yard and the big covered-in-fire area. The kids intended to catch fish from it and have a barbecue there. It sounded like an excellent plan to Kate, who otherwise risked wearing a wet bra all night. They met at Mike's, picked up dry clothes and the bits for the meal, and returned to Kate's and Jimmy's.

The kids sorted their rods and set them up on the pond's bank. Chinook sat beside them, their backs to Kate and Mike as they sorted things by the fire pit. Once everything was ready to cook up, Kate gave Mike a beer and excused herself to change her clothes. She went into her bathroom, flung off her wet clothing, and jumped into the shower to freshen up. Slipping into an off-the-shoulder chiffon dress, she went into the bedroom to apply perfume. The windows to the bedroom were all open. She was sure they'd been closed that morning but brushed it off, her mind still electric from that afternoon's close encounter. She returned to the kids and Mike.

The kids were busy discussing what they'd caught in the pond while they enjoyed the barbecue. They moved the two sofas facing each other in the fire pit so that one was facing the roaring fire, the other facing the table where the kids were sitting. Jimmy and Jake were deep in conspiracy theory discussions with Kelly. She'd fished out an old wallet with a male Swedish driver's license in it from the pond. It shocked all of them. From the information on the license, it would have been there for at least seven years. The wallet held nothing else.

Mike promised to give it to Dan so he could trace it back to its owner. The kids couldn't stop trying to figure out where it came from and how it got there. It was the principal topic while they ate.

The lazy sun was quickly gobbled up by the trees when Jimmy asked if they could watch DVDs. She gave her approval as they rushed off to the house, calling out that there was microwave popcorn in the pantry if they wanted any.

***

Mike poured Kate another glass of wine and sat on the couch next to her. She moved slightly, re-adjusting closer to him. He could feel her warmth on his skin. They sat in silence, enjoying each other's company while the fire blazed, the spark of the fire reflecting in her eyes. Mike was awestruck at how beautiful she looked, bathed by the firelight. Her black hair gently framed her big green eyes and rounded cheeks, and her plump lips glistened temptingly. Her dress followed the line of her shoulders and displayed her breasts perfectly, the fire throwing shadows on her cleavage. She brought her wineglass to her lips, making his heart beat faster. He looked into the fire, willing his temptations away. She's married, and he just met her. Why was he having these feelings? How did he fall for the little lady so quickly?

She lay her head on his shoulder, his eyes showing pure contentedness. She was the best woman he had ever enjoyed spending time with. Forgetting that she belonged to someone else, he kissed her head.

The moment was so intoxicating that they never noticed the two figures looking out at them from the plantation. If the firelight had not blinded them, they would have seen one wearing a gray hoodie and the other wearing Luke Dalton's hooded bush shirt.

PART 2

| **35** |

The Call

The call finally came at four-thirty in the morning, on a Friday, five and a half weeks later. She answered groggily after the second ring.

"Hello?" Her voice was still rough from sleep.

"Kate, it's Nick."

His voice rattled her awake. She bolted upright. "Nick, I didn't know if you were alive or dead. Why didn't you call me sooner?" she said, her voice thick with disapproval.

"I've been flat out, Kate, on the mine site, which was a waste of time. Same old bullshit again. I took a job in South Africa. It pays a ton, and you and Jimmy will be safe living in a compound." He sounded excited.

Kate reeled. A compound! He acted like he'd left yesterday to go to Australia, not five and a half weeks ago. She responded to him calmly, fighting back the urge to yell.

"We won't be living in a compound in South Africa, Nick. No way will that be happening. You need to slow down. You can't be happy anywhere for more than a few weeks. We can't follow you every time you have a whim. You've left us high and dry too many times already." Her voice was cracking, and she struggled to contain her emotions.

He lashed back furiously. "I didn't get married not to live my life, Kate. It's my life. I only have one, and I will live it on my terms. Either you follow, or you don't."

His words stung, but the confidence she had found during her journey in the past five and a half weeks shielded her from their intended effect.

"We won't be following Nick. We won't be following you."

"Right, well, if you are going to be like that, I don't see a point in us continuing the relationship. It's over," Nick said, unwilling to compromise. "Best of luck to you. I'll get the paperwork sorted when I return to New Zealand in a few months."

The phone went dead. Kate was numb. She barely spent time with Nick since they got together five years ago. It was a long-distance romance from the start; unfortunately, distance helped end it. It was usual for him to be gone for three or four months, only coming home for a week to ten days, but this time, it was different. He promised to settle in New Zealand. He'd been the one to pick the country. He said he was sure this time.

Throughout their globe-trotting relationship, she always remained faithful to him. This time, faithfulness proved to be the biggest test. Her attraction to Mike and how she enjoyed his company, accompanied by heavy sexual tension, made staying true to Nick difficult. The chemistry was so strong, the attraction so fierce, that both knew something special was growing between them. She made it clear to Mike that she needed to talk to Nick to set things straight before anything happened between them. This call clarified the situation. It was over between her and Nick.

She couldn't sleep anymore after that call. She got up and jumped into the shower, the warm water soothing her body as her mind raced. How could Nick do this to her? She couldn't help thinking of Dan and the resemblance with his situation.

The past five weeks had been sad ones for Officer Dan. Kate often wondered why Lorraine left so abruptly. Dan said they flew back to the UK. Lorraine didn't want to live in New Zealand anymore. She hated their house and felt safer living in their home country. Dan considered taking legal action to reclaim custody of Jeffrey but knew that a single father on call as a local police officer without another guardian at home wouldn't fare well in the courts. It pained Kate; he looked like a broken man trying his best to do his job.

Jimmy started walking across a few paddocks to reach a bus stop at the last pickup point before school in the morning, affording him a bit more time to sleep. Dan hadn't called in for a real catch-up since they gave him the Swedish license plate and wallet they found in the pond. Dan tracked down the individual on the license and found out that someone had reported him missing seven years ago.

Christchurch headquarters were testing the bones found in the plantation for DNA. The results should be available in a couple of weeks.

Dan suspected the poor soul had fallen victim to Luke Dalton's homicidal intents. She shivered, thinking of how many people may have perished near or on the land occupied.

Jimmy adjusted quickly to his new school. Jeffrey's sudden departure saddened him, but he rapidly made friends with Callum, who lived down the main road. The school had organized a three-night camping trip up to Wooded Gully Campsite at the base of Mount Thomas. They were leaving Friday morning and returning on Monday afternoon. He was excited about it going ahead. The school only confirmed the trip when the weather forecast ensured the Nor'Wester wouldn't show its face. Fortunately, the wind would only arrive the following week. Kate thought of the gear she needed to pack as she showered.

***

"Sorry, I'm late." After dropping Jimmy and his equipment at school, she arrived at the farm a bit later than usual. Mike was waiting for her outside his shed.

Mike smiled and laughed. "You're fired," he mocked through the driver's side window. He jumped in the passenger seat.

"We need to head to Matt and Melissa's. I've fed the lambs already," he said, biting a toothpick between his teeth.

Kate headed toward Matt's farm when Mike asked if Jimmy was off to school camp that day. She looked at him and smiled.

"Yeah, that's the reason I was late."

"What will you do for three days alone in that big house?" Mike teased her, looking out the window.

She couldn't see the concern on his face since it was turned away from her. She giggled and blushed, relieved they were arriving at Matt and Melissa's place.

They shared a coffee before the men set out to the yards, Melissa taking Kate to wander in the garden.

"Okay, sister, what's going on?" Melissa asked, noticing a difference in her friend's demeanor that morning. Kate told her about her conversation with Nick and how relieved she was that it was over.

"I see…" Melissa said, her eyes glinting wildly. "There isn't anything stopping you now. I've seen the look you give each other sometimes, and… yeah… everyone can see it."

Kate blushed and made a funny face at Melissa. Both burst out laughing and went back to join the men.

| 36 |

Lost

Dan sat alone on his deck, holding a cold coffee, overlooking the distant lush green hills. He had aged tremendously in the past few weeks. The sense of duty he always prided himself on was gone; there was no one to prove himself to.

Lorraine had called when she reached Buckinghamshire. She'd taken up residence with her parents until she could re-settle herself and Jeffrey. The one thing she was definite about was that she was not coming back.

He racked his brain for hours during many sleepless nights, thinking of everything he could have done differently. He missed them tremendously, finding himself near tears when driving past Jeffrey's old school and seeing children his son's age. He should have been stronger and a better husband to her. He realized too late that his wife needed help. He should have been more compassionate.

Dan slowly got up and chucked his coffee on the lawn. He had a lot to do at work today, with the investigation into Luke's death still not completed. They found multiple body parts in various stages of decomposition at Paterson's place. The DNA concluded they were all from separate individuals. Whatever happened in that plantation involved multiple homicides. Was Luke the monster that Shannon made him out to be? Dan kept track of her whereabouts from afar.

She'd gone to Greymouth as she said. Luke's family arranged for his body to be moved to Hokitika. He had a simple funeral. Shannon and the children didn't attend.

A week later, she left her daughters with her sister on the West Coast, moved back to Canterbury, and shacked up with a low-life mechanic named Barry, who lived in a dilapidated complex of old sheds and scrap vehicles.

From what he knew, Luke and Shannon had been together for at least the best part of a decade. He found it odd that she'd moved on so quickly. Dan quickly reminded himself that he didn't know women well, and there might have been a reason for her to have done so.

He stopped in the bathroom to brush his teeth before leaving for work and stared at himself in the mirror. Deep lines creased his face, and his eyes were bloodshot and vacant. He desperately needed sleep and, ironically, started seeing things in the house.

The French doors rattled during the night, and he thought someone was trying to break in. He stumbled through his dark home to the hallway, where he could peer over the door frame to see the intruder. No one was there.

He thought of Lorraine and her apparitions and dismissed the thought immediately; there wasn't anything in the house to fear.

Dan approached the French doors, seeing nothing to explain the rattling sound that awoke him. He turned his back to them and returned to bed, thinking the wind was playing tricks on him. He felt a presence to his right, on the far side of the dining room.

Standing in the corner were two hooded men, lost in the shadows. He jumped and rushed to turn on the lights. When he looked back into the dining room, they were gone.

"I'm losing it," he thought, grabbing his head. Lack of sleep and the guilt of letting his wife down poisoned his thoughts. He went back to bed to his wild, sleepless contemplations.

Dan looked at his reflection in the mirror and sighed. He needed to get going; otherwise, he would be late for work.

The morning light hurt his eyes when he hopped into his cruiser and went to the station. The heat of the day was already setting in heavily. He scolded himself as he drove.

"Snap out of it, Dan. A Nor'wester is coming, and you'll need to be on top of your game."

He grabbed his coffee cup and took a large swallow.

The trees created a flickering pattern down the empty road. Dan could see the heat radiating off the pavement, even at this early hour. It was going to be a hot day. He looked up at the sky. The sheer layers of barely discernible clouds crawling in showed the wind was coming.

The knot in his stomach grew tighter.

| **37** |

Bliss

The temperature reached a scorching thirty-one degrees Celsius by one-thirty that afternoon. The sun baked the landscape dry as the women returned from feeding the lambs at Mike's. Everyone voted to get out of the heat and cool down as Kate and Mike entered the truck. Matt spoke to Mike through the open window of the Navara.

"Thanks for your help, mate. I needed to get those things sorted before the Nor'wester comes in next week." Matt had an elbow on the door, tipping his hat to his mate.

"No worries, cobba," Mike responded, flicking the brim of Matt's hat.

Mike and Kate drove off to Melissa and Matt waving, the dry road creating a cloud of dust behind them.

***

"So, what's next, boss?" Kate asked Mike, wondering where he was going. He grinned and looked at her from the corner of his eyes. The air coming through the open truck windows was so enjoyable that Kate closed her eyes to savor it. She opened her eyes when Mike turned off the paved road.

"Fancy a swim?" he asked.

She nodded to signal her approval.

They drove in silence as they got closer to the swimming hole. Surprisingly, they were the only ones out for a swim that hot afternoon. They had the entire riverbed to themselves.

The trees had grown since they last visited, enveloping the swimming hole. Their long branches reached over the water, shading the entire pool from anyone's prying eyes. Kate looked back at Mike when she heard his voice.

"It will be nice and cool in the pool. We are taking Friday afternoon off for staff appreciation day. It'll be great to cool down with a swim before we head to the Lodge for our usual pizza night. Matt shouted me a few cold beers," Mike said, handing Kate a beer.

He was so relaxed she couldn't help but follow suit. Mike placed his beer on the stone wall of the pool, kicked off his boots and clothing, and entered the cool water wearing his familiar tight black underpants. He made his way to the stone ledge at the back of the pool and sat looking content under the shade of the trees, his muscular arms stretched out, the water reaching the middle of his chest.

Kate placed her beer next to Mike's. She could see Mike was about to go on with the '*I'll turn around*' spiel he did last time. She stared him into silence and quietly unbuttoned her shirt. His gaze transfixed on her; Kate could feel his eyes devouring her as her shorts fell to her ankles.

She stood there majestically in her pale pink bra and panties, long tendrils of her black hair cascading over her shoulders. The light the swaying tree branches allowed in danced on her body.

She reached behind her, let her bra fall, and wiggled out of her panties. She slipped into the cool water.

Her eyes locked with his. She floated closer to him, the cool water exhilarating her. He slipped back into the water to join her, drifting closer, never letting go of her eyes. They met in the pool's middle.

Kate whispered in his ear. "He called. It's over."

She looked at him, telling him with her eyes what that meant.

Mike placed his hands on her hips, bringing her closer to him.

The way his powerful hands felt when he pulled her close made her gasp, the warmth of his muscular body contrasting deliciously with the coolness of the water. She could sense his arousal pressing against her, making her tremble with desire. Her lips lifted to his, instantly igniting a passionate fire too intense to extinguish. She savored the way their tongues mingled.

Wanting to have him next to her, primal in her need for him, she hooked her thumb in the front of his underpants and dragged them down slowly.

Mike kissed her arduously, his passion for her making his body quiver. Fully uncovered and pressing against her stomach, she knew he'd waited long enough for what he desired. She lifted herself slightly, kissing him feverishly as she wrapped her long legs around his waist and slowly slid down to be filled by him. Both gasped at the wave of pleasure they shared, their eyes locked, holding each other tightly.

He reached the mossy side of the pool underneath the trees, holding her close to him. Lifting her out of the pool, he lay her wet body on the thick moss. He took his time kissing her mouth and neck, delicately caressing her breast, parting her long legs, and nuzzling her gently. She climaxed quickly. Mike took her as she lay basking in the glow.

| 38 |

Barry

The air was thick with smoke, floating in waves through the filthy room. The yellowed wallpaper, torn and dirty, hid a sadder brown wallboard underneath. An old picture frame barely held on to the wall, a shadow displaying where it originally hung. The place stunk, but it didn't bother Shannon or Barry; they smelled just as bad.

"You can't stay here for free, Shannon," Barry whinged as he took a long hit from the crack pipe.

Shannon, dressed in an old bush shirt and worn-out jeans that hadn't seen a washing machine for a few months, lounged on Barry's old, stained sofa. She had arrived at Barry's without the kids a few weeks ago. They binged on meth the first few days and had a good time. She presumed he was content with their arrangement; he got to fuck her as much as he wanted in return for a share of the drugs. It wasn't working out for Barry.

Since high school, no woman had come close to his hairy, overweight body. He had let himself go, rarely showering or shaving and only doing his laundry a few times a year.

He grabbed the pipe and took another hit. The drug hit his nervous system like an electric shock, energy vibrating throughout his body. He thought he would have slimmed down from the effects of the drug, but his marijuana use gave him constant munchies. The years of drug and alcohol abuse and imbibing on a diet of mainly pies and sausage rolls had taken its toll. Barry was a disgusting, dirty old man.

"Do you want to fuck me again?" Shannon slurred as she sat up, wobbling from the effects of her high. Barry cringed. He would need to be much higher than he was to come close to her putrid body odor.

"Nah, this isn't working out for me, Shannon. We don't work together anymore. You have nothing worthwhile to offer me. You're not worth anything."

Shannon sprung up wildly, her arms flailing. "Fuck you, Barry. I have more than you think. I still have the land in Okuku..." She bit her lip, regretting what she said.

Barry thought about it. Luke had a sweet shed on that property, his mind's eye envisioning the hangar-sized building. If he could close the garage to keep prying eyes out, it might be the perfect place for his meth lab. They would have to deal with the council first. Shannon had been fined for improper waste management.

"Yeah, Shannon, you do," he responded, signaling her to sit. He handed her the pipe. Barry got up and went to the back door.

He exited the decrepit home, a derelict shack he turned into living quarters, and proceeded to the far wall to piss in the corner.

The locals thought he made his money selling car parts. He'd collected too many vehicles to count. His cars lay scattered on his twenty-hectare land between Tai Tapu and Motukarara south of Christchurch. He looked out at the mechanical graveyard in his backyard as the night fought the last fragments of the day.

If he could get the council off her back, he could gain access to the shed, he thought, finishing his piss. Helping her pay for the mess they created on that land might be worth it. He looked around his property. He wasn't as bad as they were, he thought; he didn't have a shit pit.

The faster he could get the heat off that property, the quicker he could take over and make serious cash without being overtly implicated. The land was still Shannon's, so she would be responsible if they got busted. He would claim he didn't know what was going on. He hatched a plan by the time he reached the back porch. He would keep that smelly pig around a bit longer.

| 39 |

Rage

Gin spilled from her glass as she slammed it on the polished tabletop.

"How dare he?" she screamed, still fuming about Kate feeding the lambs in Mike's shed.

She'd gone on and on, bad-mouthing Mike and treating Kate to vulgar accusations. Kevin didn't care. She was paying for the trip to Queenstown, and as long as she put out and he had coke to numb her constant whining, he was good as gold.

He thought their trip was a bust because of Mona's bad mood, so he suggested they return home early. Mona wouldn't have a bar of it. She wanted to wait until the kids were back at school before coming back. She didn't have time for their boring ideas; they reminded her too much of Mike.

They spent their three-day break lost in the fog of Mona's anger. She drank profusely at each meal and embarrassed him at the restaurant. Their days in Queenstown had ended with her taking the bed and Kevin sleeping on the couch.

Her jealousy and hatred hadn't dissipated since her return. Instead, she continually watched her ex-husband and that Canadian woman play about on the farm.

"He's going to pay for this," she said as she looked toward Mike's place.

Her vendetta was growing and had turned into an obsession. Mike had done so well keeping out of her way that Mona needed to hide in surrounding bushes to spy on him. She patiently waited for them to get intimate so she could jump out and accuse him of infidelity. She hadn't caught them yet, but it was a matter of time before he slipped up. That would guarantee her everything. The courts would award her the entire property because of his adultery.

Her situation was different. Mike's inability to provide her with the life she deserved pushed her to Kevin. She resolved she wasn't responsible for her adultery.

"He lent her his truck," she screamed while wrecking the shed's side with an ax. Kevin left her to it and sipped gin and tonics while he worked on his tan in the front yard.

***

At six on Saturday morning, she set out to spy on Mike. She barely slept that night; visions of them poisoned her thoughts, jealousy consuming her. His Navara was there, but so was the Land Rover. Her heartbeat quickened, noticing the vibrations it caused in her body. She needed to get closer to see what they were doing. The shed was dark.

A loud noise filled the air. Mona grabbed her ears. Still making her way toward Mike's place, she held her hands tight to the side of her head, trying to block out the humming noise.

Movement in the window caught her attention. Mike was getting a glass of water from the faucet. She could make out his bare chest through the shed's kitchen window. Still clutching her head, she watched him. Her jealousy flared, noticing how well-built and strong he stood compared to Kevin.

Her inner turmoil brought the hum to a crescendo. Incapable of taking the noise any longer, she headed the shortest way home, by the pigpen, stumbling. Her eyes teared, she could barely see, the all-consuming noise making it difficult to breathe. The intense pain in her ears made her feel faint. Mona dropped by the pigpen, holding herself on the gate post.

Half dazed, she could hear the pigs grunting. She tried to focus, but everything was blurred and fuzzy, the hum vibrating her vision.

She could barely see the profile of the hooded man standing next to her, blocking the sun. A croak escaped her lips instead of a scream. His shadow consumed her. She could hear his laughter mix with the hum.

Mona held her ears, closed her eyes, and cried as pain shot through her legs. Barely conscious, she could see the pigs eating something familiar. Her blurry mind, overcome by the clamor, couldn't understand or make sense of what was before her. The pain intensified, pushing her to the point of despair. Mona passed out next to the pig pen in the shadow of the hooded man.

| 40 |

New Life

Her eyes opened to see his powerful arms enveloping her, his smooth, sun-kissed skin sprinkled with soft, golden hairs. She could feel him breathing, his chest nestled closely in her back, the warmth of his loins on her bare buttocks. She didn't want to move, content in her world, surrounded by the intoxicating smell of his skin.

How long has it been since I woke up next to a man feeling like this? Nick was absent so often and for such long periods that it took time for them to get reacquainted when they came together. Nick often left before they could be intimate. The chemistry hadn't been there.

She cherished the pleasure she was feeling. Mike stirred slightly, his arms readjusting themselves to ensure he didn't lose grip of her, and lightly moaned his satisfaction. She could feel his eagerness growing, pressed firmly against her.

***

Mike opened his eyes, the sunlight entering the cabin slowly waking him to his new reality. In his arms was the woman he'd grown to love in such a short time. The frustration of being unable to touch or hold her seemed to go on forever, never expecting Nick to wait five and a half weeks before calling. She'd given up on her husband but wouldn't entertain anything until she talked to him and cleared the air.

Thinking of their afternoon at the swimming hole, he felt himself swell. Kate was so beautiful, so perfect. He snuggled into her hair, breathing in the sweet smell of her skin, his hand running down the edge of her rounded hips.

"Good morning, baby," he whispered in a scruffy, sleep-tainted voice and buried himself inside her.

***

They spent the rest of the day enjoying each other, only coming out to watch the sunset off the porch. Dressed in one of Mike's bush shirts, Kate sipped her ice-cold beer. She looked up to the sky; the eerie patterns the clouds were making made her nervous.

"Do you reckon it's going to be a bad one this time, Mike?" she asked, referring to the impending arrival of another Nor'wester.

"Not sure, Hun, you never know how long or how bad they'll be. They're always different and unpredictable. At least we don't have the lambing to worry about. It's done now for this year." He sat on an old green cushion-covered bench, his legs spread out lengthwise.

She sat beside him, her head on his chest, splaying her long legs on his. Instinctively, he wrapped her under his arm.

The need to feed the lambs had drawn to a close; they'd grown strong and been released to join the others. Kate decided to buy an old car and give him back his Navara, but he insisted she keep it, telling her he would appreciate her continuing to help in return for using his truck. She felt relieved, not for the continued use of the car but to have an excuse to spend her days working in paradise next to him. The look of horror on his face when she said he would no longer need her help cemented her feelings for him. He made it clear, without many words, that he wanted her to stay.

They sat there, happily entwined until the sun was nearly retired. Something caught Mike's attention in the left paddock. Kate followed his gaze to see Kevin waddling around aimlessly, looking for something and wearing oversized gumboots. He was scouring the paddocks, dressed in a light blue velour tracksuit.

Kate laughed. "That man could never look at home on a farm," she said under her breath, shaking her head.

"What's that silly fucker doing now?" Mike whispered. They both giggled at the spectacle. Kevin crossed the paddock and headed toward the pigpen.

Somewhat wondering if everything was all right, Mike yelled out to Kevin. He'd yet to hear the pigs being fed today.

"Best you check on your pigs, mate; they'll be hungry," Mike said, calling out to Kevin, shaking his head disapprovingly.

Kevin looked at them and waved like he was greeting them from afar.

Mike sighed, holding Kate tighter.

***

They spent the next day and night savoring their time together. Mike knew Jimmy was coming home on Monday afternoon. Kate would be spending her nights in that godforsaken house without him. Unfortunately, she was stuck there for the time being. He couldn't ask her to live in the shed with him; she deserved far better.

Daydreaming of their future while his arms held her tightly, he decided he needed to build a house worthy for them to come and stay within six months. He brushed her long, silky hair with his hand, knowing he would do anything for her.

| 41 |

Imminent

Monday came after another weekend from hell, the lack of sleep leaving Dan shattered. Things had been relatively quiet apart from a missing stock report, which turned out to be nothing, and a few alcohol-related offenses. He would have considered that a great weekend, but now, with Lorraine and Jeffrey away, the weekends were hell, especially the slow ones. He depended on his work now; without his family, he was a shadow of his former self, relying on his appointment to fill his time.

The sleepless nights and apparitions transformed him into a zombie. He contemplated discussing it with a professional until he realized it would interfere with his job; they don't take kindly to cops seeing things that don't make sense.

He brought it down to guilt. It was like Lorraine cursed him to see the man she saw. Worse yet, he'd seen two men, making him question himself.

It wasn't the first time that Dan doubted his sanity. It happened once before, a long time ago, when they lived in the UK.

He'd left the Thames Valley Police Force after an incident contributed to severe post-traumatic stress. He couldn't afford to have another mark on his record. His mind re-lived the horror as he drove toward Rangiora.

***

He and his former partner Gerry were assigned to work on one of Thames Valley Police Force's most heinous crimes. They'd worked it for four months when he got called out that night. Told it was related to the case, Dan left the station unaware he was driving himself into something that would change his life forever.

The partners had found mutilated bodies in crack dens and drug houses for nearly six months. The autopsy reports indicated the victims had been tortured to death before high doses of heavy drugs were injected into them, their bodies left on display like effigies warning others to stay away.

Something wasn't right. If it was a straightforward drug deal gone wrong, wouldn't the culprits take all the drugs with them after the dealer died? Why inject the victims with the drugs?

Gerry had done the hard yards of visiting the junkies in the community to warn them of the killer preying on them, a courtesy to Dan since he had a family at home. Gerry lived the single life of a dedicated officer.

They asked him to investigate suspicious activity at a drug den. When Dan arrived at the house, its haunted, dirty Victorian facade made the scenario even more distressing. He made his way up the front steps to peer through the rotten curtain. From his perspective, the place looked empty; there wasn't any movement inside. He turned the doorknob and entered cautiously. Gerry was already there, dressed in torn, dirty clothing.

"Did you get called out painting your boat?" Dan asked, chuckling at Gerry's attire. Gerry had a look of wild excitement in his eyes.

"Look at all of them." he motioned with this hand to the far corner of the room behind Dan.

Dan looked beyond the rubbish-strewed floor to a collection of old urine-soaked sofas and chairs.

Four dead junkies had been trashed apart; their body parts were threaded onto pieces of wood to form macabre statues. Dan approached the scene with horrified fascination. The killer was progressing fast; the montage was more demented than others they had previously found.

Severed heads leaned precariously on their wooden tower, some with their privates shoved into their mouths. Their eyes were stapled open, their eyeballs begging to spill out of their sockets. Dan looked at his partner and shook his head. The way he grinned made Dan uneasy.

Something was wrong with Gerry. Why was he acting this way? He knew better than to come to the scene dressed like he was and what was going on with the mad look on his face. Gerry wordlessly walked down the corridor to the basement. Dan's hackles were up. Something wasn't right.

He slowly followed Gerry, shuffling the piles of used needles and food wrappers from this path. As he descended the steps to the basement, the single light bulb in the middle of the room shed light on a horror scene.

Someone had set up a craft table to build human sculptures. Miscellaneous body parts were strewn haphazardly on the table, blood oozing from the severed edges and spilling on the floor. Dan noticed Gerry's badge and gun lying on the table, but why were they covered in blood? Gerry pounced at him, knocking him to the ground.

*****

A violent shiver rocked Dan, and he gripped the steering wheel tighter. He tried to force himself to stop thinking about that life-altering night. He still had issues coming to terms with what transpired.

The killings had been the work of his partner, Gerry. Having enough of the stresses of police life dealing with junkies, Gerry had taken it upon himself to rid the plague by taking the matter into his own hands.

A struggle ensued, which saw Gerry take a knife to Dan and Dan fatally shoot his partner. The investigation outcome shed no additional light on the horrific incident, stating that something in Gerry had snapped. It made Dan's blood run cold.

The Nor'wester was bound to arrive tomorrow. Dan observed the long ribbons of clouds forming in the high altitudes. His stomach churned. Tonight would be his last chance to get the sleep he desperately needed before the wind came. He made a beeline to the coffee shop for a triple shot.

| 42 |

The Stink

On Saturday evening, Kevin found Mona unconscious, covered in filth, next to the pigpen. Initially thinking she was dead, he panicked. Where would he go? What would he do? He'd gotten used to living in her country mansion and being cared for by Mona.

She was a nutcase, but she paid for everything. At least Mike did anyway; Mona hadn't worked a day in her life. Not having to pay rent in town meant he could afford more cocaine. He snapped back to reality when he heard her groan.

She lay next to the pig pen gates; half her body had been dragged in with the hogs. He pulled Mona away from the enclosure and tried to rouse her. How long had she been lying out there? He concluded it must have been since early morning. She was already out of bed and away when he woke and hadn't seen her all day. It was when she didn't show up to make dinner that he started worrying.

She sprung to life, her eyes popped open, her expression wild.

"Get me up, you piece of shit," she spat at him violently.

He struggled to get her on her feet. Blood mixed with mud and pig excrement covered her legs and stained his pale velour tracksuit.

He dragged her into the house, his frail stature preventing him from carrying her in his arms. He set her down in the bathtub to tend to her wounds. She grimaced in obvious pain. Kevin ensured the water from the faucet was at the correct temperature and used the hose attachment to spray off the filth covering her wounds.

"What happened, Mona?" he asked, looking at the bite marks she had on her legs. Mona was delirious, her eyes rolling in her head.

"Get me some coke, you useless piece of shit," she said, squeezing his wrist tight, pushing her fingernails into his skin.

Taking another quick look at her wounds, Kevin left the bathroom to gather the cocaine and grab a bottle of whisky from the liquor cabinet. Returning to Mona, he obliged her with the cocaine and waited until the drug took effect before spilling the whisky on her wounds. She rocked back and forth from the pain running through her, rousing her to full consciousness.

"Your fucking pigs tried to kill me!" She pointed her finger at Kevin accusingly. "You wanted those disgusting animals, didn't feed them right, and they almost killed me." She stared at Kevin, hatredin her eyes.

Kevin, reeling, backed off from her and stood beside the tub.

"How did you end up in the pigpen, Mona?" Kevin asked, incredulous at what happened.

"Mike is trying to drive me insane with his bloody noise machine he keeps attacking me with. I don't know what he's rigged up in his shed, but the constant humming drives me demented. He's purposely trying to drive me out and replace me with that Canadian slut," she said, grinding her teeth in rage. "The noise got so bad I must have fainted next to the pigpen."

He could see her trying to process what had happened in her mind. "But... why were you at the pigpen, Mona?" Kevin asked again, still confused. She made it clear when he first got them she would never come close to the disgusting animals. They were his responsibility.

"I was trying to catch Mike and that Canadian bitch in the act. He's going to pay, Kevin. Mike's going to lose everything, and it will be all mine," she said, signaling to him to bring the coke mirror closer.

Kevin was sick of her madness but put on a look of fake compassion. He dared not cross her, fearing she would take his comfortable lifestyle away. His ever-growing cocaine addiction meant he needed a more lucrative job to keep him comfortable. The car sales wouldn't do.

The business was a farce. Kevin's company only sold enough cars to pay the yard's rent and his employee minimum wage. He didn't know if he had it in him to work the yard. He'd gotten so accustomed to his free time.

He scanned her injuries attentively. The dirt and grime were gone, but her wounds glowered with an ominous purple tinge, indicating the start of an infection.

"You need to go to the hospital, Mona," he said, trying to lift her out of the tub. She fought back like a scared animal, her strength surprising him.

"Let go of me. There is no way Mike is getting the chance to take over this house. I'm staying here whatever happens," she screamed, flicking dirty water at him.

Kevin looked at her and sighed.

| 43 |

Power

Mike was pacing inside his tiny kitchen. It was Monday evening.

He had to face his first night without Kate since Friday. It made him ache. He kept looking out to the pine plantation separating them and wished so dearly that it didn't exist so he could have a clear line of sight to her house.

The Nor'wester would arrive on Tuesday evening. By Monday afternoon, he had secured the farm to prepare for its arrival. He pulled his eyes off the plantation, finished his beer, and headed for bed, knowing his mind was too occupied with thoughts to allow him peaceful sleep. He couldn't wait to see her tomorrow.

***

The sudden force of the blow shook the shed and rattled the windows so fiercely it startled Mike awake. He couldn't grasp that the wind and not a semi-truck had hit his hut, the impact nearly knocking him out of bed. The building shrieked as it resisted the assault. He could feel the twisting on the structure, nails popping as they broke. As quickly as it came, it dissipated, leaving Mike panting.

Before he could catch his breath, the walls groaned, and the roof squealed a death cry as another gale pushed the boundaries of human construction. The Nor'wester had come in strong and unexpectedly in the middle of the night. Facing the impossible, knowing he couldn't secure his roof should the wind decide to devour it, he sat on his bed, praying it would hold.

He looked outside, noticing his kitchen window had cracked from the torsion generated on the building. The night sky looked like ink. Mike could hear buildings succumbing to the invisible force in the distance. The outside motion sensor light went dark; the power had gone out.

He boiled with worry, thinking about Kate and Jimmy. The guttural sound the wind made as it raced down the land made him nervous, its dry, arid heat cooking everything in its path. Estimating the current holding at least 120 kilometers an hour with substantially stronger gusts, he thought of his stock and hoped no harm would come to them. He rose to look through the side window, scanning his land. The mass of white indicated they moved under the shelter belts, safely huddled together.

The night sky barely afforded illumination, making noises seem louder. The horrible symphony of sounds made him anxious; it howled like the devastated wail from a grieving mother. Another strong gust hit, taking no mercy on the shed.

| 44 |

Blow It Down

The devastation was revealed when daylight came the following day.

Driving slowly, Dan surveyed the damage in awe. The Nor'wester's sudden arrival during the middle of the night ripped the roofs off houses and sheds. It toppled farm buildings and overturned a few parked buses and caravans.

The destruction was extensive. Cleaning up would be impossible until the wind ceased its torment.

He drove past Mike's shed, shock and horror kicking him in the face as he studied his friend's property. He pulled over to the side of the road to take it in.

Mike's shed was severely damaged. A large branch from a tree many meters away had come crashing down on his roof, causing it to jut out and tear off in a large portion, exposing his living quarters. He feared for his friend's life and rushed down Mike's driveway, praying he survived the storm.

Mike was sitting on the ground where his porch had stood. Head low, his body took the battering of the strong wind. Dan couldn't see Mike's face, but from the way he was sitting, Dan knew what his friend was feeling.

"Get in the cruiser, mate," Dan requested of Mike as he helped him to his feet.

"Everything's destroyed. I'm lucky to have made it out alive, Dan. When that roof came down, I thought I was a goner. We need to check on Kate and Jimmy," Mike demanded, fastening his seat belt.

"Heading that way right now," Mike assured him as the vehicle sped down the dirt road, the wind pushing against it, rocking it. They arrived at Kate's driveway. Mike rushed out of the cruiser and ran toward the house.

Dan scanned the damage the night bestowed on the Paterson place. Four mature pines had fallen, blocking the drive. The fourth one had come precariously close to hitting the garage and the Navara, lying between both in a jumble of tree branches. A quick inspection proved the house had done well that night; he couldn't see any damage. Dan checked the home further while Mike negotiated his way to Kate, climbing over the downed trees.

Seeing his absence, Dan thought Jimmy must have made it to the bus that morning. He observed how Mike and Kate embraced and immediately noticed something profound had shifted between them; they'd grown closer. Dan was happy for Mike; his friend deserved something positive after everything his life had thrown at him. He climbed out of the cruiser and went to the couple, holding his hat for fear of it blowing to a faraway land. Kate waved him inside the house, where the wind's interference lessened.

"That was such a scary night!" Kate exclaimed, pouring them coffee. "I thought the whole plantation would come crashing down at one point. I didn't know how lucky we were until morning," she said, beaming gratefully and then switching to concern. "What if it's worse tonight?"

The men both looked at her without saying a word. No one knew what the Nor'wester would bring.

Dan broke the silence.

"Kate, you'll need to do a good amount of chainsaw work to get this place working again," he said with a spry look. "At least you won't run out of firewood anytime soon."

Kate looked at her hands, looking helpless. She knew there would be no way she could tackle the job without help.

"Well, Mike, you might want to barter Kate's spare bedroom and help her out with this mess until the wind dies and you can fix your shed," Dan said, downing his cup.

Kate went to grab his empty cup to make him another one, but Dan waved her off.

Mike gazed into his coffee. Dan knew he yearned to be with Kate and wished he'd been close during the night to protect her, but he couldn't fathom sleeping at the Paterson place.

Mike made his feelings clear about Paterson's place years ago when he first met Dan. All the long-term residents felt the same about the property; they wouldn't be caught dead spending the night.

Mike was going to have to make a decision. He had nowhere to go for the next few days until the weather cleared. He could always stay at Matt and Melissa's place, but that would leave Kate and Jimmy alone. Mike placed his hand on Kate's and looked up at her sheepishly.

The severity of the situation hit her.

"Oh no, Mike, how bad is the shed?" she asked. "Of course, you can come and stay here," she added before he could answer, automatically putting her arm around his shoulders to comfort him. Dan knew it was time for him to leave.

"Right, well, you lot are sorted. I've got to keep moving. A ton of damage has occurred, and we must ensure everyone is safe." He tipped his hat as he opened the front door, exposing the rapture the wind was unleashing, and stepped outside.

| 45 |

Rubbish

Barry stayed up all night, unable to sleep with the clamor the wind choreographed around him. Loose sheets of tin, rusted car parts, and ancient door hinges all creaked and moaned. Ironically, the house was more robust than it looked; it stood in all its derelict grandeur in the morning. He looked outside wearily, trying to determine if he lost anything in his yard to the wind's tantrum.

He stepped out, the wind whipping at his thin, sweat-stained shirt and dirty overalls. He looked around, squinting, as tiny particles of sand interfered with his sight.

Dirty Nor'wester, he thought to himself, rubbing at his eye sockets.

His face shielded from the swirling sand-filled air, he made his way to the back part of his property, overlooking the extent of the night's damage. He made his way to the door of his main workshop and forced it open against the howling wind.

The building was gone; only the facade remained standing. Barry couldn't believe the hangar-sized workshop could have crumbled upon itself, the roof collapsing after the windows had blown out, pushing the walls down. There was nothing left.

He returned to the confines of the house, cursing the invisible enemy.

****

He looked at Shannon, stretched sloppily on the filthy sofa. She'd finally crashed from being up for days and was unaware of what the night brought. She repulsed him; her smell, looks, and bad attitude grossed him out. She couldn't even get him hard anymore. He had a significant issue on his hands now that the roof had collapsed on his shed; he needed to keep her around.

The front of the shed housed what looked to be a regular mechanic shop, with a greasy hoist and tools scattered on the benches. Barry wasn't much of a mechanic, and he'd only set it up to meet the approval of wandering eyes. The real money-maker was the back storeroom where he housed his meth lab.

The game had started innocently enough. Barry grew a few marijuana plants to sell but quickly progressed to meth as the demand was more substantial and was much easier to hide. He couldn't afford to be out of business for long. The project he envisioned with Shannon's shed in Okuku would need to come together quicker than he'd planned.

| 46 |

Fester

Mona opened her eyes to a veiled version of her world. Everything was hazy, making the bedroom shimmer with an ethereal glaze.

She shifted slightly, re-adjusting herself on the pillow. The agony exuding from her legs cursed through her core. Mona forced her body to sit. She swooned, dizzy from the fever cooking her internals. Her hand pulled the amber-colored stained sheet away, exposing her lower half.

Dark purple marks surrounded the raw red flesh where the pigs bit her. She had a nasty gash next to her ankle, four more on her thigh on the left side, and two on her calf on the right side. They oozed a viscous bile-colored liquid, the jagged skin flaps showing no indications of wanting to conform to their original location.

The nightmares she conjured during her comatose slumber still fresh in her mind, she looked apprehensively around the room. The hooded man wasn't there. She took a deep breath, relieved.

A wave of nausea blew her over, and she lay back onto the pillow, hoping it would subside. Her stomach spasmed, lurching her forward involuntarily, her legs responding with lightning bolts of pain. Mona dry-retched uncontrollably, her nausea fuelling the pain coursing through her. It subsided as quickly as it started, allowing her to scream out to Kevin.

***

Kevin came running, his eyes automatically taking in her wounds. He grimaced in disgust and tried to focus on her face, his stomach threatening to retaliate. Mona was covered in sweat, her pale skin displaying a greenish cast. He could see the infection winning over her immune system.

"Mona, you've been sleeping for hours. You're burning up with a fever. Please let me bring you to the hospital to treat those wounds," he begged, hoping she would see reason and leave the house. Her obsession with hurting Mike was killing her as fast as the infection.

"Screw that. Get me those antibiotics on the top shelf of the bathroom cabinet, some Dettol, and the coke." Her voice was hoarse as she barked out the directives.

Even in this state, she incited fear in Kevin. He made his way to the bathroom, going through the pill bottles to find the ones most likely to be what she was asking for. He found three bottles out of the seven he reckoned could be antibiotics, although all were expired by a few years.

Kevin grabbed the bottle of Dettol household disinfectant from the bottom of the sink, picked up a few towels, and laid all the items on Mona's bedside. He returned downstairs to get her the cocaine mirror he had on the living room table, ensuring he got his fill before heading back.

Her predicament didn't prevent her from serving herself. She quickly cut up four lines and inhaled them through her abused nostrils. Quivering from the effects of the drug, she felt bulletproof. She grabbed the bottle of Dettol and soaked her wounds in the harsh liquid. If her pain flared, she didn't show it, wasted in her drugged haze. Shaking from her body's intense shock, she swallowed a pill from every vial and lay back in bed.

Kevin was beside himself at this point. He couldn't afford to lose Mona for fear of losing his lifestyle. Would those dirty wounds kill her? There was no way of calling an ambulance for her; she'd stated in fury that she wouldn't leave the house, thinking she would potentially be giving Mike the upper hand. If he disrespected her wishes, it would most likely get him kicked out of the house.

He checked on her a while later. She was sleeping, splayed in an uncomfortable-looking position, beads of sweat at her temples. He decided he should pick up proper bandages from the Rangiora Pharmacy. She needed to get on top of the infection if he had a chance to get out of his mess. He hopped in his Mercedes and headed toward town, the wind flinging stones at its shiny exterior.

Mona's house hadn't suffered any damage from the night's fury, but Mike's shed had fared poorly. Only a minor section of the shed still had a roof, the improvised home he'd built in the shed on full display. His belongings were scattered on the grass where the sheep should be. The shelter beds protected the placid animals as they inquisitively looked toward their owner's abode.

Driving past the property, Kevin couldn't help but feel bad for the poor guy. He didn't deserve Mona's abuse. Mike was a good guy, always ensuring Mona and the kids were cared for financially. He giggled. Mike did such a good job she could afford to keep Kevin in the lifestyle he'd come to depend on.

Kevin thought he should have hooked up with Mike since he was paying the bills and wasn't nuts like Mona. He chuckled to himself. The thought wasn't that far-fetched for him; Kevin had no preference. Female or male, he didn't care as long as there was something in it for him.

Just before Mona, he dated Richard, a burly, overweight exporter who was married but wanted his toy on the side. Richard paid well until he counted the benefits Mona could give him and quickly broke it off with the man. He threatened to tell his wife the truth about her husband if he didn't give him $10,000. The money didn't support him for long but was adequate to ensnare Mona for himself.

His face grimaced, sour at the realization that he was now the trapped one.

| 47 |

Wait

Mike didn't want Kate to help him in the yard; it was too dangerous. The hot air currents barreling down his fields peeled layers of roofing from the shed like onions shedding their thin, dry skin, the metal's sharp edges threatening to slice anything it touched.

Debris covered everything. Mike hurried to gather as much of it as possible to ensure the stock's safety. A loud crack from where the roof clung to its partnered walls made him look up nervously. He sighed with relief when it remained affixed.

He counted himself lucky to have moved the motorbikes to the main shed before bed, his last-minute decision saving them. The open hut that usually stored them no longer stood, another casualty of the wind.

Heartbreak clouded his vision. Only hours before, he had dreamed of building a house so Kate and Jimmy could stay; now, he didn't have a place to call his own. His heart heavy from the sting of reality, he set off on the motorbike to clear the paddocks of debris, his thoughts turning to the Paterson place.

***

Kate was relieved when Mike decided to wait out the storm with them in the big house they were bound to. It was a large enough house for a family of five, overkill for her and Jimmy. She struggled with the house's eerie vastness, preferring smaller, cozier homes.

Kate grabbed linen and went to prepare the bed in the spare bedroom. Jimmy had been told what happened with Nick and didn't seem bothered. It perturbed her since they'd been close. She guessed it came down to the extended separation. They'd been apart for longer than they'd been together. Jimmy couldn't see a change in the dynamic and didn't grasp that Nick wasn't returning this time.

His response saddened her, and she wondered if she'd done him a disservice with her decision to follow Nick.

She sighed heavily. It was too early to be open with Jimmy about the physical relationship she and Mike shared. Separate bedrooms would be the way forward for the moment. The situation would be a challenging one, she thought, her mind replaying images of their time together.

***

The wind strewed debris everywhere in her yard as well. She was picking up the pine branches that peppered the yard when she heard Mike's motorbike. He looked parched, his skin dry and dusty. She led him into the shed's wash basin so he could wash his hands and splash water on his face.

The first thing she got from him was the rundown of the damages on the farm and what he needed to do to protect the stock. When she asked about the house, he went silent. He looked at her, his eyes showing how heartbroken he was. There was no other option apart from starting over. Insurance would cover a part of it, but it was for the shed and not the dwelling inside.

Mike paused, deep in thought, then grabbed her hands and apologized, his eyes misty.

"I'm so sorry, Kate. I was hoping to make it into a real home..." At a loss, he looked to the ground, beaten.

She pulled him to her forcefully so he would know she meant business and looked him directly in the eyes.

"We'll rebuild it together," she said, her words barely audible in the noise brewing outside.

The pine branches from the downed trees made screeching noises when they rubbed against the garage. Mike felt what she said more than he heard it. His insides were drenched with warmth at her support.

He kissed her passionately, holding her close. His overwhelming need for her took over. Grabbing her buttocks, he sat her on the washing machine, intent on having her for lunch.

She squirmed with pleasure, excited by the mastery he was showcasing and at the sudden, unexpected lovemaking session.Feeling her approach her threshold, he stood up, freed himself from his confines, and plunged into her warmth. She reacted quickly and reached her peak with only a few thrusts.

Her physical reaction was so intense Mike could no longer hold himself. He closed his eyes in response to the rapture coursing through his loins as the first wave of passion made way for the second. Mike opened his eyes and glanced out the window. Standing in the yard, a few meters away, were two hooded figures facing the shed.

Another wave of pleasure hit him, and he delightedly closed his eyes. He re-opened them and scanned the yard.

The ecstasy he was feeling replaced itself with fear. The backyard was empty.

| 48 |

Brothers

Matt and Melissa's property fared well from the midnight gales the Nor'wester conjured to make its arrival known. His brother, Eric, hadn't been so lucky.

Much of his milking shed roof peeled off, and his grain silo shifted, now sporting a dangerous lean. The erratic stock was lamenting their displeasure, their cries ringing in the distance. They had to delay morning milking until the shed was safe to use.

Seeing the gargantuan task, Matt jumped into his truck to ask Mike for help. On his way, he came to the Paterson Place driveway, opening like an eye through the thick green of the pines.

As far as he could see, the place only suffered a few downed trees. Mike wasn't there. He drove down Harper's Road to find the main road junction.

The sight before him made his heart ache. Mike was driving around on his motorbike, trying to pick up the guts of his shed. The wind had strewn them in the paddocks, blowing them around like insults.

Matt stopped the truck. He knew all too well Mike would leave everything to help him. His home needed tending to first, then Kate's place. He backed away without Mike catching wind of his presence and drove back, intent on asking for his help later this afternoon if needed.

***

Eric was a sour guy, his personality more suited for business than farming. His wife, Jeannine, was happy when they first got married, but the death of their father changed Eric. He became greedy and spiteful. The longer the drawn-out legal battle to have the will overturned went, the darker Eric became. He developed a fierce paranoid streak, and his unpredictable behavior progressively drew his wife away from him. One day, a year and a half after Eric had taken over the farm, Jeannine left. Matt hadn't seen her since.

"Jesus Christ, Matt, are you going to sit there doing nothing or help?" Eric growled at his younger brother.

"Mate, I'm making sure nothing more flies off. Would be a shame if a cow got hit," Matt said as he secured the structure. It was already a big job, but the wind's force made things even more difficult. His shirt flapped wildly as he struggled with his task.

Eric came to help steady the temporary anchor. Once satisfied it would hold, they headed inside for lunch.

***

"The bloody thing is hitting us hard. It usually skips off Mount Thomas and spares us, but this time, it's headed straight for us." Eric spoke as if only to himself. He grabbed the radio and called the farm workers to gather the cows. They'd missed their morning milking and were uncomfortably full, making mastitis a real threat.

"How's Melissa doing?" Eric asked.

Matt was surprised his brother asked about his wife, usually paying no attention to her. Melissa had taken ill during the night with one of her strange migraines. They'd started when she was just a tot and always appeared when the Nor'wester arrived. Something about atmospheric pressure, he'd been told. He had tried to get used to it throughout his years by her side. Seeing her suffer and grab at her ears wildly, complaining of a loud hum, made him feel helpless.

A loud crack interfered with the smooth flow of tea Eric poured, hot liquid splashing on the table. Both men hurriedly looked out the window.

Another part of the milking shed had torn off, exposing the milking platform. Matt told Eric to call on any mates available. He was going to get Mike to help secure the structure.

***

Matt sped to Kate's place, relieved to see Mike's motorbike up the drive. He parked as close as he could to the house, the driveway still impassable from the downed trees.

He'd been right. The property once again escaped damage. Most reckoned the place was cursed, and they were probably right. Matt felt the same as Mike about Paterson's place. They'd grown up next to it. It wasn't right then, and it wasn't right now.

He thought he saw Mike and Kate in the backyard past the shed and waved to them. Making his way through the maze of pine branches, he emerged, surprised to see no one in the yard. He spied them again deep in the forest. No, it wasn't them. It was two men with hoods on. He climbed his way through the maze of branches to reach the forest. When he looked for them, they were gone. It made him nervous.

He decided he must be imagining things and knocked on the front door. The dissonance from the forest and the blast of hot air pummeled the house like a jet plane at total engine capacity. No answer.

He walked to the garage door, concern blooming in his gut. Where were they, and who were those guys in the forest? Matt wondered as he opened the shed door.

He regretted not having knocked.

Matt looked away, embarrassed, catching his mate in the act.

Mike stood with his back to him, still holding Kate, her legs wrapped around him, his shorts down to his sock-covered ankles. The only grace saving his dignity was his bush shirt falling long enough to hide anything down to his lower thighs. Matt cleared his throat.

"Ummm, I'll give you guys a minute," he said, exiting the garage.

Mike and Kate burst out laughing at getting caught. He kissed her passionately before uncoupling from her grasp and pulling his pants up. She also pulled herself together, tugging at the front of her shift dress to straighten it. He opened the door to let his mate in, his smile fading when he saw Matt's troubled expression.

"You alright, mate?" Mike asked, putting his cap on.

"Mate, a big chunk of the milking shed roof has fucked off with the wind, the rest is about to go, and we haven't been able to do our morning milking." Matt's whole body was visibly rattled with distress and anxiety. "I could really use your help," he begged.

"No worries, mate," Mike replied, putting his boots on.

"Can I be of help?" Kate asked, hoping she could assist the men.

"Melissa has taken ill. I'm too busy to look after her. Can you check on her and maybe make smoko for the boys coming to help?"

She promptly agreed, worry for her friend apparent. She would take the motorbike and join them later.

The men made their way to Matt's truck, once again climbing over the trees in their way. The rattle the branches made subsided in the enclosed cab of the Hilux, making conversation possible. Matt stared directly ahead of him as he drove.

"So… got any news to tell me, old boy?" Matt asked, taunting Mike. He felt he gained permission to ask after catching him and Kate in the act. Mike smiled and looked at Matt from the corner of his eyes, acknowledging Matt's suspicion. He'd fallen for Kate.

"She's a pretty cool chick, mate," Matt added approvingly.

"Too bad the bloody wind took my place down," Matt heard Mike say as he drove.

"What's your plan, mate?" Matt was intent on helping his friend rebuild as soon as possible, but he would need a place to stay.

"I'm staying at Kate's until the wind dies down," Mike said, looking out the passenger side window, averting Matt's gaze.

Matt looked at him. He would never spend a night at Paterson's old place.

| 49 |

Sickness

Dan caught wind of the dramas at Eric's dairy farm and volunteered to help. Most callouts would surround Stewart's farm, the area hit hardest. He would be readily available to anyone requiring help. His off-duty workmate joined them. Word spread like wildfire in town. The farm was in danger. Every man who could help should make themselves available.

The officers arrived to see a crew of workers desperately trying to hold down the remaining portion of the roof. Colossal strops anchored the structure to the ground. A series of industrial-size bolts, freshly driven into the building, coaxed it back to where it belonged. Dan and his workmate silently disembarked the cruiser and made their way to the group.

"We've got to milk those cows. They need in the shed now," Eric said, frantically signaling to his worker to let the cows in.

Eric was under tremendous pressure. It was apparent in his every action, and how he spoke made everyone around him uncomfortable.

The wind lashed at the strops, straining the load they were there to secure. They were looking over the shed when they saw Kate approaching by motorbike.

"She's inside," Mike yelled, his cry sounding more like a whisper.

She waved and headed for the sanctity of the house.

***

"Melissa," Kate said softly, in case her friend was sleeping. She heard a whimper coming from the back of the house. She entered Matt and Melissa's darkened room and stopped cold, shaken by her friend's state.

Disheveled, wild-eyed, and grasping at her ears, the only thing Melissa could muster was, '*Make it stop!*' Kate immediately sat beside her friend and held her to steady her vigorous rocking.

Melissa howled in pain, incessantly clawing at her ears, trying to stop the clamor. Kate could see faint marks where she'd damaged her skin. She held her hands to Melissa's ears, hoping to calm the noise she was hearing. Melissa stopped rocking and stared directly into Kate's eyes.

"It's begun," she said, her voice ragged. Melissa gasped and slumped into her pillow in what appeared to be a deep sleep.

Kate sprung up from Melissa's bedside, chills rocking her body. The look on Melissa's face haunted her. Her friend looked utterly possessed.

She tucked her in and ensured her breathing was stable before leaving her side. It looked like whatever was plaguing her had dissipated for the time being.

***

Kate went to the kitchen to prepare drinks and nibbles for the crew of workers. Once she had everything ready, she bared the elements, making her way to the clearing where you could see the dairy shed. Considering the circumstances, the mammoth roof was holding on to its foundations, and the milking seemed to be going well.

She watched the men work tirelessly on a temporary measure. They would need to rebuild the roof when the wind tired itself out. She admired how Matt and Mike worked with the other men.

Eric was screaming instructions no one was paying attention to. She could understand why; the man had no presence. His persona reflected his inner turmoil and stature; he was a small man with an immoral mind. She walked back to check on Melissa.

She'd only been in the house for 10 minutes when the front door flung open, surprising her. She jumped, holding her chest. It was Eric. She introduced herself and asked if he would like coffee or tea. Eric looked at her with a creepy smile on his face. A quiver of fear licked her. She tried to brush it away, wanting to be polite.

"Nice to meet you, Kate." He moved closer to her. "How do you like our wee farming community?"

He sounded sleazy; she didn't feel comfortable being near him. She backed up further, her back to the kitchen counter. He seemed to relish her fear and advanced slowly toward her, giggling.

Kate put out her hands to stop him from coming closer. Desperately wanting to escape him, she pushed hard on his chest.

"Eric, stop! Please don't..." she begged.

His stale coffee breath pummeled her face, making her nauseous. She held her head higher, trying to make more space for herself, away from him. He pressed himself on her. She whimpered as her back bent under the pressure of his body and the countertop.

A sob generated by raw fear escaped her. Eric's hands started moving up her thighs. She pushed back to no avail; she was pinned to the counter. His head neared hers to kiss her. She cringed and pulled her face away as best she could to avoid his advance, tears streaming down her face.

They heard the front door fly open. Eric stepped aside, still looking at her with that strange expression.

Matt entered the room, the smile on his face collapsing. He looked at his brother, then at Kate, brushing away the tears from her face.

Facing Matt, Kate shook her head, signaling for him to let the issue go. She didn't want to cause a stir.

Matt was still fuming when Mike entered the room. Oblivious to Matt's anger and the tears she had convincingly wiped away, Mike poured himself a cup of tea.

Her eyes met Matt's. She could see that he wouldn't let it go that easy.

| 50 |

Will It Come Again?

Darkness beckoned, bringing no change in the wind's velocity or warmth. Melissa was better and had gotten up briefly before they left when the humming extinguished itself. She terrified Kate. She seemed so unlike herself; Kate shivered thinking about it.

They made their way back to Paterson's place by motorbike. Jimmy had already arrived from school and was busy taking branches away from the drive. Mike dropped Kate off with her son and told her he would return with the chainsaw.

Jimmy was excited to see her. He hurriedly recounted the stories the students told him about the destruction the nearby properties had been prey to. The children at school had been spinning yarns longer than a dirt road.

They'd gotten lucky. Kate looked up at the trees, thinking the plantation might act like a shelter for the house when Jimmy said something that made her blood run cold.

"Two guys were here when I got home. They watched me work and stayed around for a while but then disappeared. They didn't say anything," Jimmy said nonchalantly.

Every hair on Kate's head stood at attention, her body tense. Few people used Harper's Road. Who could he be talking about? She faced her son, putting both her hands on his shoulders.

"What did they look like?" she asked, trying to keep her voice from shaking.

"Just like two normal guys," he replied, shrugging his shoulders. "They wore jeans and hoodies." He bent down to pick up a branch.

"Could you see their faces?" she prodded further, uncertain whether she wanted to hear his answer.

"Nah," he said, pausing to look around. "It's like they didn't have any."

***

That evening, Jimmy went to bed exhausted from the physical labor. The house's windows rattled, the wind harassing them relentlessly. Kate sat pensively in the living room next to the fire, unable to digest the conversation she had with her son in the driveway. Afraid of making him nervous, she kept her composure, telling him to find her or Mike if he saw anyone in the yard again.

It was far from cold, but the day's extreme elements and exhaustion left her chilled. If the wind bothered Jimmy, you would never have guessed it. He was overjoyed when they announced Mike would take over the spare bedroom for a few days and asked if he could stay longer. Kate was pleased Jimmy approved of the arrangement.

Mike walked into the living room fresh from the shower, running his hand in his damp hair. He flopped beside Kate on the sofa, exhausted after the day's workload. A creak in the roof from the wind's pressure made him look up at the ceiling, apprehension making lines appear on his forehead.

Kate snuggled closer, more pensive than usual.

"Are you okay, Hun?" he asked, running his hands up and down her smooth legs.

"Yeah, I guess…" she wasn't sure how to bring it up. "Jimmy saw two men wearing hoodies watching him today in the yard." Her mouth was dry, her voice cracked, making the last word of her sentence inaudible. Mike shifted to give her his full attention.

"I think I saw them too," he said, holding her hands. "When we were…you know." The look he gave her told her when.

"I looked out the window; they were there, then gone," Mike said, shaking his head.

"Kate, I've got to be honest with you. This house freaks me out. We thought this house was haunted when we were kids, probably because we saw how uneasy our parents were about the place.

Old man Patterson had a huge family, his wife giving birth to twelve children. When the Spanish Flue hit, all except the youngest perished in the pandemic. The heartbroken parents buried their children on their land, the lot the Daltons occupy now. The Paterson's owned the entire block back then."

"That's horrible. Those poor people," she said, looking at Mike in disbelief.

"The farmer and his wife tried their best to get past the tragedy and raise their youngest, but something wasn't right with their boy. At first, they thought the grief of losing his siblings made him act strangely. He would speak to them while he played in the yard, insisting that he saw them. The child was two years old when they perished, too young for him to remember their names and faces, yet he could describe them accurately. His parents were bewildered."

Kate listened intently, wide-eyed. Mike continued with his tale.

"The old man struggled to get the farm work done without the help of his older children. His fields soured, his stock suffered, and less than a decade after losing most of his family, he was found hanging from the old macrocarpa at the driveway's entrance."

Kate covered her eyes with her hands in disbelief. "That's dreadful. I'm never going to look at that tree the same again. What about the wife and young boy?" Kate asked, sitting at attention.

Mike's mouth was dry. He took a sip of beer before continuing.

"They kept on living in the house, keeping to themselves mostly. Her son was odd, not wanting to play with other children and only talking to his lost siblings. Eventually, they became recluses, removing themselves from society altogether.

"One day, when the young man was fourteen, his mother's extended family visited from Marlborough. They found the mother mummified in her bed. She had been dead for a few years. The child lost his mother but kept on as if nothing happened, living in the house alone. The family blamed his behavior on trauma, having lost his entire family.

"They tried to bring him north, but he refused, stating he couldn't leave his family behind. He claimed they were still with him, joining him when the Nor'wester blew, walking the land he grew up on. The family gave up and left him to it. Things were different back then; at fourteen, you were considered a young man, capable of caring for yourself."

He took another swig of beer, uncomfortable with where the story was going. Kate kept quiet, listening.

"He never married or had any children. The house fell into disrepair, the land overrun by weeds, and no one could figure out how he fed himself or made any money. No one wanted to ask either. They determined him to be mentally unwell and avoided the strange man.

"The Nor'wester roared one night when Paterson was himself an old man. For years, he'd managed to keep to himself on Harper's Road, his nearest neighbor living a few paddocks away from Matt and Melissa's.

"The neighbors had come from a high-ranking family in Christchurch, settling in Okuku after purchasing a sizeable parcel of land. The night the storm hit, the wind blew the roof off their home. The husband had no choice but to ask the old man for help, seeing that his wife had just given birth to their son two days prior and was still frail.

"When he got to Patterson's place, he saw the old man standing in the yard, surrounded by ghostly figures swirling around him in the wind. He seemed to feed off them, consuming their energy while they fed on the gales. He returned home swearing never to return; they moved away a few weeks later after telling everyone what he'd seen at Patterson's place.

"People have committed suicide, been killed in freak accidents, or murdered during the Nor'westers in these parts for years. Many residents still believe the spirits join the Paterson family's ghosts, roaming the land in Okuku, ready to feed on the living when the wind blows.

"It explains why so many keep their curtains drawn when the storm peaks. They say you can hear a loud hum when they are near, even when you can't see them. It made us listen to our parents when they told us to go to bed: Paterson's ghost would get us if we didn't." He averted her gaze, knowing the truth about her home would scare her.

Another strong gust shook the house. She clung closer to him, shielding her face. She finally looked up at him, her hand holding his tight. She told him about the man in the gray hoodie she saw in the forest and on the deck.

"Melissa said she heard loud humming; I heard the humming the first day I was here. There's something not right with this place, Mike. We need to leave."

Mike gave her a side glance and silently shook his head in agreement.

Unwilling to face going to bed separately, they fell into a broken sleep, holding each other on the sofa, the remnants of fire flickering light across their bodies.

| 51 |

Scavenger

At nightfall, Shannon drove Barry to the shed in Okuku. She knew he was growing tired of their deal and wanted something more; he wanted the shed, but it might not be easy. Shannon knew there was still heat on her, the police coming to her mother's place in Greymouth and Barry's place to ask her questions.

Barry went wild at her when the police arrived early one morning. He had a lot to lose and didn't want anyone snooping around, especially not the fuzz. The council also contacted her, fining her for the pit. She had no means to pay and didn't care about their stupid fine.

Shannon was surprised the shed still stood, considering the trail of destruction they'd driven through. After measuring it, Barry walked the garage perimeter to ensure no prying eyes could interrupt his plans. He could vaguely see the neighboring house from the shed, so he approached the forest boundary.

The sun had not fully committed itself to rest, but it was still dark enough to see inside the home, the large casement windows allowing a full view of the living room. A black-haired woman sat on the sofa next to the fire, her legs stretched out, her silky blue robe hugging her ample breast.

She wasn't the type of woman Barry ever got the chance to see in the flesh. The better-looking women he entertained he paid for;

they would never have been with him otherwise. The rest were crack whores.

He felt himself stiffen, his hand going down to his crotch as he stared intently at her. Jealousy and rage squashed Barry's desire as he saw a well-built man sit beside her.

He would have her, Barry thought. She'd be a bonus that came with Shannon's place. He looked at Shannon and motioned to follow him into the car.

***

Barry told Shannon the trip's primary purpose was determining the shed's suitability. The other reason for the late-night trip was to raid the sheds the wind ripped open. The noise didn't carry the same in the night's dark, with the wind howling its haunting cry. It was a perfect opportunity for them to take the spoils of the previous night's war.

Shannon again proved her worth, able to run from the side roads through the paddocks practically unseen. With his wide girth, Barry couldn't perform at the same level. They raped and pillaged the wind's unfortunate victims throughout the blustery night.

| 52 |

Delay

Kevin got sidetracked while picking up bandages for Mona. He met an old acquaintance and accepted his invitation to meet him at his hotel for some whisky and coke. They shared more than drinks, and Kevin was happy to leave with money in his pocket for services rendered.

He hoped Mona was still sleeping, not wanting to deal with her wrath, especially how her wounds held her up in the house, unable to walk alone. Thinking she would most likely want a drink when she woke up, he picked up a few bottles of cheap red wine and headed back toward Okuku, bandages in tow.

The landscape had changed since the morning. The few lights always present in Mike's shed were sorely missed, the dark concealing the remnants of the building. Kevin nearly missed Mona's driveway. He looked over to the house to see it also covered by darkness. It looked vacant.

Butterflies swarmed in his belly. He parked his Mercedes and entered the house as silently as possible, not wanting to wake Mona. Kevin placed his purchased items onto the table and headed for the stairs to check on his keeper.

"Kevin," a guttural voice called from the corner of the lounge.

He froze, the mass amount of cocaine he'd ingested during the afternoon making his heart hammer wildly. He turned to face the voice. Sitting in an old wing-back chair, he could see the shadow of a woman.

"Mona, is that you?" he said, his voice getting caught in his throat.

The thing emitted a sound like a death rattle. Incapable of holding his suspense any longer, Kevin turned on the side table lamp, casting light on the chair and its occupant.

He pulled back, utterly disgusted. What was sitting in the chair was a monster.

Mona hadn't been a model of youth and vitality, but what sat before him was revolting. Wearing a short pink nightdress, her battered legs were displayed prominently. Long ribbons of dark blue veins ran up her legs to be consumed by the darkness under her nightshirt. Her arms and neck showed the same grotesque death marks.

It was her face that shocked him the most. She'd picked at it in a drug-fueled haze, her bloody nostrils matching the sores she'd created on her cheeks. Her eyes were wild with intoxication, her gaze darting back and forth quickly, reminding Kevin of a frog. She'd pulled out most of her hair, leaving a small amount of broken, dry, bleached ends sticking up randomly from her head. A putrid smell of decomposition emanated strongly from her body.

Kevin shuddered and retched.

As if trying to prove her capability, she rose slowly from the chair, her arms straining at the exertion. Mona walked toward him, pus oozing freely from the gashes on her legs.

How did she get down those stairs? He wondered, incredulous at her strength despite the infection coursing through her. The smell of her wounds wafted to meet his nose; he gagged. She didn't seem to notice his disgust. Trying to make sense of what he was seeing, Kevin moved to the light switch on the wall and flicked it on. Her image didn't improve.

What should he do? What could he do? He asked himself, ready to leave and never return, but where would he go? He'd depended on her for so long that he had no way out.

He was going to keep her hidden. If Mike saw her now, he would kick Kevin out and probably press neglect charges. Kevin took out a bag of coke and offered her some after freely snorting as much as he could.

"Come on, baby, let's go to bed."

He helped her get up the stairs.

| 53 |

The Grind

Dan tossed and turned all night.

Visions of ghostly apparitions, Lorraine's and Jeffrey's faces, and excerpts from his past haunted his mind. The wind forced its weight on the house, bullying it with constant taunting. He'd gotten up a few times, unable to shake the mental imagery dancing a macabre dance in his head.

Walking to the kitchen to get himself a glass of water in the night's gloom, his sleep-deprived eyes caught glimpses of what was not there. He jumped instinctively, his heart pounding like a jackhammer.

He needed to get a hold of himself, he thought, disappointed at himself for having dwindled to the state he was in.

Running the faucet to cool the water, he heard a scraping sound from the attached garage. He slowly turned off the tap to focus on the sound originating from the dark confines of the room.

Someone was in there.

Goosebumps erupted across Dan's body. He picked up the fireplace poker and reached the garage's access door, standing beside it, breathing heavily. Mustering his confidence, his eyes still clouded from lack of sleep. He slowly turned the door handle to enter what used to be his wife's parking space.

The darkness was more profound in the purpose-built room. Taking a few tentative steps, Dan could feel a presence to the right of him and one to the back of the room where a simple workbench stood. Holding his breath, he listened intently. He could barely disseminate a slight rattle coming from one of them.

Every nerve in his body, responding to the imminent threat, sparked with electricity. He advanced one more step, bumping into something soft. It moved quickly aside as it swung from the rafters. He pushed it away, wondering why what was hanging there smelled so familiar. A bag of laundry, perhaps?

He heard shuffling at the back corner and feet moving on concrete. A shadow moved over the window on the right wall. Someone was there, hidden in the shadows. Determined to accost whoever had breached the sanctity of his home, he moved quickly to the light switch on the wall. The entire garage was instantly illuminated in yellow light.

Dan looked where the sound came from. He could only see his workbench. No one was there. His shoulders relaxed a bit. He must be imagining things in the clamor of the wind. He turned to walk out of the garage.

What he saw tore his heart to shreds. Hanging from the rafters, Lorraine and Jeffrey's bodies swung, nooses attaching them to the exposed rafters.

He rushed to his son, frantically trying to untie him, making his head dangle at an odd angle. His young body slumped on his father as he fell to the ground. Dan looked up at his wife. Her eyes stared blankly, grotesquely glazed over. He knew she was dead.

Dan cried, holding his dead son at the bottom of his wife's dangling feet.

***

The light of day coming from the side window of the garage struck him like a blow. Feeling intoxicated, he slowly looked down at his arms, expecting to see his beloved son, Jeffrey, lying there, but there was nothing. He looked up with apprehension; Lorraine wasn't there, either.

Picking himself up, he looked around the garage to see nothing but a small oil spot Lorraine's car left months ago. The wind laughed at him, bashing itself into the garage door, sounding like a monster knocking for permission to come in. Alone in his misery, he left the garage to get ready to go to work.

He was losing his mind, he thought to himself.

Maybe he'd already lost it.

| 54 |

Brotherly Love

What remained of the milking shed roof miraculously withstood the night's battle with the wind. Matt, relieved, reached across the yard to help his brother. They'd worked hand in hand for years before their father's death until Eric got greedy.

Matt saw his brother change after losing their father and was often worried about his mental state. His temper, demeanor, and creepiness made Matt keep his distance despite their dispute. If not for the wind damaging the milking shed, he wouldn't have come close to Eric and the farm. It was still the family farm, and he would never let his dad down, even if he wasn't here to see it. The bloody Nor'wester brought an end to their months of silence.

Mike had become his adopted brother. He saw him through the dark days after his father's death and was always there for whatever Matt and Melissa needed. He cared more for Mike than he did his own brother and would do anything for him.

Matt had to put his differences with his brother aside; they would need to work together to fix the roof. He gritted his teeth, not looking forward to Eric's orders and ramblings.

"Well, she held together well enough," Matt commented as he entered the milking shed.

His brother, getting things ready for milking, paid him no attention, his back to him replacing the teat cup liners. Matt looked up at the missing section of the roof to work out how best to close it in until they could get the builders on site.

"She's nice..." Eric said randomly.

Matt looked at him. "Who's nice?" he asked, his gut already knowing what he would say.

"That Canadian lady," Eric responded with a strange look of desire on his face.

Matt's hackles went up.

"Don't mess with Mike's girl, Eric. Mike's been through hell and back and deserves a break; he hasn't been this happy since he and Mona married. I'll stand in anyone's way to prevent Mike from getting hurt again, and the last thing I want is for you to interfere with their relationship," Matt said, making sure Eric knew how serious he was.

Eric brushed him off. "How's Melissa?" he asked, changing subjects.

Matt thought he was a caring brother-in-law yesterday when he asked about her, but now Matt wasn't so confident.

A profound transformation had occurred in Eric. Since they'd started speaking again because of the roof, Matt no longer trusted him around women. He didn't want him near Melissa or Kate, his instincts telling him his brother was dangerous.

"She's good," Matt responded, not wanting to divulge too much.

Melissa was in bed, tortured by a constant buzzing.

The hum she kept complaining about didn't just affect his wife. The specialists told them many hear the strange incessant droning worldwide; the phenomenon wasn't solely happening in Canterbury.

People reported being tortured by a constant pulsing whine, keeping them awake and driving some to the brink of insanity. One family member could be severely afflicted while the remaining household couldn't hear a thing. No one could explain why it was happening or what was causing it. For Melissa, she could only hear the noise when the Nor'wester was imminent and for its duration. Matt often wondered if stories about Paterson's ghosts could be true and if that's what Melissa was hearing.

Matt left Eric in the shed and went to Paterson Place to see if Mike could help him pick up timber and plywood in Rangiora to fix the shed. Driving by his house, he thought of Melissa still sick in bed. Matt didn't feel comfortable leaving her with Eric being so close. He'd never felt this way previously, but his brother was acting too strangely for him not to be nervous. He rolled down the road and took a sharp right down Harper's Road.

He noticed the downed trees had been removed from the driveway and piled neatly as firewood near the tree line. Matt realized how much work his friend accomplished the previous day. He first cared for his stock in the morning, then picked up his belongings strewn through-out his paddocks before helping him with the milking shed. After that, he cut and piled firewood at Kate's. The legend even made time for some afternoon delight during his lunch break.

Matt laughed, thinking of when he'd walked in on the two of them in the garage laundry. The boy finally found someone that made him happy. He pulled up the drive to Mike, waving to him from the garage, a cup of coffee in hand.

"She's blowing her ass off again," his friend said. He was leaning one elbow on the garage door, looking outside, drinking his coffee. The trees bent like an archway over the driveway, screaming their lament as they danced a macabre ballet.

"Are you up for giving me a hand to pick up plywood and timber for the shed? I thought we could get some for your place at the same time. We can start on your place once we sort out the milking shed." Matt said, trying to be helpful.

He could see the wheels spinning in Mike's head.

"We'll get Eric sorted first, mate. That uptight bastard is about to blow a gasket. The milking shed is more important than my pile of shit." Mike headed inside momentarily to say goodbye to Kate before putting on his boots. The men jumped into Matt's truck. Matt paused momentarily and looked at Mike.

"Mate, I got to tell you something about Eric." Matt took a deep breath, trying to find his words. "I don't think he's alright." He looked at Mike and shook his head.

The ignition came to life; the battered truck rocked violently. Matt told Mike how Eric had been with Melissa and Kate.

| 55 |

Concern

Kate heard Matt's truck pull out of the driveway. She was alone in the house again, and it made her nervous.

Kate locked the doors and ensured the French doors were closed and latched. She looked out the kitchen window toward the plantation. It seemed so much safer out there than within the walls surrounding her. She only felt comfortable in the house when Mike was there with them. What would she do when he went back home?

She had a terrifying night. Her sleep had been interrupted by horrific dreams of the hooded man, Paterson's ghosts, and the unrelenting thunder of the wind. She'd awoken to a frightful sound, lost in her surroundings, realizing a tree had fallen close to the house. She relaxed, realizing she was in the living room, her head resting on Mike's chest. His warmth and the up-and-down motion of his chest as he breathed, soothed her back to sleep.

Getting up in the morning hadn't been pleasant; Kate and Mike were stiff from sleeping on the sofa. Jimmy woke before them. He poured himself some cereal and a glass of milk and sat in front of them with his bowl on the coffee table, watching cartoons on TV. The wee man had his morning routine down pat: get up, make breakfast, get dressed, brush his teeth, pack his school bag, and walk to the bus. He was becoming a well-disciplined young man.

Kate cringed as the gales whipped the tree branches along the side of the garage. Eerie shadows from the sun trying to break through the trees bounced off the kitchen walls.

She looked outside; a sea of pinecones littered the plantation floor. It would be dangerous to venture into the forest's depths in these conditions. Tired or misplaced branches often shake themselves off, making it a hazardous environment in these conditions. She was confident she could find enough pinecones without venturing too deep into the forest. First, she had to get the laundry done.

She picked up all of Mike's clothes and washed them this morning, ready to put them on the line. Thankfully, the clothesline was still usable. The wind swirled but didn't gather enough strength to rip the laundry off its pegs.

She carefully maneuvered the garage door to the internal hallway open with her thigh while she balanced the wash basket on her hip. The wind cracked the roof as she made her way to the hallway leading out to the lounge.

She dropped the laundry basket, frozen, unable to move. Both sets of French doors were opened and precariously swigged in the currents of air.

She'd closed and latched them less than an hour ago.

Who would have opened them? Was she alone?

Fear set in and revved up her senses. Rushing to the living room doors, she struggled against the wind but managed to bolt them shut. The dining room doors proved easier. Sitting at the dining room table, panting from the adrenaline rush, she didn't feel alone in the house anymore.

Tentatively looking around the doorways, the fireplace poker in her hand, she checked every room in the house but found nothing.

The Nor'wester brought hot air, but she could see her breath. The house was freezing. Goosebumps raised themselves on her arms as she felt something brush against her. She grabbed the laundry basket and rushed outside through the front door. Shaking, she hung up the clothes on the clothesline. She wasn't going back into that house until the boys returned.

***

After hanging the laundry, Kate grabbed an empty seed sack from the garage and went to the plantation to gather pinecones, trying to forget what had happened in the house. She decided her mind was playing tricks on her, yet didn't dare to return inside.

Picking the cones was easy, and she soon had her bag full. Proud of herself, it had only taken a quarter of an hour to accumulate a week's worth of fire starters. Straining her ears, she thought she heard her son calling for her.

That's odd, she thought; it must be the wind playing tricks. Jimmy should still be in school. It wasn't even lunchtime yet.

Bending to pick up a few more cones, she heard Mike's voice. He must be back from running errands with Matt. She entered the yard to see Mike and Jimmy waving frantically from the driveway. They both started running toward her.

"Hey, what's up guys? Shouldn't you be in school, Jimmy?" Jimmy hugged her tight, tears streaking his cheeks. When Mike reached them, she was about to ask Jimmy why he was crying.

"Kate. Where have you been? We have been looking for you for hours. You had us worried sick. I nearly called Dan," he said, panting.

"Hours?" She asked, not comprehending what he was saying. She looked questioningly at Mike.

"I've only been in the forest for fifteen or twenty minutes. You would have seen me; I only picked the cones in the first rows," Kate said, pointing to the plantation.

"Kate, it's seven o'clock at night."

She looked to the sky to see the sun low on the horizon.

"We've been looking for you since Jimmy came home from school."

| 56 |

Monster

Kevin watched her breathe, sitting on the bed beside her. Every time her chest expanded and contracted, she emitted a creepy gurgle.

Her fever had broken through the night. The mixture of random antibiotics, whisky, and coke must be a magic potion because he expected her to be septic by now. She groaned as she moved her legs. Her wounds stuck to the thin white sheets, leaving grotesque yellow and brown stains. The putrid smell wafted in the air, filling the floral wallpapered bedroom.

She'd terrified him yesterday, her transformation so otherworldly he barely recognized her. He'd pleasured her as best as he could until she fell asleep, unable to rise to the job's demands. The memories of their encounter were guaranteed to reappear in his nightmares.

She clung to her ears in her sleep, pulling out more hair as she did. She was out cold, and Kevin expected her to sleep for the next few hours. He made his way downstairs to the kitchen.

I'm up shit creek now, he said under his breath, contemplating the situation that he was in. He would come up with something else that would work for him. Mona would no longer do.

***

An hour later, after a few lines of coke, Kevin was sitting on the front deck sunning himself. Clad in a pair of pink cotton shorts and a white polo shirt, sipping a gin and tonic, he looked like a guy who didn't have a care in the world. The sun was a pleasure; the wind was not. He'd religiously worked on his tan and wouldn't be deterred.

Hearing activity in the house, he got up, put down his drink, and opened the front door. He stood there, half in, half out of the house, straining to hear over the wind's pounding. Nope, he couldn't hear anything. He relaxed, turning to make his way back to the lounge chair.

Kevin's heart jumped out of his chest. Mona was right beside him. Dressed in jeans and a pink blouse, her eyes moving sporadically, she looked at him with a crazed smile.

"Mona," he stuttered. "How did you make it down the stairs alone? How did you get dressed?" Her miraculous recovery chilled him. He wondered if she was even human anymore, possessed by something otherworldly. She shouldn't even be conscious with that infection coursing through her.

"Nothing's wrong, Kevin. Why do you ask?" she crackled her response, further alarming him.

She didn't sound like herself anymore, her voice belonging to a lifelong cigarette smoker.

Sitting down on the lounger next to his, seemingly unaffected by her recent injuries, she sipped his drink before offering it back to him. Kevin waved her off. She could keep it. He didn't want to expose himself to whatever the hell she had. The wind tickled the bits of pulled-out, broken hair; it reminded him of tendrils of smoke coming off a burnt-out fire.

"We should go upstairs for some play time, darling." She spoke in a deep tone, trying to be seductive. Any provocative effect was lost with the hard crackle in her voice.

"I'm feeling quite randy," she said, the movement of her eyes manic.

Kevin felt the bile rise in his throat and forced it down. He couldn't say no.

He hated himself.

| 57 |

Break-In

Making his way past the police station reception counter and the desks covered in paperwork, Tewano opened the office door without knocking and rushed in.

"Looks like there were eight break-ins last night, all of them hit by the wind the night before," Dan's co-worker, Tewano, announced.

He hadn't been on the force long and was out to impress. His ulterior aspiration was to land a detective job in Auckland. That meant years of climbing the ladder. He needed to start somewhere, and the Rangiora police department was as good as any.

"Whoa! Are you alright, mate?" he said in shock. Tewano's jaw dropped at the sight of his supervisor.

"You look like death warmed over. What the hell is happening to you? You need time off."

Preoccupied with Dan's unhealthy, drawn-out state, Tewano sat on the worn-out leather chair in front of Dan's desk.

Dan didn't raise his eyes from the paperwork before him, entranced by its words. He considered speaking to Tewano and telling him the things he was seeing, the visions. He thought it best he didn't and looked over his reading glasses.

Abruptly, Tewano arose, nervous he might have overstepped his boundary and pissed off his boss.

"Mate, no one can blame you if you need time off after what happened. You never skipped a beat after Lorraine and Jeffrey left. You should have taken time for yourself when it happened," he said, trying to comfort Dan.

Dan took his time digesting his friend's advice and eventually nodded.

"Yeah, it's been a few hard weeks. I have annual leave owing to me. I might consider it, but first, we've got to sort out the break-ins." Dan said, leaving his desk and walking to the patrol car, Tewano following him.

"Random stuff was taken, chainsaws and generators mostly." Tewano gave Dan the rundown as they drove through the countryside, the trees scattering their discarded branches and leaves all over the road.

"Oh yeah, Mike McEwan's TV, stereo, and laptop were stolen. Poor guy's stuff was all over his paddocks." Tewano knew Mike and felt terrible for him.

"Damn, that's no good." Dan shook his head.

"He said he wasn't too bothered because they were crap anyway," Tewano said, sadness shading his words.

"Where are we heading anyway?" he asked, looking up from his files to Dan. He knew he should be driving instead of his exhausted co-worker, but he didn't want to aggravate his boss.

"I've got a hunch," Dan whispered while they turned off the main road and headed to Dalton's old place. He pointed the cruiser down the drive, parked the vehicle, and disembarked.

Tewano followed suit.

Dan investigated the areas not brushed smooth from the wind. He lifted his head and looked at Tewano.

"Someone's been here recently. We'll go lift prints at the crime scenes and compare them. I've got a hunch. I reckon we get a list of those missing items and pay Barry, that bloke that Shannon has been shagging, a visit."

| 58 |

Boiling Point

Melissa slowly went to the kitchen, holding on to whatever she could to keep her balance. The burning in her head blurred her vision. The constant humming, now in tune with the wind, threatened to drive her insane. Dressed in her nightgown, she got herself a glass of water and looked out at the strange clouds in the sky.

The episodes started when she was only a child. It baffled the doctors since they couldn't find anything abnormal in her medical tests. She could feel the Nor'wester brewing better than any meteorologist could predict. A few days before it arrived, she would start seeing glimpses of things that weren't there in the corner of her eyes. As the pressure built on the other side of the mountains, she would start hearing a hum as the wind picked up.

Her horses felt what she was going through, acting erratically, easily spooked. As the buzz increased, the pressure in her head became unbearable, giving her crippling migraines. Matt had known her since primary school and was used to her being tortured during the wind. It broke her heart to see the helplessness in his eyes.

Melissa spied Eric wandering near the gate while scanning the front yard. She'd only seen him twice during the past few months, both times he was driving. He made a point of staying away from them, which suited her fine. She found him to be mean and understood why her sister-in-law left. The separation hadn't done him any favors; he was undernourished and strung out on caffeine.

The pain her brother-in-law caused her husband by shutting him out of the family farm could never be forgotten. Melissa feared them getting violent a few times and was thankful for Matt's ability to control himself. She often wondered what he would have done in those instances if she hadn't been present. Everyone knew the boys hated each other, some betting it was just a matter of time before they took to each other and settled things once and for all.

Eric was fiddling with the gate at the front entry, the door falling off its hinges as he tried to adjust it.

"What's he doing?" she asked under her breath.

He lifted his head like he heard her, looking directly at where she was standing.

"Oh, no! He's coming to the house!"

Dread filled her. She tightened her bathrobe around her, instantly uncomfortable. She heard the door open.

He hadn't bothered knocking on the door. Melissa couldn't believe his arrogance. She heard him make his way in. Every fiber of her body screamed at her to run away when she saw him coming through the hallway to the kitchen. He had that creepy smile, his wide eyes sparkling like a madman.

"Hey, Melissa. Good to see you're doing better." Eric said, his voice not matching his expression. He sounded happy and jovial but looked demented and evil. She stared at him and tightened her bathrobe, her head throbbing.

"Yeah, coming right," she responded feebly.

Picking up on her unease, he cocked his head like an attentive dog and slowly ran his tongue over his teeth. Melissa looked at the door leading out of the kitchen to the yard. She looked back at him, her head still spinning. She gagged involuntarily, the pressure in her head making her feel sick.

Oh my God! I need to get out of here, she thought as she rushed to the door. She turned the handle the instant her hand grasped the cold metal and pulled, her heart thumping so arduously it made her vision vibrate. She caught a sliver of light from the door opening before feeling a pain in her head and falling.

***

She opened her eyes. A deep ache radiated from the side of her skull.

She shook her head, trying to clear her mind. The reality of her situation came flooding back to her. Melissa looked up, terrified.

Eric pulled her onto her feet. She felt his hands snatch her by the waist, shifting her body to face the kitchen counter. He started grinding himself on her buttocks, making her gag uncontrollably. She closed her eyes and screamed as hard as she could, hoping to alert Matt and scare Eric off. It did neither. The wind was screaming louder than she was.

His hand slipped inside her bathrobe and roughly cupped her right breast. She screeched from the pain of him squeezing her so savagely, knowing then that if he were to have his way, she would never be the same. Rage grew inside of her as she struggled to get away. He lifted her bathrobe, pulling down her panties with one hand while still clamping her breast tightly.

Her crying stopped momentarily, her survival instincts taking over. She lurched hard to the right, surprising Eric. He released his grip on her, shocked by her odd movement. Melissa grabbed the butcher knife from the knife block and stabbed wildly above and behind her head. She felt the blade enter his flesh. In shock, he backed away enough for her to escape his grasp.

Eric was bleeding heavily from his forehead. His demented eyes rolled up, trying to see his wound as the blood dripped down his face. He laughed, then slumped to the ground in a sitting position.

Melissa grabbed at the door handle to escape. Knife still in hand, she crossed the threshold.

He plunged for her, his hand gripping her ankle and pulling back hard, making her fall. She bit her tongue, her chin hitting the step. The taste of blood sickened her, stars swimming in her vision made her dizzy.

He pulled her closer. Melissa's stomach lurched; she was sure she would throw up. She snapped to an abrupt sitting position, his hands pulling at her thighs while she retched violently. He moved away, revolted.

In an arc of light, Melissa's right arm barreled down on Eric, the knife entering the left side of his head so forcefully that its blade snapped, leaving her holding the handle.

Eric gurgled. His eyes stopped their demonic dance and glazed over, his movements slowing like a battery at the end of its life.

He fell on his side, eyes open.

| 59 |

Overprotective

Since Kate emerged from the forest after disappearing, Mike hadn't let her out of his sight. He watched her picking pine branches while sitting on the front deck drinking his coffee.

"Don't go too close to the forest, sweetheart… please," he called out, reacting instantly as he saw her pick up a branch in the shadow of the first row of pines.

He knew something was wrong when he saw Jimmy walking around the yard, calling for his mother. In tears and near frantic, Jimmy melted in his arms. He tried his best to not feed Jimmy's fears with his concerns as they looked through every single nook and cranny of the property and surroundings, thinking she might have gone for a walk to the pub. He thought of calling Dan. His panic turned to terror when she saw her walk out of the forest they searched. It was impossible.

She joyfully walked out, proudly displaying her bag of cones. Even Jimmy looked dumbfounded. They searched the entire forest. There'd been no sign of her. He wouldn't let that happen again; the woods would devour her if she went back in.

She didn't believe she'd been in the woods most of the day, adamant she'd only been picking cones for a quarter-hour. Where had she gone? You could easily see through the first three or four rows of pines since their trunks stood bare and tall. They should have seen her. Kate wasn't in the plantation when they searched for her. None of it made any sense.

He took them out to the Lodge for pizza. Kate didn't seem affected by her disappearing act. She was her usual, happy self, claiming they were playing a prank on her. Jimmy seemed to have healed from the fright of losing his mother, downing enough pizza to feed a grown man. Mike's mind was elsewhere.

***

He despised living in the house, constantly feeling like someone was watching him, especially in the shower. He often opened his eyes, shampoo stinging them, feeling like he wasn't alone. The fog lay thick everywhere in the bathroom, unaffected by the fans or the open window. He couldn't figure out why it wouldn't dissipate.

Once, he saw a handprint appear outside the shower's glass doors. He automatically shut off the water and opened the shower door, hoping to surprise the joker playing tricks. There was no one there. His gut told him something had been there, and he didn't want Kate close to it.

When they returned to the house, Mike's apprehensiveness came back to slap him when the Navara turned into the drive. They parked on the couch to watch a movie. He couldn't concentrate. Restless, he left them to enjoy the movie's end while he ran Kate a bath. He picked lavender from the front garden and lit the scented candles. He heard her coming up the hall, having tucked Jimmy in bed for the night. She peeked in and smiled, coming over to him slowly.

"I hope you are joining me," she said, looking at him meekly, placing her arms around him. His desire flared like a fire flamed by the wind blaring outside. His lips met hers eagerly as he pressed himself subconsciously on her, his hunger fueling his body's actions.

Kate pushed him away gently, her eyes glittering in the candlelight, her cheeky smile teasing him. She closed the door, turned to face him, baring herself off her clothing, and approached him seductively. Her gaze bore through his soul. He knew she'd won him over.

***

They sat intertwined in the bath, listening to the wind howl. He stroked her arms as she nestled on him but couldn't relax.

The bare window beside him was black from the darkness outside; Mike couldn't see out. His gut told him that something was lingering close to the house, something atrocious. They needed to get out of the damned place.

Having to live in the house terrified him after knowing its history, although he believed more horrific things happened at Paterson's place than those he'd heard of. Mike felt the dark despair soaked in its walls, evil surrounding him constantly. It felt like the house was alive, the land its skeleton. The place would never be right. The longer they stayed, the more they risked falling prey.

He needed to move them, but where?

| 60 |

Busted

Dan and Tewano fingerprinted the locations where goods had been stolen a few nights previously. One set of prints was common to all the scenes. A search of the database at the station hadn't pulled up a perpetrator, but Dan's gut instinct was still betting Shannon Dalton was involved.

Tire tracks and footprints indicated two people had gone to Dalton's. The weather severely hampered the evidence, and they could cast only a small portion of a tire track and partial footprints.

Tewano had no reason to deny Dan's instincts. Looking at his friend's deteriorating condition, he felt he should go with him to visit Barry and see if Shannon would answer their questions. They drove in silence, Tewano glancing at Dan every few minutes, anxious he might fall asleep at the wheel.

Dan had taken his advice and applied for his annual leave. He accumulated his full four weeks but decided two would be more than adequate. He kept enough leave to fly back to England to see Jeffrey and Lorraine, although he wasn't sure if Lorraine wanted to ever see him again. Dan called often to see how she was doing, but she never spoke to him for longer than getting Jeffrey on the phone. It made his heart ache, the lack of contact with her. He still loved his wife and wished he could fix things.

He also decided to speak to a doctor regarding his insomnia, wanting to get a prescription for sleeping pills while he was on leave to get back on track. He hoped sleep would be enough to stop him from seeing the disturbing visions plaguing his nights.

***

The hour-long journey brought them to Barry's run-down property. A graveyard of scrap cars sat at the mercy of the wind, loose parts singing a ghoulish song led by an invisible conductor. Dust swirled at their feet. Apart from a few weeds near the base of the buildings, no greenery was present, making the property feel post-apocalyptical.

They made their way to the back of the house, where the porch was located. Dan pointed out that the workshop had caved in on itself. It didn't surprise the men. The derelict structure had seen better days and might have succumbed to the same faith, with or without the wind's influence.

They knocked on the weather-beaten wooden door leading to Barry's house.

Dan turned to speak with Tewano after their initial knocks went unanswered. They would need a warrant to investigate further. They were only here to ask questions, Dan explained.

Deep in conversation, they both jumped when Barry finally appeared at the door.

"What the fuck do you want?" he answered gruffly, holding onto the door. The smell of his filthy body and clothing wafted toward the officers; they both scowled.

"We need to ask you a few questions, Barry," Dan said, trying to look inside past the big man.

"About what?" Barry said, eying them suspiciously.

"We have reason to believe you and Shannon might have something to do with the stolen property a few nights ago from Loburn and Okuku," Tewano said but was immediately cut short by Barry.

"I have nothing to do with it," Barry responded. "Not sure what the hell Shannon is up to. Ask her," he said defiantly.

"Can we talk to her, please?" Dan asked politely.

Barry nodded and went back to the lounge to fetch Shannon.

The men stayed on the porch, not permitted to enter the house; they could venture no further. Dan's blood ran cold when they heard Barry yell out.

"What the fuck, Shannon? Get up! What the fuck!" Barry sounded terrified. "Shannon, wake up!"

The officers looked at each other and rushed inside to assist.

They were in a dingy living room, littered with bottles and ashtrays overflowing with cigarette butts.

Shannon, lying in an uncomfortable-looking position, was unresponsive on the disgustingly dirty sofa, a strong smell of urine filling the air surrounding her body.

Barry, sweating profusely now, pushed her violently, screaming, "Get up, bitch!".

How her body moved when Barry shoved her told Dan this was more serious than just a drug trip. He quickly checked for a pulse but registered nothing, catching the scent of decomposition on top of her usual stink. Shannon was dead.

Tewano called an ambulance while Barry was being held by Dan's continuous questioning in the cruiser. Barry was adamant he'd not gone to the Dalton's or had anything to do with the robberies or Shannon's death.

Dan made the call to arrest him after spying on a crack pipe shoved in the folds of an old recliner with a meth stash tucked in next to it. He sat a handcuffed Barry in the back of the cruiser while he spoke to his partner.

"Forensics are heading in to search the property," Dan told Tewano as the ambulance arrived.

They explained to the attendants what they'd found and needed confirmation of her death. The coroner was only a few minutes away and would assist with the extraction of the body. The mandatory ambulance crew quickly rushed inside to assess for any signs of life. After a few moments, they came out to confirm the woman was deceased and had been for at least a day or two.

"I'm bringing him to Christchurch station for processing," Tewano offered, while Dan decided to wait for the forensic crew and coroner.

"When he's booked in, I'll return for you." He tipped his hat and got into the cruiser.

"Thanks, Tewano," Dan said, feeling less tired from the adrenaline coursing through his veins. "I'll start looking around the place."

***

He went back inside after Tewano drove away. Scanning through the rubbish, Dan noticed a few items in the living room didn't fit the general soiled look of the place; they looked too clean and new. His feet clung to the sticky carpet as he made his way to the rather clean-looking television. It was the same brand and size as Mike's missing TV. He looked around and found a stereo unit looking out of place, also matching Mike's missing one.

He shuffled around the trash on the living room floor and found a laptop. He opened it to a password screen with a personalized screen saver, a photo of Mike's farm.

Pushed underneath the sofa, a dozen or more used needles lay on the floor. Dan was willing to guess they'd sold off the stolen chainsaws and generators and binged on drugs, Shannon taking more than she could handle.

| 61 |

Accident

Matt drove in with a load of plywood in the trailer. As he approached the house, he knew something was very wrong. Eric's truck was parked in front, the gate lying in the grass. He drew a sharp breath, got out of the Hilux, and ran toward the house, intent on getting to Melissa as fast as possible.

He opened the front door, raced down the hallway, and stopped dead in the dining room. Melissa was on the kitchen floor, clad in a blood-spattered bathrobe, crying softly in her hands. His brother lay lifeless, glazed eyes staring blankly, a knife blade in his head.

Matt approached his wife gently, helping her and holding her close.

A nasty gash on the side of her head matted her hair with blood. Her voice, when it came, mimicked a child's. She timidly recalled the horrifying events that led to the disturbing scene. As she spoke, his rage grew. If that bastard wasn't dead already, he wouldn't hesitate to kill him, even if he was his brother. Grinding his teeth, he tried to calm his fury.

"I'm going to go to jail, Matt. Everyone around here knows we don't get along with Eric. They'll think I did this to get back at him for taking your half of the farm. They won't believe me when I tell them it was self-defense." Melissa burst out crying at the enormity of what occurred. "What will we do?" Her mind raced while sobbing heavily.

"It will be an accident, sweetheart. Don't worry, I'll take care of it," Matt reassured his wife, rocking her gently. "Let me take care of it," he repeated a few times, trying to convince himself he could fix the mess his brother caused, his mind thinking about how to dispose of his brother's body quickly and plausibly.

***

He wore Eric's cap, took his truck, and drove to the effluent pond, his brother's body in the back of the car, covered by a tarp.

Matt used pliers to remove the knife blade from his brother's head. It took some work to get it dislodged from his skull. Melissa had put substantial force into her blow.

The bloody effluent pond had been a thorn in his side since their dad had gotten sick a few months before his death, becoming Eric's responsibility when he took over the dairy operations. The original liner was deteriorating and needed to be replaced. Eric's answer had been to cover the banks with a new liner so it would look like they'd refurbished it while neglecting the portion that couldn't be seen. It would save them a ton of money, he said.

Matt was unhappy with his brother's illegal solution. He was even more disappointed when he got the intricate metal causeway system built instead of refitting the pond correctly. The workmanship was extremely shoddy. Old metal parts had been used, creating sharp edges waiting to cut anyone coming within its grasp; they were everywhere on the yellow atrocity.

He left the vehicle and looked around, the wind stinging and drying his eyes. Nothing more than dusty fields around them. He took his brother's body out of the truck and dragged him to the stairs leading to the causeway, taking each step first and then hauling his brother's dead weight up with him.

The platform at the top of the stairs had the most significant safety hazards on the causeway. A large piece of rusted metal that had been at one point a post, sharp and jagged, stood like a monolith in the whistling gusts. Matt took his brother's head in his hands, eyed out his knife wound, and pushed his brother's head on the rusted metal implement.

Trying to match the knife wound in his brother's skull, he drove the spike deeper, ensuring the post had adequate blood to act as evidence.

He pulled his brother's head from its metal toothpick. A sucking noise exuded from the wound, making Matt heave. He looked at Eric briefly and threw him in the pond. His body momentarily hugged the side of the pool, then slowly slid into its liquid grave. When he completely vanished, Eric descended the stairs and started walking home to Melissa, leaving Eric and his truck at the effluent pond.

PART 3

| 62 |

Change

Matt's brother's death stunned Mike; however, his friend didn't seem too bothered. The rift that had grown between the men somewhat explained Matt's coldness toward Eric's tragic death.

They declared Eric missing the following day when the staff arrived for work. Matt was shifting the cows in his paddocks when they asked him to look for Eric. They searched the farm to find his truck parked at the effluent pond without a sign of him. The police were called, and Tewano came in to investigate as Dan was on leave.

They searched the area around the pond, each fruitless minute leading to a dreaded thought: Eric might have fallen in. Tewano noticed blood on a rusted, torn-up pipe and requested they empty the pool of filth. Sure enough, Eric slipped on the causeway and impaled his head. He'd fallen in the effluent pond, becoming pinned close to the pump, keeping his bloated body from surfacing to the top.

As they pumped the effluent out, Tewano noted the ruse Eric had pulled to con the environmental officers.

Matt stood by Tewano, looking silently over the pond where his brother's body had been found. His solemn voice broke the silence.

"Don't worry, Tewano. I'll get the pond fixed and certified before we store any more effluent," Matt said, his voice croaking. Tewano was compassionate to Matt's immense shock and pressure; he nodded, trusting Matt's word more than he would have Eric's.

***

Matt swiftly took over the dairy farm operations. The coroner's report deemed Eric's passing a tragic accident. The cause of death was determined as penetrating trauma caused by his head's impact on the jagged metal pole. A gust of wind most likely tripped him, making him fall on the sharp metal.

Mike was surprised when Matt and Melissa moved into Eric's house. The house was more extensive and modern than their farmhouse but far from Melissa's stables. They had changed since Eric's death. They were solemn and kept to themselves, even with Mike.

It had been a substantial change of lifestyle for them. The extra work of running the dairy farm, managing staff, and caring for the grazing cows wore them thin.

Mike had done his best to help Matt graze his cows while caring for his own stock and trying to rebuild his home. The damage had been extensive enough the dwelling portion had to be entirely rebuilt. He was still staying with Kate at the damned Paterson place, where he sometimes thought he was losing his mind. Not a day would go by he wouldn't hear, feel, or see something he couldn't explain, his fear growing daily.

Last night had been a perfect example of the games the house played on them.

Jimmy had woken up during the night, screaming as he ran to the master bedroom, that a herd of animals was at his window. Mike initially thought the little one had a nightmare, but when he approached the bedroom, he knew he hadn't been dreaming. The thunderous sound of a herd of deer running next to the house, their antlers hitting the walls with such force the impact could be felt, chilled him. One went right for the window, cracking it before the spooked animals scattered away.

The following day, he'd inspected the damage caused by the herd, wondering where they'd come from. There were no signs of hoof prints on the loose gravel. It was like they'd imagined the entire thing, apart from the cracked window, which he promptly replaced.

There was no sign of the chaos that shattered their sleep.

***

Mike arrived at Matt's farm earlier than usual. Already having tended to his flock, he spent a few more hours helping Matt and Melissa. They were so grateful to see him that morning, desperate for his assistance.

At smoko time, Matt waved Mike into their new abode. Mike hadn't been inside the house since Matt's father was alive. Eric spent a pretty penny completely redoing the inside of the dwelling to very high standards. He looked at Melissa preparing coffee in the kitchen and thought the top-end granite kitchen suited her. She was more cheerful than she'd been for a while. It delighted Mike that she seemed better.

"How are things with our Canadians up the road, Mike?" she asked, sitting down after serving them coffee and biscuits.

"Certainly not getting the sleep they deserve, them or I," Mike said, then explained the strange disturbances at the Paterson place.

Since Melissa grew up in the area, she knew the folklore associated with old man Paterson's place and looked at her husband with concern.

Matt put his hand on Melissa's and looked directly into Mike's eyes.

"That place isn't right. We need to get you folks out of there before something terrible happens." Matt said, pausing for a moment, looking over at his wife.

"You should move into our old house. Your place will not be ready to live in for quite some time, and things are getting scary at Paterson's. I could really use your help to manage the grazing farm. It's a minute's drive from your place, so you can keep tending your flock. No charge, mate. You would be doing me a favor, and we wouldn't worry about you guys living in that haunted hellhole of a house."

Mike stared at his friend in silence, unable to find words. The offer was not only generous, but it would also work for all of them. Kate and Melissa could hang out together during the day and help each other with minor farm duties. He hated leaving her alone at the house since her disappearance in the forest.

Jimmy's bus stop would be more accessible in the morning. He was used to crossing over multiple paddocks to reach the bus stop directly in front of Matt and Melissa's place. He desperately wanted them out of that mad house. Melissa confirmed the offer, her eyes glistening at the prospect of having her friend around.

"Talk about it with Kate, Mike. You guys could move in tonight. There's no need to bring any furniture; we left our place as it was. It would save you from spending another night in that godforsaken place. We could celebrate with a barbecue tonight." Matt rose and touched Melissa's shoulders, unconsciously massaging her.

"Yeah, mate, go off and talk to your woman and see if she is keen. She can pack her stuff, and we can move you guys in later this afternoon," Melissa added, convincing him further.

"Sounds like a great plan. I'll talk to Kate and see what she thinks," he declared, heading out the door.

Once he got back into his truck, Matt and Melissa looked at each other with knowing eyes. They could never live in that house after what happened with Eric.

| 63 |

Wellbeing

The grogginess stuck around for a few hours every morning, making Dan feel like a zombie. He hated the doctor's medication but desperately needed the rest. Sitting on his porch, his long-forgotten coffee on the grass next to his chair, he waited for the fog to clear in his head.

He sorted out the robberies that occurred in the region. His gut had been right; Shannon's fingerprints were the only ones found at all the crime scenes. Mike's missing electronics had been recovered, and multiple missing items were found in the search of the property once they removed her remains.

Dan knew Barry was involved in the robberies but lacked evidence. He couldn't be charged with Shannon's death, the official autopsy report stating she'd died of a drug overdose a few days before her body was discovered. He still couldn't believe Shannon lay dead on his sofa for a few days without him realizing it. The thought haunted him. They'd been bingeing heavily on heroin and meth, purchased with the proceeds of their stolen goods. Barry had obviously been too far gone to grasp the reality before him.

A quick examination of the fallen workshop gave them the ammunition they needed to charge Barry with a crime and lock him up, the building's debris hiding the ruins of a meth lab. After Barry was locked up, authorities took control of his property to dispose of residual drugs and cooking utensils. He'd taken leave immediately after the investigation was completed, only hearing about Eric's death from Tewano when he popped in to check on him.

***

He dutifully attended the doctor appointments he'd made. Although initially nervous, he'd found his fears unfounded. The doctor listened attentively when he explained how his insomnia had affected him since his wife and son returned to the UK.

"Do you see things that aren't there?" the doctor asked casually.

"It's happened a few times, like seeing something in the corner of your eyes that isn't there," Dan said, lying, too embarrassed to admit how bad his visions were becoming. His eyes lowered, and his hands clenched together. He hoped his admission wouldn't haunt him as significantly as the real visions he was having.

The doctor said it was typical with severe insomnia and gave him a sedative to help him sleep. She implored him to take advantage of his total leave allocation now instead of only taking a fortnight off.

"You have gone through a traumatic experience with your family leaving. What you are going through is quite normal. You kept working and never took time to absorb the life-changing event, leading to burnout. I am confident you will come right if you take your full annual leave. If you choose to go back to the force in two weeks, I'll be forced to report that I am not assured you are fit and proper to address your duties."

Dan thought about it and promptly replied that he would do as requested and take his month off. After leaving the doctor's office, Dan wondered how he would keep himself occupied for that long.

***

He finally spoke with Lorraine.

There would be no reconciliation; his not believing her ruined any chance of salvaging their relationship. She would, however, allow him access to Jeffrey. He discussed with her the leave he'd taken and if there was any possibility that Jeffrey could fly to New Zealand to spend time with him.

Neither fancied the idea of Jeffrey flying halfway around the world alone. Dan offered to pay for her ticket should she want to escort him, but she refused.

Never would she set foot in New Zealand again, she stated firmly.

She left the conversation with a promise to think about a solution. It was a futile request, and Dan's heart felt crushed until he received a call from her.

Lorraine's aunt was heading to Australia for a fortnight and was keen on accompanying Jeffrey to New Zealand. She would visit New Zealand a few days before heading to Australia and arrive a few days before the end of her vacation to pick him up and fly back to England.

Dan was elated but also fully understood the enormity of his request; Jeffrey was in school and would need to recapture what he'd missed when he returned to Buckinghamshire.

The plan was set. Jeffrey was arriving in a week and a half. Excited, Dan worked hard to improve himself and follow the doctor's orders. He needed to be in the best frame of mind for Jeffrey's visit. He missed his job tremendously but had a bigger job to do at the moment, keeping his sanity.

| 64 |

Avoidance

Kevin's anxiety flared as his Mercedes drove to Mona's house. Since her accident, he couldn't stand being around her. Although some time had passed since the pigs took to her, her wounds hadn't healed. She walked around in no apparent pain, like nothing happened, leaving large, pus-soaked patches on her clothing. He couldn't understand how she wasn't dead by now.

Her personality took a turn for the worse. Entirely obsessed with Mike, she never stopped talking about him committing adultery and how she would end up with the farm because of it. It was always the same thing, over and over. Kevin didn't want to be there anymore but encouraged her to seek a lawyer's advice to claim what she believed was hers. After all, he would benefit if he could con her into a binding relationship that would see him own half of her assets.

The day of her appointment with a solicitor in Christchurch came. She'd gotten ready for it, but Kevin begged her to reconsider and attend the meeting via telephone. Her physical appearance was no longer acceptable.

She'd put on a pretty duck egg blue dress that didn't cover her gaping lacerations. They leaked their foul-smelling juices, slowly making lines down her legs as the vile fluid pumped out of her wounds. Her frizzy, pulled-out hair and the excessive glam makeup she plastered on her face made her look demented. Any lawyer would be repulsed. Thankfully, she agreed to the phone appointment.

She took the call in the office, running her mouth at a million miles a minute, describing every detail she'd captured between Mike and Kate. The person on the other line also asked if she'd been unfaithful. She said she'd been forced into her relationship with Kevin. Mike hadn't kept up with his end of the bargain, so she had no choice but to move her boyfriend into their home. There was a long pause before she answered questions regarding the shared assets.

"Yes, the house is in both our names," Mona said, her tone full of contempt. "The farmland? No, my name isn't on it because it was his family's, but I'm married to him, so it's mine now," she said aggressively. She hesitated as they continued their questions and added, "The kids... are in boarding school. No, he pays for it. It was my decision..."

From the pitch of her voice, even if she was only responding with 'yeah,' Kevin could feel things weren't going her way.

"Well, I disagree and won't be needing your useless services. I'm taking my business elsewhere," Mona said, hanging up abruptly.

"Fuck that load of bullshit! I'm calling another lawyer," she said, raging as she exited the office.

"Those idiots think Mike and I should split the assets in half. Like fuck that's going to happen. This is mine now, all mine, and he can fuck off with his slut."

She looked utterly mad, Kevin thought, and quickly assessed how he could get away from her, even for the moment.

"I'm going to check on the pigs," he said, stammering as he hastily left through the back door.

Waddling in the oversized gumboots, he wondered how she could eliminate Mike. That way, Mona would get the entire lot she was entitled to. Kevin was usually too faint-hearted to consider violence against anyone, but he was sure he could step up if it benefited him.

Approaching the pigs, he noted that their condition had deteriorated. Kevin counted and found one of them missing. He visually scoured the smelly mess at their feet and saw the remains of the missing pig's cadaver. They'd taken to killing their own because they were starving.

Kevin hadn't anticipated how much food they would need and had thrown them a bucket of food scraps every few days. He'd lost interest in what he thought would be a simple money-making scheme and spent little time looking after the pigs since they'd bitten Mona. Kevin needed to feed the wild drove, but with what. He looked over to Mike's shed.

| 65 |

Home

Kate heard Mike drive in and instantly put on the jug. She hoped he would stay for a while; she didn't want to be alone in the house.

That morning, she'd sworn she saw three people in the woods while tending to the garden. Two were wearing hoods, and one had a cap on, obliterating their faces from view. Fear crippled her as they stood there, unable to move or speak. As quickly as she saw them appear from the trees, they stepped back into the shadows, disappearing but not from her mind. She knew they were still there; she felt it.

Once released from her paralysis, she sat on the front deck and cried. She wanted out of the miserable place so badly. If Mike noticed her reddened eyes as he walked into the kitchen, he didn't show it. His beaming smile and sparkling eyes showed his excitement as he grabbed her to kiss her.

"I have something to talk to you about, sweetheart."

She listened on, intrigued.

"Matt and Melissa have offered us their house for my help on the farm..."

Her reaction cut him off. Her eyes went wide and watery, her hands covering her mouth, surprise and relief overwhelming her. Tears ran down her face as she squeezed him tight in her arms, quietly sobbing on his chest.

"I'm guessing you are okay with the idea," he said, chuckling as he pulled her away slightly so he could see her face. She meekly wiped her tears and shook her head up and down, her grateful approval obvious. In a small voice, she asked when they could move.

"We're not sleeping here tonight, Kate. We're moving this afternoon. We can leave the furniture here, pack your stuff, and anything you might need for tonight. We can always return to pick up what you've left behind."

She kissed him excitedly, melting into him. She felt the familiar fire start inside him, but he pulled himself away. If they were setting up a house at the Stewarts's tonight, he had a lot of work to do before they could shift.

"Pack up what you need. I'll finish my jobs so I can pick you and Jimmy up when he gets home from school." Mike said, planting a soft kiss on her forehead and heading away.

Kate's mind was spinning. He hadn't stayed long enough for coffee, but it was well and truly pardoned. She headed to the garage to re-tape boxes that were in storage and set off to pack.

***

When Jimmy arrived, their belongings were in the garage, ready to be loaded. He looked sad when he walked up the drive, so she went to greet him.

"What's wrong, bud? Did you have a bad day?" Kate asked as she put her arm on his shoulders as they walked.

"Nah, I didn't want to come home," he said as tears welled in his eyes, breaking her heart. He'd been seeing things and hearing things that couldn't be explained. It was really starting to affect him.

"Look inside the garage," she told him as they approached the open door.

"Why are there boxes there?" he asked, showing no enthusiasm.

"We are going to live at Melissa and Matt's place. I know you haven't visited yet, but it's a cool place, and they have horses."

"What?" he asked incredulously. The young boy's demeanor changed as his excitement flared. "Really! We don't have to stay here tonight?"

The question sounded more like a plea. Kate stopped walking and hugged Jimmy.

"No, hunny, we are leaving."

Hearing Mike's truck coming up the road, she smiled at him and added.

"We're leaving right now. I packed all your books and everything in your room. If we forget something, we'll come back and get it."

"Are we going to live with Mike, Mom?" he asked. The look on his face begged for a positive answer. She gestured yes, smiling. Jimmy hugged her tightly.

Mike pulled up the drive to see Kate and Jimmy embracing in front of the open garage door.

***

The look on Jimmy's face as they arrived at their new home was priceless. Jimmy was not impressed by the quaint farmhouse surrounded by mature weeping willows that swayed gently in the breeze. Something else made the place special to him.

"Mom, I know this place. It's right in front of my bus stop," he laughed merrily.

They were unpacked in no time. Since Eric's house was fully stocked, Melissa hadn't taken any linens or kitchen items. Jimmy loved the spare bedroom, and it was a relief to both Kate and Mike that his room was closer to theirs.

They'd decided to share a bedroom since Jimmy was comfortable with their relationship. They helped him sort his bedroom, unpacking his models, and putting his books on the shelves.

He thought the decor was perfect. His room had blue walls, blue and gray plaid curtains, and a matching bedspread. He had a wooden desk with plenty of shelves and a big window he could sit by. He was overjoyed. They left him to explore his new room while they set up theirs.

Their room was light and airy, with a high ceiling and a substantial bay window. Opposite the enormous handmade wooden bed was a fireplace, two chairs, and a small side table. The bedroom also had French doors going out to a balcony.

Kate brought in her bedspread and sheets, preferring to use her own. The charcoal bedspread complimented the light gray walls, and the boldly striped black and cream curtains added a touch of old-world charm. Kate put their clothes in the wardrobe while Mike unpacked in the bathroom. They came together in front of the fireplace for a quick kiss before they went to the Stewarts for a barbecue.

***

They celebrated more than they'd planned at the barbecue. Matt kept the drinks flowing until Mike raised his hand to stop him.

"We've got the early shift tomorrow, mate," Mike reminded him before things got out of hand.

Matt seemed amused as he passed him another beer. Mike shook his head.

"I've asked the staff if they could switch tomorrow so we could sleep in tomorrow morning." Matt smiled broadly, signaling to Kate with his eyes. Color blossomed on her cheeks.

Mike, catching what his friend meant, raised his beer. "Cheers, mate!" he said jovially. They laughed a bit harder than usual, the alcohol loosening their inhibitions.

Kate handed Melissa a glass of wine when she emerged from the stables. She'd taught Jimmy how to brush the horses and muck up the stalls. He was indeed in his element, loving spending time with the horses as much as Melissa did.

"Thank you for doing this for us," Kate said, tears fighting her eyelashes, the alcohol making her more emotional than usual. The trials of living at the Paterson place had worn her down. She was overjoyed not to be living under that roof anymore. Melissa approached her and hugged her friend.

"It's our pleasure, and it works for all of us," she reassured her. "I'm happy you guys are out of that house."

Everyone nodded in unison. They raised their drinks and drank to new beginnings.

***

Jimmy had worn himself out when they arrived at the house. Both Kate and Mike were feeling quite festive with the alcohol they'd consumed and retreated to their bedroom as soon as Jimmy was asleep. Mike had started a fire in the bedroom fireplace while she tended to Jimmy. She softly closed the door when she returned to their room.

He couldn't wait any longer to kiss her and brought her to him swiftly, his hands caressing the small of her back and the tops of her buttocks. As her hand moved down his hip, he groaned lightly and acknowledged her desire. Stripping her red sundress off, he unhooked her bra and pulled down her panties.

Gripped with lust, he couldn't care less if he was still dressed. He lay Kate's warm body on the chair near the fireplace. Her long black hair spilled to the ground, her body glowing as he touched her tenderly.

By the firelight, Mike recaptured the strength he'd lost withstanding all the years of Mona's madness. He knew things would differ from now on. Mike found a new family when Kate entered his life. All three kids would be living under the same roof with both of them as soon as he could arrange it.

| 66 |

Patience

Dan was thankful for Tewano's visits. They helped keep him in the loop while he was on leave and warded off insanity. His co-worker was the only one who visited.

Dan probably seemed overly keen during his last visit; it had thankfully taken him away from pruning Lorraine's roses. He didn't know what he was doing but couldn't find any other yard work, so he tried mimicking his wife's skills. There was only so much lawn mowing and house cleaning to be done at the end of the day. He feared the break he took to regain his sanity would do the opposite.

Thankfully, Tewano came to the rescue.

***

The men sat in the sunshine while they grilled a venison fillet on the barbecue. The smell of roasted corn and potato enhanced the aroma of the cooking meat. Dan felt comforted by it. He'd not relaxed in a while, and this was the best he'd felt in a long time.

He told Tewano about Jimmy coming over and how he was finally sleeping better. Unfortunately, vivid dreams were part and parcel of taking the sleep medicine he was prescribed.

His co-worker gave him a rundown of what was happening at work. A few break-and-entering charges were laid against individuals Dan and Tewano, earmarked as possible suspects. Someone tried to steal the eggs at the McPherson farm but got bitten by their dogs. No charges were laid.

Tewano laughed and said the exciting stuff only happened when Dan was there. Dan sipped his beer and chuckled at the irony with his friend. They got on to talking about Dalton's place.

"So, what do you reckon will happen to it?" Dan asked.

Tewano had been a local for many years and knew the history of the land.

"We never found out why old man Paterson gifted that parcel of land to Dalton. Luke had no money and couldn't keep a job if his life depended on it. Out of the blue, the old man who stayed away from everyone suddenly gave Luke a large part of his land. I've often wondered what Luke had on the old man, what he knew, or if he saw something. Whatever it was, it must have been something big."

Dan listened to Tewano intently.

"Yeah, suspicious, isn't it? What was Paterson doing with that part of the land when he transferred it over?"

Tewano looked at him with his eyebrow raised.

"It was the family's private cemetery," he responded dryly.

Dan was incredulous. He sat at the edge of his chair, staring at Tewano. "What? No way, we searched that place and didn't find any headstones."

Tewano shook his head, his voice showing disgust.

"Luke knocked them down when he took over the land. The graves should still be there, but from what I could see, he built his shack on top of Paterson's entire family. Old man Paterson refused to leave the land, stating they were tied to it. When I was a kid, the local said he joined them in spirit form to roam the land of the dead when the Nor'wester blew."

"Wow," Dan shuddered. "That's heavy stuff. Did Paterson know Luke desecrated his family's graves?"

"Yup, he must have. I drove past the house and saw the headstones strewn on the side of Paterson's drive. As far as I know, the old man said and did nothing about it. Whatever Luke had over Paterson was huge," Tewano trailed off, then added as an afterthought. "Since both are gone, we will never know."

Dan nodded, looking in the distance, his mind still trying to process the information.

***

Tewano left when the sun was setting. Dan felt genuinely tired, not accustomed to having company over, and still recuperating from his insomnia affliction. He packed the food, put the dishes in the dishwasher, and threw away the empty beer bottles.

He was about to shut the outside light when he saw them, the sheets on the line. The forecast called for rain during the night. Dan made his way in the growing gloom to the clothesline, holding a laundry basket he'd picked up from the laundry room.

It was the right thing to do to take a break, get medical advice, and rest; Dan felt much better. He unpinned the clothes pegs, waves rippling its surface, the breeze tickling it. He reached out for the other sheet. It waved more violently, giving him a glimpse of what lay behind it.

No, it couldn't be, he thought, his throat tight. The sheet lifted again. Three shaded figures were standing behind the clothesline, facing him. Shivers showered his body. He struggled to breathe, the pressure in his throat choking him. He pulled the sheet down hard, the pegs flying away.

There was no one there. Dan scanned his yard. He was alone. He picked up the laundry basket and headed into the house, going directly to his bedroom.

As the last of the light was lost to the darkness, the faint outline of three bodies standing a few meters away from his bedroom window could be seen.

| 67 |

Stolen

Mona watched him driving around the paddocks, tending to his sheep. He was younger and more confident than she remembered him.

Hidden in the hedges, concealed from view, she sat in misery. She examined her pant legs; the vile yellow fluid escaping her wounds had seeped through. Grabbing at the thin cotton with her fingertips, she felt a chunk of meat dislodge from her calf and stay stuck to her pants. She pressed down on the material, hoping to cement the flesh to its proper place. It didn't hurt. She no longer felt pain, not from her legs anyway.

***

He saw her crouched in the hedge, her appearance shocking him so profoundly that he almost toppled off his bike. Mike adjusted his cap, squinting to make sense of what he'd seen.

Was that Mona? What the hell happened to her?

He couldn't understand what she was doing there and why she looked like she'd escaped from a horror film. He approached the invisible boundary they'd set by agreement and turned off the motorbike.

"Mona… Are you okay?" he asked cautiously.

She growled at him like a wild animal, her eyes darting from side to side.

What the hell is wrong with her? Mike thought to himself. He'd known she'd dabbled in drugs with Kevin; could that have been the reason for her horrifying transformation? She bolted upright and screamed.

"I wish you would drop dead and leave me what I am due, you piece of shit! You can't be frolicking around with that skank without repercussions. You are going down, Mike!" she screamed while pointing at him with her finger, her other hand pulling erratically at her broken hair.

He noticed the large patches of wet pus on her legs and shook his head. She wasn't the Mona he'd known. This version of her was worse. His first thoughts were of his children. He couldn't let them see their mother like that.

"You need help, Mona. I'll drive you to the hospital. You aren't well," he said, extending his hand to steady her swaying body. She slapped it away, hissing.

"Fuck you, Mike! You are not playing this game with me. I'll see you go down. Mark my words."

She turned her back to him and headed toward the house. Still in shock, Mike could only watch her walk away like she wasn't afflicted by her horrible wounds.

Something dark had crawled inside Mona, something darker than what she was before.

***

Mona had devised a cunning plan while sitting in the bushes that morning. Those precious lambs Mike constantly tended to would be the best way to get to him.

Since his shed had been damaged, she noticed he was always absent from the farm in the late afternoon. Mona waited until Mike left, then went to the paddock where the lambs had been separated from their mothers. She climbed over the fence with difficulty, the flesh near her wounds taking the impression of the wire, gushing their juices on her pants. She didn't notice the material sticking to her legs as she rushed a lamb into the corner and wrangled it.

The young animal fought back as she held it close. Finding strength she didn't know she had, she lifted the lamb over the fence to have it fall with the pigs. The starving pigs broke into a frenzy, quickly making it their meal.

| 68 |

Life

The first few weeks of life at the Stewarts were filled with joy and wonderment. Kate had all but forgotten the strange occurrences at the Paterson place. As she took the clothing off the line, she contemplated how fortunate she and Jimmy had been to meet Mike.

Jimmy was benefiting from the constant male companionship. Mike would pick Jimmy up at his bus stop after school to help shift the cows. Jimmy learned to fix a water trough and how to check the current on the electric fences. Rain or shine, the routine stuck, and they'd become inseparable.

Mike was distraught not to have his children near him. Kate clarified to him that there was more than enough space for them at the new house, and she would love for them all to be reunited. Mona stopped Mike from making the move; how would the children react to her condition?

Kate was shocked when he told her about having seen her. She knew he didn't exaggerate, but it didn't sound like he was describing the woman who berated her a few months ago. He blamed her drug use, but Kate wondered if something more was happening. She heard Mike's truck pull up and made her way to the house, the laundry basket at her hip.

"What's up? You look worried," she asked, the concern on his face moving to hers. She dropped the basket in the laundry room and entered the kitchen, Mike following her.

"You know when I told you a few weeks back that some lambs had gone missing? Well, even more have disappeared. Thinking that stray dogs were responsible, I called on the neighboring farmers to see if they'd caught wind of what was happening to my stock and if they'd suffered losses themselves. They couldn't help but be compassionate with my situation, but none reported losses.

"I tell you, Kate, I have never seen this happen in all my years farming," he said, removing his cap and scratching his head.

"Any sign of where they could be going?" Kate asked as she poured him a coffee.

"Nah, they disappeared. It's doing my head in. Prime quality stock doesn't go missing unless it's stolen or killed. I don't get it."

The exacerbated look on his face showed the full extent of his frustration.

She stepped behind him as he sat at the table and bent down to hug him.

"It will be alright. I'm certain we'll sort it out," Kate said, trying to reassure him. He put his hand on hers and pressed down, thankful to have the support of his woman.

"Listen, Kate, the kids are having a break from boarding school for a few days and are going on a tour of Tekapo to visit the hot springs and the observatory this weekend. It's been arranged through the school. Since a few spots are vacant, Kelly and Jake asked if Jimmy would like to go with them. I told them I would ask you before we talk to Jimmy."

Kate, touched by the kind invitation, wished they could come together as a family soon.

"I'm sure he will love the idea, Mike. I'm all for it," she responded, thinking she would need to return to Paterson's place to pick up his overnight pack.

"Ask him when you pick him up to do chores this afternoon. You can tell him I'm all good with it."

"Cool, babe, listen, maybe we can have a night out on the town when we drop him off. It would be different for us; we haven't left Okuku since we got together."

"Hmm, whatever would we do alone in Christchurch together, Mr. McEwan?" she said, teasing him as he got up from the chair.

"Oh, I'm sure we could find something to do," he whispered close to her ear, his hands already on her hips, his lips meeting hers. He pulled her close and looked wantonly into her eyes. "Done deal, sweetheart, leave it to me," Mike said, kissing her again. He put on his cap and waved goodbye at the door.

Mike was sure Jimmy would jump at hanging out with Kelly and Jake for a weekend in Tekapo. He had to get a plan into motion and impress his girl. He decided to brainstorm with Melissa before returning to his mowing.

***

"Good day, Melissa," Mike boomed in, tipping his cap, excited. He sat next to Matt, who was finishing his break.

"Looks like Jimmy and the kids are off to Tekapo for the weekend. I want to wow Kate with a stay in the city."

Matt looked at him with a sly smile on his face.

"Well...Well..." Matt exclaimed, taking the piss out of Mike. Melissa smacked her husband playfully with a tea towel.

"Friday, mate," Mike responded, oblivious to Matt's teasing. Matt perked up, about to keep on with his taunting, when Melissa decided to speak up.

"Why don't you use mom and dad's cabin in Akaroa? It's sitting vacant most of the time. Mom and Dad moved above the restaurant. It's easier on them, and they have a great view from the balcony. They would love to have you. I could check if it's available."

Melissa was pleased to help Mike; he'd been in her family since they were teenagers. He helped her parents relocate the cabin from her mom's family farm in Hamner Springs to the large, wooded lot overlooking the ocean in Akaroa. He'd also helped them refit the restaurant when her parents bought it a few years ago. She never imagined her parents would have owned and managed a French restaurant in a quaint tourist town, but with friends' help and family's support, they made it grow into something special for locals and tourists alike. They loved Mike and would be delighted to see him happy again with a new love.

"That would be perfect, Melissa," Mike said, smiling bashfully as he looked down at his hands.

"Tell you what, since you need to bring Jimmy to Christchurch on Friday to catch up with the kids, why don't you and Kate stay there until you need to pick him up on Sunday? I can manage here with the staff, and I'll shift the sheep in the morning and make sure everything is sorted," Matt said as he chomped down on the last bite of his biscuit.

"Be careful, mate. Last time Melissa and I spent a weekend there, I was sure she would return with a bellyful of bubs."

Matt laughed heartily as he looked at his wife. Melissa smacked his arm with the newspaper this time, making a face at him.

"Right, Melissa, if you could check with your parents, I would be grateful. Let me know what they want for the few nights, and I will square them up," he said, nodding to her.

"Now, get your ass off that chair and get back on the job. We have another Nor'wester coming soon." Mike said, hitting Matt's baseball cap rim, instantly covering his face.

Matt's laughter could be heard from behind it.

***

When Kate heard Jimmy scream 'whoo-hoo' at the top of his voice, she immediately knew Mike had told him about the trip to Tekapo. She looked out the window. He was hugging Mike and jumping up and down simultaneously, making it necessary for Mike to stretch his neck out to keep his chin from being hit. He said something to Mike, and Mike nodded, laughing.

Jimmy sprinted to the house, screaming, "Mom!".

The front door swung open. Jimmy rushed in to hug her.

"Mom, I'm going to Tekapo with Jake and Kelly," he said, clinging to her like glue, excitement pulsing around him.

"Yes, you are, buddy! I'm so excited for you," she said, bending her knees slightly to see him eye to eye and kissing his forehead. "You're going to have a great time. Now, go help Mike with the chores. You can do your homework before we have tea," she said, giving him two spinach, feta, and sun-dried tomato muffins.

"Give one to Mike, okay," she called out as he ran down the deck stairs.

Mike waved to Kate before the boys headed off together.

***

Melissa saw him moving the trough with Jimmy and ran out of the house to announce the happy news.

"Mike! Mike!" Melissa called as she ran toward them at the back of the main paddock. As she ran, she noticed her head pounding every time her feet hit the ground, vibrations making her ears ring from the impact.

Oh no! she thought in despair. It's coming again. Her heart fell, realizing she would soon be in for a week of pain and agony. She slowed down and waved at them.

"Melissa!" Jimmy called as he ran to hug her.

She used to mourn not having children, but with Jimmy around, he filled a void her heart would be forever grateful for.

"Buddy! How was your day in school?" she asked, ruffling his hair.

"Good, but not as good as when I came home. I'm going on a trip with Jake and Kelly to Tekapo the day after tomorrow." He couldn't stop jumping, his exhilaration like electricity.

Mike laughed as he straightened himself from attaching the ballcock to the trough.

Melissa smiled brightly, excited to tell him the great news.

"Mike, my parents would love to have you and Kate this weekend. They won't hear of you paying. They said they are still in debt toward you for all your help throughout the years and making them feel like their daughter has a big brother watching over her." Melissa said, pulling Mike aside as they walked to provide more privacy.

"Listen, Mike, Mom's overjoyed at you finding love again and being happy. She's thrilled and wants this to be extra special. Your meals and drinks will be delivered to the cabin; you only need to call and order. If you want to eat at the restaurant, call in, everything will be taken care of. Dad's loaning you his cabin cruiser so you and Kate can get on the water. They are as excited about doing this for you as you are about this weekend's getaway. It means a lot to them."

Taking it all in, Mike had the look of genuine happiness in his eyes.

"Thanks, Melissa."

| **69** |

The Visit

Tomorrow's the day, Dan chanted happily as he dusted the shelves in Jeffrey's room. Dan was overjoyed to be undertaking the chores he was engrossed in. He'd washed and dried Jeffrey's sheets, aired out his room, and tidied his shelves. After they'd left for England, Dan had collected all the toys his son left behind and placed them on the shelves in his room, a makeshift shrine waiting for the missing owner's return.

A crisis that could have been disastrous had been averted. Lorraine called to say her sister had taken ill and she couldn't escort Jeffrey. His heart immediately sank, but as if Lorraine could feel his pain, he quickly responded.

"I'll call the airline and see what we can do. I don't want to cancel the trip. It will break Jeffrey's heart," she promised.

True to her word, she'd called back and assured him the airline would dedicate an attendant for Jeffrey, and the trip was going ahead. He was overjoyed and so thankful to Lorraine for her understanding.

***

Once he completed his work, he went to the kitchen and opened the fridge to get something to eat. Perusing the boring sandwich options at hand, he made the snap decision to treat himself to lunch at the pub in Rangiora. He needed to go grocery shopping and stock up for Jeffrey in town anyway. He locked everything, snatched his keys and the grocery list from the small table at the entryway, and headed out the door, securing it as he left.

Driving toward Rangiora, the sun beaming loudly over the land, he looked out to Mike's farm, hoping to see him, wanting to share his news about Jeffrey and set up a get-together for the boys.

Scanning the land, he spotted him on his bike at the far end of his farm. He took a right turn on the road leading to the lodge and met with him.

"Good to see you, mate! Been a long time," Mike belted out, happy to see his friend.

Dan greeted him at the fence. They shook hands enthusiastically as a truck roared down the road beside them.

"How've things been going, mate?" Dan asked, paying no attention to the passing vehicle.

"Been pretty good," Mike told him how well staying at the Stewarts was working out for them.

"Sounds like nothing could be better," Dan said, expecting Mike to agree, but a shadow cast across his friend's face.

"My lambs are disappearing; I don't get it," Mike grumbled, "Have you seen anything weird around, like someone who didn't have stock suddenly having lambs? Half a dozen are gone. I'm not sure where they are going?" he said, visibly pondering the situation.

Dan felt his gut point in one direction.

"Any chance Mona and Kevin are taking a few for food?" he said cautiously, hoping to not upset his friend. Mike's face changed, and his features showed shock and revulsion.

"Dan, you should see Mona. She's mutated into a monster. I don't want the kids to see her that way. It's like she's possessed or something."

He described the strange encounter he had with her. Both men were silent as the wind tickled the trees.

"I don't know what to do, Dan. I'm not allowed out there, and she won't talk to me."

"Well, mate, you can always try to talk to Kevin to see what the hell is going on. You can't get charged for going onto your property to check someone's well-being. She never succeeded in getting a restraining order against you," Dan said, advising him.

Mike nodded and paused for a moment to shake off his thoughts.

"So, what's been new in your world, Dan? Enough of Mona for today."

Dan's news flowed out. Mike could see Dan's anticipation and pride; he was getting his son back and couldn't wait.

"We should get them together, the boys, for a barbecue one night sometime soon," Dan suggested, knowing the boys would enjoy catching up.

"Jimmy would love it. He's headed to Mackenzie Country with Kelly and Jake this weekend. We'll get something sorted out next week. Jeffrey would love taking care of the horses with Jimmy," Mike said as they returned to the cruiser. They shook hands, and Dan drove away.

***

He took a seat at The Barrel pub and grabbed a menu from the rack, nodding at the server when she signaled him. He loved the place. The authentic food and the fantastic service made you feel you were having lunch at Grandma's house.

"What can I get you, Officer?" The young, blond-haired server asked politely, lifting her pen to her order book. He perused his menu, unable to decide.

She picked up on it and offered. "Special of the day is freshly caught blue cod from Stewart Island, served with beer-battered chips and coleslaw. Your choice if you want pan-fried or battered fish."

That got Dan's attention: good old fish and chips like he had back home.

"That sounds like me," he said as he folded the menu and handed it to her. He ordered a lemon-lime and bitters and watched the rugby game they were replaying on TV. The bar manager, Vincent, came to keep him company while he waited for his meal.

Vincent was dressed like a character from a mobster movie, wearing white shoes, trousers, and a vest. His midnight blue pinstriped shirt and silver tie popped in contrast to the crisp white of his attire.

Vincent's dark, greased hair and goatee added to the authentic look he was striving for.

"Vincent, how are you today, chap?" Dan asked, waiting for his usual reply.

"Good as, bro," he said, busying himself with wiping down the counter. "You been good, mate?"

It always stunned Dan. Anyone would have expected a strong Italian accent, but Vincent, who grew up in the North Island, had the familiar regional twang of his homeland. They discussed the weather until Vincent unexpectedly brought up Dalton's place.

"I heard some talk, bro, last Saturday night. She was pumping in here, and there were many new faces, a bike gang from the West Coast. Heard them say they came to reclaim their sister's land or something like that," he said, looking around to see if anyone was listening to them.

"Didn't look like a gang anyone would fuck with, bro," he said as he put the glass he was polishing away.

"Have you talked to Tewano about this yet?" Dan asked, not noticing the waitress had delivered his meal.

"Nah, bro, been thinking about it, and I don't know..., maybe you should know," he said before he set off to serve another client.

They weren't out here and hadn't been at Daltons when he drove by. Dan wondered where they could be.

| 70 |

Revenge

They arrived at dusk. The thundering sounds from their bikes made the ground rumble beneath them.

The leader was the first to turn off his ignition. The rest followed suit in a wave of silence.

Sixteen men disembarked, removing their helmets and leaving them behind on their seats. Their leader waved for them to advance as he led them though the shambles of dusty, run-down sheds and rusted cars. The police crime scene tape flapped gently in the breeze.

The leader stopped when he arrived at the house's front steps and motioned for the group to do the same. He proceeded up the broken steps to the front door, two men by his side. They looked through the filthy windows before forcing the door open.

He walked into the living room where his sister's body had been found, his gaze on the disgusting urine-soaked sofa she'd spent her last hours on, rage flaring in his eyes. He kicked the ratty side table and made it fly into the window, breaking it. Regaining his composure, he walked out to the porch. He lifted his head and surveyed his men.

"Burn it to the ground," he said, walking toward his bike.

Like a colony of ants on a mission, they magically made jerry cans of petrol appear from their bikes and set to work dousing the place. Their leader looked on as they made their way back to their rides. He struck his lighter open. The flame flickered brightly for a moment before he threw it onto the trail of petrol near him.

The fire ran in multiple directions, following each man's path. The collection of ramshackle buildings burst into flames. They watched the complex burn for a few minutes, then set off on their bikes toward Okuku.

| 71 |

Hands

The gravel made crushing noises under her feet. Kate nervously walked down Harper's Road toward Paterson's place. She'd been procrastinating about getting Jimmy's backpack, not wanting to come close to the house for fear of something else happening. As the hours passed, she gathered her courage. Her son would need his pack for the trip.

She walked down the driveway, noting she would need to pull the weeds growing randomly between the plants. The sun shone brightly, making the water on the pond reflect with the twinkle of a million diamonds. The house sparkled; it looked inviting and pristine, and for a moment, Kate thought her mind had made the nightmare up.

She unlocked the front door and stepped into the sun-filled home. She placed the envelopes she'd gathered from the mailbox on the kitchen counter and opened the windows and doors to air out the house. A cool breeze washed through the space, livening it up. Kate turned her attention to the mail.

Apart from a school newsletter and a copy of the rent receipt, the only other letter was from Nick's attorney.

Nick petitioned for divorce in Australia and sent her a copy of the divorce papers to sign. She knew how quickly Nick could move when he made up his mind. She made herself a cup of coffee and read the paperwork at the dining room table.

Appreciating the division of assets, he was leaving behind all the furniture and the few thousand dollars in the joint New Zealand bank account. He wished for a quick resolution as he was setting out for a contract in the Middle East and would be difficult to contact.

After re-reading the entire document, she signed and dated her portion and inserted it in their provided envelope.

Kate looked at the clock and was shocked at how much time had passed. She got up and headed to get Jimmy's backpack in the garage rafters. The shovel handle was enough to dislodge it. She let it drop to the floor, not wanting to get close to the dust and the cobwebs it had collected during the past months. Shaking it off, Kate inspected it and found it clean enough for Jimmy to use; the outside was a bit dirty, but the inside was brand new.

Coming back into the house from the garage, she looked toward her bedroom. She knew they were going away for the weekend, but Mike hadn't told her where they were going. It didn't make the job of dressing for the occasion any easier.

She entered the closet and started packing her fancier dresses and heels.

The bedroom door slammed shut.

Kate held her breath, her heart pounding; she tried to convince herself it was only the wind. Echoing through the house, she could hear the doors to every room slam one after another.

She peeked out of the confines of the wardrobe to look around the room, noticing the open window. Picking up the backpack, she crawled slowly toward it, hoping to not attract the attention of whatever was causing all the ruckus.

She reached the window and relaxed, the breeze kissing her cheek.

The window crashed shut as if someone had forcefully pulled it down. Kate gasped and rushed back to the wardrobe, clutching the backpack to her chest, rocking back and forth in disbelief.

Kate screamed. The windows in the house slammed shut one by one.

Hidden in the wardrobe, she observed the light from the window darkening; clouds were moving in. An unexpected storm must have blown the doors and windows shut, she thought, trying to justify the petrifying phenomenon she was trapped in. The wind must have picked up. Nothing sinister was going on.

The glass on the bedroom window started to rattle. Kate's thoughts went from a storm to an earthquake as she heard the thunder of the windowpanes resonating throughout the empty house.

It was darker; the light had dimmed substantially. Kate peeked out of the wardrobe to the bedroom window to see what was happening. The glass panes rocked violently.

More than a dozen dirt-covered hands pounded on the window-pane, trying to get in, the vibrations nearly pushing the panes out of their frames.

The hands parted.

A demonic, screaming face with black eyes looked directly at her.

Kate shrieked and ran back to the corner of the wardrobe, fearing she would never leave the house alive. The racket continued for an eternity until all went silent, her beating heart the only thing she could hear.

She slowly crawled out of the closet to peek at the window. It was shut; there was no sign of anyone having been there.

Incredulous, she stood up and gingerly walked to the window to look outside. The window was latched shut. She'd unlatched it with difficulty, the hook stiff with the pressure the paint put on it. How could it be locked? She was alone in the room.

She slowly opened the bedroom door and entered the hallway. All of the doors in the house were shut. Her breath became visible; an icy chill filled the house. The hairs on her body stood at attention, terror coursing through her.

When she arrived in the kitchen, she gasped. The windows and doors she opened had been shut and latched. She glanced at the dining room table; her mail was gone.

The front door was open; its rusty hinges squealed as the wind played with it.

Kate walked gingerly toward it and stepped outside. Her correspondence was stacked neatly under a large rock, restraining it from blowing away in the breeze.

"I did not just imagine that!" she screamed, frustrated by the cruel joke the house played on her. She leaned her head on the house's brick facade, dizziness threatening to take her legs. Looking out toward her bedroom windows, she could see it. It was subtle, but it was there.

Each window had a handprint in the middle of it.

| 72 |

Madness

Kevin panicked when he saw Mike coming up the drive.

Oh shit, this must be when I get killed, he thought, hurrying to hide his coke. Kevin was high and didn't want to have to deal with him. Mona was still sleeping off what was happening to her or taking over her body; he didn't know anymore. He wiped his nose and made his way to the front door. Kevin opened the door before Mike knocked.

"What can I do for you, mate?"

His whiny voice sounded like a prepubescent teenager; it made Mike wince.

"Listen, mate, I don't want to intrude, but I have serious concerns over Mona's health. I saw her in the bushes yesterday and almost didn't recognize her. I think the drugs might be too much for her. She's losing it," Mike said, shaking his head.

Kevin relaxed. Mike wasn't there for him. He was there because of Mona.

Kevin led him off the front porch so they could talk by the truck, far from Mona's ears.

"I don't know what happened, Mike. She had an accident and became," he paused to find the words, "messed up."

Kevin tried to explain the events that led to Mona's downfall. "Honestly, I would have brought her to the doctors to tend to those pig bites," he said, trying to make him look like he held no responsibility.

"The pigs bit her! Kevin, what were you feeding those pigs, and how often?" Mike asked, now convinced he was incapable of caring for the herd.

"Food scraps from around the house, about a bucket a day," Kevin said, thinking this was adequate.

"Mate, you have a dozen in the pen. They need to eat substantially more than your food scraps to survive, that's for certain. Get in the truck. We'll check on them and see if we can sort them out," Mike said, grinding his teeth.

Kevin got into the truck, wiping his seat of the thin layer of dust to prevent his pale-yellow velour tracksuit from getting dirty. They drove the short way to the pen in silence.

When they arrived, Mike immediately jumped out of the truck to examine the mob. Ten pigs were left; one was missing entirely, and the other was barely recognizable as the famished others tore their bodies to shreds.

Evidence of where his lambs had gone was apparent, their skulls and wool pelts strewn in the mud.

Mike was flabbergasted. Never had he seen such abuse of animals.

"What the hell, Kevin! You've been feeding my lambs to the pigs? These pigs are in such a bad state they have taken to killing and eating themselves. You have two pigs missing!" The veins on Mike's temples throbbed, and his jaw clenched tight. He restrained himself from punching Kevin out.

"Mate, I never fed the pigs your lambs! I couldn't catch one, even if I gave it my best shot. It must have been Mona. She's been out in the paddocks, spying on you every day for weeks," he said, aware he was incriminating Mona.

"What the hell, spying on me? What the hell for?" Mike asked, his mind reeling at the information. Why was Mona interested in what he was doing for the first time in the past twenty-two years?

"She's obsessed. She thinks she can win you over in court because you committed adultery with that Canadian chick and get the entire farm to herself."

"Get this straight, Kevin. I've gone to the lawyers. She'll only get half the house, and the trust will pay her out. I paid off her credit cards when she got in trouble; there's still $75,000 owing for that mess.

Not much would return to her from the house after everything. The land was mine since before I met her, nestled in a trust. I have signed testimonials from multiple individuals to testify she never had any involvement. Both lawyers I have spoken to have clarified she would walk away with barely anything, and I could reclaim the house and farm."

Kevin's face showed what his slimy mind was thinking: the end of his party was near.

"Kevin, tell her you spoke to me. I won't be paying her the weekly support anymore. I have half a dozen lambs that went to feed your pigs, and she needs to reimburse me. I've also started to pay for the kid's boarding school directly. They called to say the account was in arrears; the money I gave her to pay for the kids stayed in her pocket.

I've had enough of her bullshit. I'm filing for divorce and getting my kids and my house back," Mike said, pointing his finger at Kevin.

When it came to Mona, he always bowed his head and was obedient to her wishes for fear of her taking his children. Kevin knew Mike didn't have to worry about that anymore; Mona was unfit.

"Get this shit sorted. I want these pigs off the property within twenty-four hours; otherwise, I'll call the authorities," Mike said, hissing at Kevin.

Mike looked at the pigpen. "Any more missing lambs, and I'll call the police and get you and Mona arrested for theft,"

Mike thundered, his anger on full display as he climbed into his truck and sped away, leaving Kevin with his pigs.

Kevin's high was working against him. He looked over at the dead carcasses in the pigpen and retched. Unable to hold the contents of his stomach, he spewed his lunch, the mess splashing on his white tennis shoes and pale yellow pants.

He headed toward the house, hoping that Mona was still sleeping. It was time for him to make his move. She wasn't worth anything, and he would soon lose his free accommodation. He also didn't want to be part of the mess she was about to find herself in now that Mike regained his balls.

The deal was off.

He was leaving.

| 73 |

Headquarters

They rolled in at dusk, their thunder resonating in the shadows of the trees. Twenty bikes and a few trucks carrying building supplies rolled into Dalton's property. James parked his ride, the gang following their leader. He disembarked and walked around the property, silently scrutinizing the land his sister lived on before Luke's death.

James always hated Luke. He was a weak, sniveling little shit that never amounted to anything. It embarrassed him his sister married such a loser. Although they'd tried to pull them apart, she wouldn't be deterred and stood by her dead-beat husband.

Shannon suffered from poor taste in men, but Barry, for God's sake, how could she go there even to quench her need for the pipe? He shook his head silently. Barry, now that was a waste of space.

He'd heard from a brother in prison that Barry had gifted his land to a local rival gang to use as a meth lab.

No way would James let that happen. Barry desecrated his sister. James wouldn't allow him to seek favor in a rival gang. His attempt to secure protection inside the slammer backfired; Barry had no assets left to barter. They'd all gone up in flames.

James's attention turned to his brotherhood. The men accompanying him lost no time getting their gear together, building walls to enclose the shed. He toured the site, looking over to the only neighbor he could see in the gaps of the trees. When he learned of their proximity, he'd initially thought they could be a problem, but he couldn't perceive the slightest sign of life at the property. They might not be an issue at all, he grinned.

The shack was pathetic, and he wouldn't consider it fit enough for an outhouse without them doing work. He decided it would become the ablution block and toilets. James would set up the septic system properly this time.

She'd left such a mess he needed to pay restitution to the council for the work they did to secure the site. He'd played the game well, walking into the council office in a shirt and jeans, his hair neatly combed back. The attendant was easily charmed; she also changed his name on the title from the paperwork he submitted.

He walked into the local building center and paid for a complete septic system. He also got enough timber to build a new shed and close off the one already on the property.

James looked like a regular guy until he hopped on his bike and donned his colors. Having flown under the radar, he hadn't raised any suspicion they'd arrived to claim their own.

By nightfall, they would have another headquarters for their new chapter, the wind picking up and abusing the tops of the pine trees. They were lawful occupants of his sister's land, and there was nothing anyone could do about it.

| 74 |

Vacation

Holding the hand of an airline attendant, Jeffrey appeared from the depths of the airport. Dan's heart felt like it would burst at the sight of him, tears clouding his eyes. When the young boy's eyes found his father, he bolted from the airline attendant's hold and ran to his open arms.

The attendant came to greet Dan, carrying Jeffrey's bag.

"He described you well, Officer Talbot. Jeffrey's been such a brave boy. I've been caring for him since we left London. He spent most of his time watching movies, playing games, sleeping, and eating," she said, her laugh echoing off the walls. Jeffrey jumped into the conversation excitedly.

"They have the best cookies, Dad. You would love them," the young boy said, smiling at the attendant.

"I slipped a few extra ones in your care pack," she said, winking at him.

Jeffrey beamed and gave her a big hug.

"I looked at your return flights to the UK, and guess what? I'll be bringing you back home," the attendant said as she smiled and bid them farewell. Dan shook her hand and thanked her for her service.

He hugged his son again, looking him over. Only a few months had passed, but he'd grown and changed so much. Even his glasses were different.

"Did you get new glasses, buddy?" he asked while leaving the airport.

"Yeah, I accidentally stepped on them," he replied, his embarrassment apparent.

"That's okay, buddy," he comforted his son.

They got into Lorraine's car and headed home.

***

"Look at all the bikes, Dad," Jeffrey said, breaking the silence and pointing toward Dalton's place.

It was getting dark, but you could see a hub of activity near Luke's open-walled shed. Dan slowed down to have a better look.

They were closing in the shed. Twenty or so bikes gathered in a line with their headlights on, the illumination essential to complete the work in the forest's darkness. Dan wondered if they might have a new chapter moving into the neighborhood. Picking up the pace to avoid suspicion, he kept driving down the road until they were home.

Jeffrey jumped out of the car and ran to his sandpit, enjoying the long-lost toys Dan had taken out for him before his arrival. Dan followed him, switching on the outside light and calling Tewano on his mobile simultaneously.

"Dan, what's up, man?" Tewano asked when he picked up.

Dan covered his mouth to keep the conversation from Jeffrey.

"Listen, mate, Dalton's place has some company of the two-wheeled kind, a good group. It looks like they are closing in the shed. I don't know who or where they are from, but they could be the biker gang Vincent told me about at the pub. It would pay to investigate. It looks pretty organized."

He listened to Tewano speak.

"What, you're kidding. Dirty Barry's place. Burt down. Wow! Not much of a loss, really," he said, pausing and looking at his son while Tewano spoke.

"Yeah, check with the council and rock up there tomorrow. Everything might be legitimate, but we definitely have new members to our community."

Dan finished his call and joined his son at the sandbox. Jeffrey was busy making roads with his dozers and diggers, the sand the only evidence of the vision he had in his head.

Dan sat in the chair next to his son and watched him play.

***

They ate lasagna, salad, and fresh bread for tea, all purchased pre-made at the grocery store deli. Dan didn't have Lorraine's cooking abilities but wanted to feed Jeffrey properly.

They watched the start of a movie before Jeffrey fell asleep on his lap. He didn't want to move him, engrossed in watching his innocent face relax with sleep's caress. Dan felt content and whole once again.

He thought of Lorraine. She'd sacrificed to make this happen and stepped out of her comfort zone. He was surprised about Jeffrey's new glasses; she hadn't asked him for money, even though he'd offered to pay for all of Jeffrey's needs.

He took Jeffrey to his room to tuck him in.

When he was positive Jeffrey had settled soundly, Dan checked the time on the kitchen clock and called Lorraine to set her mind at ease. Their son was doing well and had a good flight.

The phone rang and rang. Dan nearly gave up when the line picked up.

"Dan? Is that you?"

"Hi Lorraine, yeah, it's Dan. I wanted to let you know that Jeffrey had a great trip; they cared for him well. He's all tuckered out and sleeping, but I'll get him to call you tomorrow so you can talk to him. Listen, Lorraine, thank you for doing this for us, for me. It means so much. I missed you both more than you will ever know." Dan said, his voice cracking. He was having trouble containing his emotions; the tears running from his eyes could be heard in his voice.

They talked for an hour, the conversation pleasant and uplifting. Lorraine wished him a good night and hung up, promising to talk when Jeffrey called her the next day.

Dan gazed into Jeffrey's bedroom. His son's young face looked angelic in the glow of his nightlight. He watched the rhythmic movement of his breaths, his body entirely relaxed.

Dan failed to see what the curtains were hiding. Three faceless men stood centimeters from the house, their hands pressed to the glass. A woman stood next to them.

Getaway

The wind was only supposed to arrive at the start of next week, although random gusts gave the impression it was imminent. Mike looked over his pastures and decided to mow off the ones getting to heads when he returned from their trip to Akaroa. Matt could use extra tucker for the cows; he had more than enough for the sheep he cared for.

Hopefully, the lambs would stop disappearing now that Kevin and Mona knew where he stood.

Thinking about their upcoming trip, Mike smiled, a warm feeling washing over him. He wanted Kate to know what she meant to him; he was a new man because of her, and Mona no longer had a hold on him.

The back gates needed securing. His eyes perceived movement toward the house as he approached them. Someone was moving the Landcruiser, and the Mercedes was on the front lawn, in direct access to the front door. Maybe that idiot is moving out, he laughed.

He put the truck in gear and drove away.

***

Kate hadn't told Mike what happened at the house. He'd asked her not to go to Paterson's place alone without him, and she had. She regretted that now. No way was she going back there alone ever again, she promised herself.

When Melissa called her to the porch, she'd finished packing hers and Jimmy's stuff for his weekend trip to Tekapo.

"Come on in," Kate said, calling out merrily to her friend.

"Nah, it's a gorgeous day; you come out," Mellisa said, as happy and bubbly as usual.

Kate wondered why Melissa refused to enter the house, always avoiding it. She brushed it off.

"Are you all ready for your big romantic trip?" she asked as Kate joined her on the porch.

Smiling broadly, Kate looked at her friend from the corners of her eyes.

"Wish I would know a bit more about what he planned so I could know what to pack," she said, complaining but still smiling.

"Come on, Melissa… Please…" she begged. Melissa laughed heartily.

"No way, my dear, I'm not ruining Mike's surprise. It's special, Kate. I have never seen Mike like this. You were good for him from the start; now, he's stronger than ever. I hope you plan to stick around Canuck."

Kate looked at her friend and nodded, the sincerity in her eyes reassuring Melissa she wouldn't dare hurt her big brother.

***

Jake and Kelly stood by the school bus, waiting for Jimmy. Jake shot out from the small crowd and ran to meet him when he saw his dad's truck.

"Mate!" Jake said as he high-fived Jimmy and grabbed his pack. Kelly followed, greeting her dad with a huge hug and then hugging Kate, complimenting her on her fitted yellow floral dress. Kate promised she could wear it the next time they came over.

"Kelly, how would you feel about coming home and attending school in Rangiora?" Mike asked tentatively, hoping for a favorable response.

"Dad, we were ready to live with you in the shed, but Mom wouldn't allow it. We would love to go home. I'm sure Jake would say the same. We haven't heard from Mom since before we came to visit." Kelly said, briefly looking down at her feet and then at her father.

"Could we live with Kate and Jimmy, too?" she asked, smiling but biting her lip simultaneously.

"If they want to," Mike said, glancing at Kate.

Kate smiled and indicated yes with her head.

Satisfied, Kelly gave Kate a big hug.

"I'll take care of them," Kelly said, her eyes darting to the boys standing at the truck's rear.

Kate mouthed, thank you.

They packed the bus and waved the kids away when the bus pulled out.

***

The air was electric, just the two of them alone in the truck. Butterflies fluttered in Kate's belly. Her excitement spilled from her pores as she rested comfortably in the passenger seat while looking at Mike.

He looked so handsome in his white shirt and dark jeans; it suited his athletic body perfectly. She felt like the luckiest woman in the world. Her thoughts came to the envelope in her purse.

"Mike, I need to pop something in the post. Can we stop by the nearest post shop, please?"

He looked quizzically at her and nodded. They stopped at the post shop in Little River. She popped out for only a few seconds, returning with a smile.

"Tell me what was so important you couldn't wait until we got to Akaroa's post shop," he teased.

"I was going to tell you later, but now I can't wait," Kate said, beaming. "Nick sent the divorce papers. He's headed for the Middle East and wants to get it sorted before he leaves. It was pretty cut and dry, so I signed them. I should get the divorce certificate by the end of next month."

His eyes sparkled.

Nothing could stop them from starting their new life together.

***

Kate's eyes could not contain her wonderment.

It was her first visit to Akaroa, and the French influence the quaint community displayed amazed her. The street signs, shop names, and cuisine made the quaint seaside town feel like home. They turned off the main road and headed up a heavily wooded drive. Tucked in the middle of mature native trees, a small wooden cabin emerged from the foliage.

"Oh, wow, Mike, it looks like it belongs in a fairy tale. It's divine," Kate said as she left the truck. Mike followed her, wrapping her in his arms while they took in the paradise that was their weekend getaway.

"How did you find this, Mike?" she asked, leaning into him as he wrapped his arm around her waist.

"It's Melissa's parents' place. They are lending it to us for the weekend. Pretty incredible, isn't it?"

Kate nodded, looking at the aqua water of the harbor twinkling between the tree trunks. She turned to look at the cabin, Mike leading her to the front door.

A small covered-in porch sheltered two Adirondack chairs and a large cast iron bath in front of the bedroom's French doors. Nothing could have prepared her for what she found inside. The wooden walls and floors made the perfect backdrop for an antique brass bed covered in exquisite fur pelts recycled from the owner's past hunting trips. Sheepskin rugs warmed the cold of the wood floors. Next to the bed was an elaborate fireplace, the hearth a monument to a time long past. The fading light dancing through the lace curtains made the cabin even more beautiful. She noticed the kitchen was missing.

"Marshmallows and hot dogs for tea?" she giggled, grabbing a stick and pointing to the remnants of a campfire near the porch.

"No, my dear, Melissa's parents own a French restaurant in the village. They've told us to order what we want from the menus on the table, and they will deliver it to us. No charge."

Her mouth fell open in awe. "Surely not, that's more than generous."

"I've known Melissa's parents since I was a kid and have helped them whenever needed. I never expected anything back; they have always been like family. Melissa assured me they wouldn't take no for an answer. So, my beautiful angel, we can order in tonight or go to the restaurant and meet them for tea."

"Oh Mike, such a gift! What wonderful people. I'd love to meet them and thank them personally. What do you think?" she asked hesitantly.

"Sounds perfect, beautiful," he responded, pulling her again into his arms.

| 76 |

New Chapter

James was directing the delivery driver to the hole they'd dug during the night when Tewano arrived in his cruiser.

James snarled.

"What the hell does he want?" he said under his breath as he instructed the driver to lower the septic tank into the ground.

"Good day, officer. Can I help you with anything?" James said, convincingly faking his welcome.

He could see that Tewano was used to forced greetings.

"Just checking in on our new neighbor," Tewano said, looking around the site.

"I'm James," he said, introducing himself and holding his hand for the officer to shake.

"Officer Tewano Montgomery. Nice bikes you have here. You guys setting up shop?" Tewano asked, shaking his hand firmly, trying to read his eyes. He could see Tewano wanting to ask why they were there but was scouting the question diplomatically. No need to get anyone's hackles up.

"We're from Greymouth. Shannon was my sister. I disapproved of how she led her life, but she didn't deserve to lose it like she did. As her next of kin, the land has been transferred to my name. I'm here to fix her mess and sort the place out." James responded, pointing to the septic tank. "Power is being sorted this afternoon as well."

Tewano seemed impressed with the work his men were doing.

"I'm sorry about Shannon." Tewano looked him in the eyes. James nodded, accepting his regrets.

"Listen, I'm not going to lie to you, James. I needed to check on things because this place has had real issues. I can see you have already taken some of those on board." Tewano said, nodding toward the work being done on the septic tank.

"People in this area usually keep to themselves and won't bother you if you don't bother them. There are children in the area, so drunken displays and drugs won't make you friends out here. I'm not giving you a warning, just a heads-up. You do as you please on your land, but please be cautious not to interfere with the neighbors."

James appreciated how Tewano spoke to him; he was upfront while still treating him with respect.

"Understood, officer, we don't plan on being a nuisance. We are planning a small get-together this weekend. Some mates are coming in from the West Coast, but nothing big. The only close neighbor we have hasn't been around." James said, pointing toward Paterson Place.

Tewano looked through the trees to the vacant house. "Nah, the occupants live at the dairy farm down the road. You won't wake them with your music this weekend."

"Can you please help us lift the loft frame, mate," A man from the shed asked politely.

James and Tewano followed the man back to the newly enclosed garage. They'd transformed the floor area into a parking area for the bikes and a vast bar decorated so perfectly it looked like it belonged in a biker movie.

A set of stairs leading to a loft that had been separated into small rooms for James and his crew was to the right of the bar.

Tewano picked up his side of the frame as four other men came to help move it into place. When the heavy piece was finally in position, two additional men secured it in its new home. James thanked Tewano for his help while they walked out of the shed.

"It's looking good in there. I'm amazed at how quickly you turned the place around." Tewano said, appreciating their hard work.

"Yeah, coming at it," James said as he walked to Tewano's cruiser.

"Well, call us if you need anything we can help you with. A Nor'wester is due any time now. It was meant for the start of the week, but they've moved it up. Keep alert for broken branches that could fall and hurt someone, and batten down your hatches before it starts to blow."

He got into his cruiser and looked at James through the open window.

James nodded and returned to the septic tank team as Tewano drove away.

"What the fuck's a Nor'wester? Who cares about a bit of wind," he said to one of his brothers.

The breeze ruffled the tops of the nearby trees.

| 77 |

Fishing

Jeffrey woke early that morning, still jet lagged. His internal body clock hadn't yet adjusted to the local timezone. He looked around slowly, unsure of his surroundings. It was his old room in New Zealand.

He'd been so happy to see his dad yesterday and wished his mom had come. She'd been so sad since they'd moved back to Buckinghamshire. He often heard her cry late at night, his auntie trying her best to console her.

If they hadn't come to New Zealand, they would still be together as a family, he thought, tears welling in his eyes.

Brushing them away, he tiptoed into the kitchen to make himself breakfast. Spying pre-made pancake batter, he decided to treat his dad to breakfast in bed.

Trying his best not to make a mess but failing, he cooked six quasi-normal-looking pancakes piled on a plate and doused them with syrup and butter. After pouring him a glass of orange juice, his father's breakfast tray was ready.

He ate the less-than-perfect pancakes, wondering why his father was still sleeping.

His dad was always the first to get up.

He crept to his room, tray in tow, pushing the door open. His father was still sleeping soundly. He put the tray on the dresser and pounced on his dad, tickling him awake.

Still groggy from the sleep meds, Dan's eyes opened to a haze. A wide smile came to his face as he grabbed Jeffrey and started tickling him. Giggles of joy resonated through the house. Jeffrey finally climbed off his father and went to fetch his breakfast surprise.

"What! You made me breakfast! Jeffrey, you are the best."

Dan, touched by his son's gesture, felt his eyes water. He'd missed him so much.

***

"We're going fishing, we're going fishing..." Jeffrey sang as they rode to the Okuku River.

Dan hadn't taken much time to do activities with his son when they'd been living as a family in New Zealand, and he was intent on making up for lost time.

Although not at its full force, the wind appeared early. The Okuku River had sheltered areas that would shield them from the wind and offered the possibility of catching good-sized trout.

They made their way on the side road leading down the braided riverbank, trying to spy the perfect spot to cast a few tries with the fly-fishing rods. Arriving at a natural pond formed by the braided river's flow, they stopped and analyzed their surroundings.

"This looks like a winning place," Dan said, as Jeffrey agreed, pushing his glasses up his nose. They sorted out their gear and cast their flies into the pond, hoping to be the first to get a bite. They stood on the bank, silent.

Dan's mind drifted to a story Tewano had told him when he first started on the force. A mother and her son had been found dead on this riverbank years ago. They'd been renting the Paterson place. The missing bank manager's husband had killed them.

He shivered, looking around at the riverbank in front of them.

| 78 |

Cold Truth

Kevin watched Mike leave his farm and entered the house to pack his bags. The wind whistled, announcing the impending arrival of the familiar gales. He was leaving Mona tonight. Beads of sweat formed at his temples, the stress of not knowing where he was going chewing at him. If he could get out of there early enough, he could probably meet up with a trick that had taken an obsessive fascination with him.

Kevin shuddered at the thought of the greasy, obese, balding man. He'd taken violent turns at his privates, frightening him senseless a few times, thinking he would kill him. But the trick paid and paid well.

Kevin reassured himself he could live a comfortable life during the day after a few hours of debauchery at night. If that didn't turn out, he would try to score tricks until he found a place he could call his own, intending for it to be subsidized by someone else.

Mona had done well, he thought, then laughed.

"Well, Mike did a great job of keeping me comfy," he said under his breath.

Spying the silverware set on the hall dresser, he packed it with his clothes. It should fetch a few dollars at the pawnshop, he chuckled to himself as he zipped his suitcase closed.

Mona appeared in the doorway.

"Where do you think you're going?" Mona said, snapping at him, poison in her voice.

"Yeah, Mona, I am leaving," he responded, walking by her to make his way to the hallway and down the stairs. She followed, wobbling but steadfast behind him. Mona grabbed hold of his arm forcefully and pulled to turn him. Her strength surprised him.

"Where the fuck are you going, Kevin?" she hissed, her eyes filled with anger.

"Listen, Mona, I've had enough. Mike came over this morning, and we had a good talk. You've been feeding the pigs the lambs you stole from him. He's really pissed off. He said he wouldn't be paying you anymore, that you owed him for the lambs. What the fuck were you thinking, Mona? For God's sake, feeding the pigs live lambs. Fuck! That's so fucked!"

She reeled back as if he had struck her. She'd done him a favor feeding the pigs.

"Those are my lambs, Kevin, and I can do whatever I want with them. All of this is mine," she said, gesturing her arms to indicate the vast property they could see through the window.

"No, Mona, it's not, and you won't be living here for very long. Mike grew his balls back when he hooked up with that Canadian chick. He told me he's gone to see a lawyer, two actually. You are only entitled to half the house's value. The trust will pay you out, so it won't hurt Mike's financials at all.

"Before you think you'll get a big chunk of cash, remember he paid your $75,000 credit card debt. He plans on deducting that from the cash he's giving you for your share of the house. The farm is his and his only. You never contributed to the business. You're screwed, Mona. You're broke, messed up, and about to be homeless. I'm not going down with you," Kevin said, averting her eyes.

"Like fuck that's going to happen, Kevin, Mike won't do anything if I have control of the kids. He won't risk me taking them away from him," she said as she pounded her fist on the table.

"Think again, Mona. You spent the money Mike gave you for the boarding school, and he found out about it. He's been footing the bill for a few months now. He wants to move back into the house with the kids and wants you out. Look at you. You aren't fit to be a mother. You've lost Mona."

He finally looked at her, his revulsion apparent in his expression.

She grabbed at him as he picked up his coke kit to pack it in his backpack.

"What about the coke you owe me, you piece of shit," she asked, panic apparent in her face. She paid the money for him to get the coke, but she didn't know who his contact was. She knew she would have issues getting her supply sorted. With no source of income, it would be harder for her to buy it, even if she found a dealer.

"I don't owe you anything, you dumb bitch," he said, growling at her as he headed out the front door to his car.

In a frenzy of anger, Mona picked up the ornate cast iron doorstop and struck Kevin hard on the back of the head. Kevin froze, blood spilling from the large open gap in his head. He turned, his eyes wide with fear and incomprehension.

Her fury turned into hate. She kicked him in the groin, making him fall heavily to the ground. Confused and unable to focus, his head injury spilled a large amount of blood, making him feel faint. He struggled to breathe. Raising the door stop high in the air, Mona brought it down on Kevin's face, splitting his skull.

Mona hit him repeatedly, the doorstop making a sucking sound as it came away from the putty of what was now Kevin's face. His face was unrecognizable, an open mess of blood and cartilage. One of his eyes had fallen out from its broken socket. Kevin was dead.

Grabbing the bag of coke from Kevin's backpack, she disappeared into the house, leaving his bloody body lying by his Mercedes.

"How dare he treat me like that," Mona said, screaming at no one.

She unpacked the paraphernalia and drew herself four thick lines of coke, imbibing them without hesitation. The drug struck her head, instantly making her feel powerful and in control. She snorted loudly and wiped her nose, a smear of blood staining the back of her hand.

What the fuck was she going to do with that lazy fucker's body?

Feeling no remorse for her actions, she started planning the logistics of his disappearance. The pigs, she thought, ecstatic in her madness, they could make Kevin vanish.

Seemingly unaffected by her injuries, she grabbed the motorbike from the shed, pulled him across the back wheel rack, and made her way to the pig's pen. The wind picked up as his lifeless limbs bounced with the cadence of the track. Not having thought past her initial plan to feed Kevin to the pigs, she paused to contemplate, then dumped Kevin's body onto the ground.

Returning to the small shed close to the house, she gathered pliers, a chainsaw, and an old, rusted hunting knife. She got back onto the motorbike and went back to Kevin's body.

The best way to get rid of him was to cut him with the chainsaw into manageable chunks and then use him as pig feed. She could drive his Mercedes to Christchurch, leave his stuff in the car park, and take the bus back to Rangiora. Hitching a ride back home would be easy, claiming her car had broken down. She had it all sorted.

He should have known not to fuck with her. She laughed out loud.

She heard pigs could digest anything except big bones, teeth, and hair. Grabbing the pliers, she mounted Kevin and pried open the mess that was his mouth. Grabbing his front teeth, she pulled her hardest until they came loose. She took care to collect them in a pile as she removed each one.

The job accomplished, she took the hunting knife and hacked at Kevin's always luxuriously coiffed hair. Her grip was strong enough to pull the hairs from their follicles. She didn't care if she cut him, as large chunks of hair and scalp fell to the ground at her feet.

Enough of this, she mumbled to herself, grabbing the chainsaw.

The surrounding trees howled at the gusts of abuse, obliterating the sound of the saw. She felt elated, full of power. She almost lost her grip on the saw. Not having ever used one before, she was clumsy and unpracticed with the dangerous machine.

Bringing the spinning chain to the fold where Kevin's body and leg met, she gasped and let go of the throttle. She hadn't been prepared for the rush of blood. It covered her face and dripped off her arms.

Too late now, she thought and dug the bar deep into the hole she'd made in his body. The spinning chain quickly separated Kevin's leg from his body. Pretending it was a large branch, she cut it into firewood-sized pieces, her entire body thickly covered with blood and gore.

The whites of her teeth flashed in contrast with her crimson face. She smiled devilishly, her eyes glowing as she picked up Kevin's severed foot in one hand and his shin in the other and threw them into the pigpen.

The starving pigs were feral. They grunted and thrashed about wildly, like a pack of piranhas. Mona watched, entranced by their hunger, as she threw in his thigh.

Her grip on the chainsaw felt slippery; blood covered everything in a slick film.

"What will I cut next?" she asked out loud, deciding to cut his head off. The spinning chain hit his spine. She felt resistance as the saw bogged momentarily.

Pressing down harder, she moved to give herself added leverage. Her foot slipped in the pooled mess at her feet. Mona fell, landing on the saw's hungry chain.

| 79 |

The Bar

Tewano's visit hadn't made a dent in the work schedule that James had planned out. Evening fell on their first day at his sister's place, his place now, he reminded himself. They'd accomplished a lot in a short time.

He'd scored a portable ablution block in Rangiora and had plumbed it into the septic system. It would take time to get the toilets, showers, and sinks plumbed in; the ablution block would do the trick in the meantime. Rows of strung light bulbs illuminated the yard, giving it a relaxed biker pad vibe. He nodded as two men held their gang colors above the barn doors as they installed their patch on the shed.

"Fix it tight, boys, this bloody wind feels like it's out for a vengeance," James said, screaming, his words whisked away from him.

He entered the shed via the side door, the gale's abuse quieting.

There was space to park at least twenty bikes. James's ride was parked beside the door opposite a huge wood stove in case he needed out quickly.

The firebox had been one of the first things they'd installed when they heard a storm was brewing. A 'Nor'wester,' the police officer had called it. He'd expected it to get colder. Instead, he was perturbed by the heat of the growing wind. The Nor'Wester wouldn't be a typical

West Coast storm, he chuckled, thinking of the heavy, relentless rain and cold that would trash his home patch. He was used to worse.

"James!"

He heard his name being called and turned to look toward the bar where the voice was coming from.

"Adele, baby, you made it," he said, walking up to her and sweeping her into his arms, her tiny frame engulfed by his broad arms.

"Snake brought me in on his bike. You were in Rangiora when we got here. This is a cool place, bro." Adele said, hanging onto his arm.

As they approached the bar, a middle-aged woman with tattoos and a leather vest welcomed them.

"What can I get you, doll?" she asked Adele, looking at James to get his order.

"Cold beer would be great, Mom. Nothing too hard for my baby sister, okay," he said, turning his head and looking at his sister from the corner of his eyes.

"You be a good girl, Adele," he said, teasing, slapping her bottom. He couldn't afford to lose another sibling.

A man came in, the side door banging after him. His leather-bound body reached the bar where he stood by James and nodded to Mom. She immediately picked up a glass from the chiller and poured him a cold pint of beer. Before he could bring the glass to his mouth, James looked at him and asked.

"What did you find out?"

Crank, his second in charge, responded in a deep voice.

"Nothing there. The owners forgot to lock the side door to the garage, so we walked in. They haven't been living there. The only clothes we could find in the wardrobe were a few boxes of men's cloth-ing, winter jackets, and shoes. No food in the fridge and only a few essentials in the pantry, like coffee and sugar," he said, James listening intently.

"How many bedrooms?" James asked. "Is it worth us crashing out there?"

Crank nodded, "Three bedrooms with beds and two sofas in the lounge."

"Right…" James said. He pondered, tapping his fingers on the bar top.

"We'll watch out and make sure they don't show up tonight. If they don't, we might claim the place for the weekend."

James raised his glass to Crank.

Crank followed suit in silence.

***

Guards stood watch at the property's perimeter; their job was to keep away any curious visitors. The pine trees howled around them, their tops twisting from the pressure the warm air unleashed.

Kenny, one of the four guards, hated the trickery the wind was playing on them. Having joined the gang a few months back, he was still considered a prospect and always got stuck with the crappy jobs while everyone else was having fun.

He looked over to the shed they'd just covered in; he could hear music coming from inside. The low thump of the bass would have echoed loudly in the night if it weren't for the wind. It made such a suitable buffer he could barely make out the song playing.

He shuffled his used black leather boots in the bed of pine needles. His jeans were so stiff with dirt that they could have stood alone. He could smell his body odor, trapped close by his leather jacket.

Kenny sighed heavily. The entire thing felt like a mistake to him. He wasn't sure how long he could be their bitch.

His vision caught something moving toward the neighbor's house. When they asked him to report any movement at the place, he thought he would be staring at a deserted house all night. His excitement grew as he looked on.

"What the fuck?" he whispered, looking over at the seven people standing in a line on the front deck.

How did they get there? he wondered, not having seen a vehicle approach for hours. They were looking toward him. He could feel their stares penetrating him even if he couldn't make out their faces.

They know I'm here, he thought in a panic. The thick bushes hid him well. They shouldn't be able to see him. He backed away, ensuring he held his cover and ran to the shed.

James saw him entering and noticed his nervous look. He motioned to Crank, both men leaving the bar to join Kenny.

As Kenny opened his mouth to speak, James grabbed him by the arm and pulled him out the door. Their hair danced erratically as the wind swirled its wand.

"Six people are standing on the neighbor's front porch. They didn't drive in. They must have walked. Listen, something isn't right. Four men and two women were standing on the deck in a straight line, looking directly at me. I swear I was hiding. They couldn't have seen me." Kenny said, trying his best to explain.

James and Crank looked at each other.

Crank opened the shed side door and waved at Snake. A moment later, Snake joined them. They stealthily made their way to the perimeter, led by Kenny.

"There's nothing there, mate," Crank scolded Kenny.

"Why the fuck are you disturbing us with this shit?" Snake said, punching Kenny in the shoulder.

James lifted his hand to silence his men.

"We'll go out there and see for ourselves. If we meet up with the neighbors, we'll say we were concerned with the music bothering them and wanted to check in," the leader directed calmly.

The band of men left the protectiveness of the forest to walk across the open yard. They searched everywhere and couldn't find a sign of anyone being at the property.

"You're seeing things, Kenny, there's nothing here. You're imagining stuff." Snake glowered at him. "I'm going back. The last thing I need is for Adele to get herself into trouble," he said, shaking his head in disgust.

James nodded and looked around the yard, straining to see anything in the shadows of the trees.

"I think you're losing it," James said.

It came as a cold slap to Kenny. Sensing his horrible predicament, he tried to persuade the men that he had seen something. Kenny knew they would never believe him again. He could kiss his chance of receiving his cut goodbye.

"Come on." Crank slapped Kenny across the head.

He lowered his head and walked behind James and Crank, still feeling the presence of the six people he saw on the deck.

| 80 |

Honeymoon

He lounged in the warm water, her soft body lying on him, breathing in the sweet smell of her hair. They looked up at the stars in silence; the only sound surrounding them was the slight rustling from the leaves.

Mike lit the fire, the cabin's soft glow spilling through the French doors to illuminate their antique cast iron tub. She shifted slightly to pick up her wine glass and delicately put her lips to its edge to savor its contents.

"I have something I need to talk to you about, Kate," Mike said, his voice barely above a whisper.

She turned to look at him, worry in her face.

"I've consulted with lawyers. I'm divorcing Mona and taking the house back. I want the kids to move back home as soon as possible; they've been away for far too long already. The thing is, Kate, I don't want to live without you and Jimmy. I know this is soon, but..." Mike said, his eyes moist from the intense emotions he was feeling.

"Would you be with me, in my house, with our kids as a family? I promise I will always love and respect you and never harm you. I need you, Kate. You make me a better man, a stronger man." Mike asked, fighting back tears to protect his dignity.

She looked into his eyes, spontaneously shedding tears of her own.

"I won't leave you, Mike. Wherever you are is where I will be. All five of us stay together from now on," she said, leaning in to kiss him.

They fell back together, looking at the stars, pure contentment enveloping them.

***

They woke to the light waltzing through the lace curtains. The sunlight through the trees created a kaleidoscope effect, the breeze constantly changing the patterns.

Honoring the change in their lives, they celebrated by feasting on each other until breakfast was delivered. Kate loved how Mike devoured his crepes and blueberries. He'd earned his appetite. She delighted in her pain au chocolate while she sipped on her café au lait.

"Feel like going for a spin in the boat? We could explore the coastlines," he asked, finishing his coffee.

"What... a boat?" Kate asked, surprised.

"Yup, Donna and Keith have graciously lent us the cabin cruiser for the weekend. It's moored at the harbor."

She couldn't believe it.

"Hell, yes! That would be outstanding," she said, popping up from her chair and hugging him.

"Right, we'll pack a day bag and snacks and head out," Mike said, his enthusiasm on full display as he took his last bite of crepe.

***

Time stood still on the boat.

She lounged on the luxurious deck, taking in the sun while Mike maneuvered the vessel around the pristine native coastline. They set anchor and tried fishing, their passion for each other eventually taking over, ruining their chances of a catch.

***

The light of day fading over the harbor was their meal's backdrop through the restaurant windows. The candlelight sparkled on their wine glasses as they savored the exquisite lamb chops and tender vegetables. The fire crackled, casting its warm glow.

She couldn't have felt better. Her heart was full and satisfied, the man responsible for her happiness sitting in front of her.

"I love you, Mike," Kate said, the words tumbling from her lips.

His eyes met hers.

"I love you too, Kate."

He reached out and gently grabbed her hand.

Both could feel the commitment they'd chosen to make to each other.

| 81 |

Discovery

"What the hell?" Matt said aloud as he arrived at Mike's farm to tend to his stock.

The wind was howling like a mad witch. He had to hold his cap for fear of it flying off.

When he looked after Mike's farm yesterday, he saw Kevin's Mercedes with the trunk open. No one in their right mind would leave their doors, trunk, or hood up in these conditions, random gusts of wind threatening to fold the metal into origami.

The car hadn't moved, and the boot was still up. Matt promised to check it out after he finished tending to the stock.

The Nor'wester came way earlier than expected, and Matt looked forward to getting Mike's help. Melissa's headaches had started again. Although she was faring better than usual, he hoped it wouldn't worsen for her. He hated to see her suffer.

After securing the gates and ensuring the water troughs were filled, he drove by the remains of Mike's home. It would need a complete rebuild before he could entertain living there again.

He parked the motorbike, got into his truck, and made his way up the drive to Mike's house, not looking forward to dealing with Mona and Kevin.

The front door was open, and the Mercedes parked in front of it. A few suitcases were in the boot.

"Hmm, maybe Kevin decided to bail," he said, laughing.

Looking around, he saw the motorbike had been taken out.

Impossible to keep his hat on, he took it off and held it in his hand. Walking to the end of the lawn, he put his hand to his eyes to avert the sun and scanned the horizon. In the pigpen, he could see the motorbike parked there, a flash of red in a green backdrop. He started walking toward it, looking back at his truck, second-guessing his idea of walking in the gales. Approaching the pen, he saw what looked like a red blanket on the ground.

"Did those fruit loops decide to picnic next to the pigpen?" he said, shaking his head as he walked closer.

Terror engulfed him, his gut screaming as bile rose in his throat.

Mona was lying on what was left of Kevin. His leg was missing, and his head had been chewed off by the chainsaw stuck to Mona's face.

He gagged, willing himself not to throw up as the smell of blood wafted to his nostrils. Matt turned around and ran back to his truck.

Matt called the police and begged them to come immediately, his heart pounding. Strong gusts of wind shook his vehicle like a baby's cradle while Matt waited. He couldn't get the visuals out of his head. He stepped out of the truck, gagging.

A police cruiser appeared, its lights flashing brightly.

Signing for them to follow him, Matt jumped into his Hilux and drove toward the pig pen.

Tewano rushed out of his cruiser, stepping back when he realized what lay before him. He grabbed for his radio, his hands shaking.

"Station, we need to secure a crime scene and get forensics at Mike McEwan's place as soon as possible," he said, his voice cracking.

"Jesus, what the hell happened here?" Tewano asked Matt.

"No idea, mate. I came over yesterday and noticed the Mercedes was parked on the lawn with the trunk open. I decided to check in when I saw the car hadn't moved with the boot still open, something only an idiot would do in this wind. The motorbike was missing, so I walked over to see what they were doing. I didn't touch anything. Looks like Kevin was packing his bags. There are two suitcases in the car's trunk." Matt said, pointing to the car parked in the distance.

"Where's Mike?" Tewano asked.

Everyone knew how much grief Mona had given Mike and how Kevin had torn down his dignity, replacing him in his own house. It was clear to anyone that the man had plenty of motive.

"Mike and Kate are in Akaroa," Matt said. "They dropped Jimmy off to meet the kids on Friday for their Tekapo trip and went to spend the weekend at Melissa's parent's place. That's why I've been coming over for the past two days. I agreed to take care of his farm for the weekend."

Tewano transcribed what Matt said in his notebook.

"Anyone in Akaroa able to substantiate his whereabouts?" he asked, not looking up from his pad.

"He's been wined and dined since they arrived at Donna and Keith's. They delivered their meals to them. He took Kate out on the boat yesterday; Melissa's mom said she packed them lunch. They have a GPS in the cabin cruiser, so you can check exactly where they went. I haven't told him yet. I called you first. How the hell am I supposed to explain this mess?" Matt said, signaling toward the bodies with his hand, his tone desperate. "I haven't even told Melissa."

"When are they expected back?" Tewano asked, still writing.

Matt understood that Tewano needed to follow the procedure to get the facts. It didn't matter that he knew Mike would never be capable of the atrocities before him; it was a homicide investigation.

"The kids get back at one this afternoon. They'll have lunch in town and make their way back with Jimmy. I don't want to call him now and have him rush back only to return to Christchurch to pick up the kids. The kids! How are they going to deal with this?" Matt's eyes filled with tears, thinking how the awful situation would affect them.

"Okay." Tewano said, finally looking up, "Probably best he isn't here anyway when we do the initial investigation. We'll tell him when he comes back and interrogate him as per protocol."

He looked over the bloody pile and sighed.

***

The coroner was quick to determine what had happened. Everyone stood silently as he explained his findings.

"Looks like Kevin died of blunt force trauma," he said, pointing at the enormous gashes practically obliterating his facial features.

"From the amount of blood on Mona, it's safe to assume she wielded the chainsaw to Kevin's leg, fed it to the pigs, and was in the process of doing the same with his head." He moved around the pile to point at the smudge marks in the bloody mud close to where her feet were resting.

"Looks like she slipped and fell forward onto the chainsaw, and it chewed through her head. Ironic, isn't it?" he said, laughing.

Tewano stared at him, his mouth open in shock. The man was obviously more used to these scenes than he was.

"She'd planned it out well. See that pile of teeth? She pulled Kevin's teeth out and chopped his hair; pigs don't digest those body parts. She was making sure he would disappear for good," the coroner said, grinning, writing everything down in his notepad.

A crime scene officer approached the group.

"The only prints we found were Mona's and Kevin's; no other prints were found anywhere near the scene, the motorbike, the house, or the shed. It looks like Mona lost it when Kevin was packing to leave her. She killed him, then accidentally killed herself when cutting him up to feed him to the pigs. We found a bloody door stopper near the Mercedes and quite a big bag of coke on the dining room table."

Tewano shook his head, disgusted. "Yeah, I wouldn't put it past her. She was that type of woman. I've never known her to be physically violent, but many have seen the abuse she could spew from her mouth."

***

Matt went home to explain what happened to Melissa. She looked at him in disbelief, feeling sad for Kelly and Jake. When Mike called to let them know they were inbound, he left to wait for him by the side of the road. He looked nervously down the street, sighing when he caught sight of the Navara. Matt flagged them down.

"What's happened?" Mike asked nervously, seeing the distress on his friend's face.

"It's Mona and Kevin, mate, it's bad. You should drop off Kate and Jimmy and return to talk to the police. Melissa's waiting for them."

Mike did as he was told, asking no further questions.

It Blows

Dan had gotten a visit from Tewano Sunday evening. He was desperate to debrief with his friend and co-worker. Dan listened, unable to do anything more than shake his head.

"Do you reckon it was the drugs?" he asked tentatively.

"Yeah, anyone who carries just under a kilo of coke, not parted out for sale, is a huge user. Mona didn't resemble herself. She'd pulled out her hair and had gangrenous wounds on her legs. I don't know how she could walk or ride a motorbike in the state she was in. The coroner reckons she'd have to be high like a kite to pull off what she did, but we won't have confirmation until the toxicology report comes in."

"Shit, that's bad," Dan replied softly. "How's Mike doing with all this?"

"He's excluded. None of his prints were found at the scene. He was out having a dirty weekend in Akaroa with his new lady. Both had a rock-solid alibi for the entire time they were away.

"Mike's in shock. He admitted having told Kevin of his plans to divorce Mona and pay her out of the house but saw none of this coming. He's more concerned for the kids and asked if we could help with a counselor. We are going to be done with the house tomorrow. He's free to move back in, probably sooner rather than later, considering his shed blew away. I feel bad for the poor bugger," Tewano said, scratching his head.

Dan took another swig of beer. "Matt must have been quite shaken up. What a thing to find when you think you'll be only shifting sheep on a Sunday morning," Dan said, his voice tapering off.

Both men sat in silence; their gaze focused on the wood table, deep in inner thoughts.

***

Jeffrey had fallen asleep on the sofa again, the racket the wind was throwing outside not affecting him. Dan picked him up and tucked him in bed, leaving the night light on.

Walking back to the kitchen, Dan could hear the front gate swinging wildly; it had broken free from the latch holding it in place. Annoyed, he stepped outside his front door to walk down the driveway.

Dan was about to flick the outside light on when the door slammed shut, sparing him from injuring his hand but leaving him in the darkness. Hoping the noise hadn't woken Jeffrey, he made his way down the driveway, struggling against the invisible assault. Finally, he reattached the gate's latch and returned to the front door.

It was locked.

"Fuck," he swore out loud and walked to the backyard, where he knew the glass doors to the dining room were unlocked.

He stopped dead in his tracks.

Standing before him were six figures, their faces unrecognizable in the dark. They stood in a line, equally distanced, their heads down.

Every hair on his body stood alert, his eyes searching for an adequate weapon to defend himself. His heart picked pace as he saw them step toward him in unison.

Thinking of Jeffrey, he picked up a rake he'd left next to the roses and placed himself between them and the entry to the house. No way were they going into the house, he swore, ready to take them down.

They took another step closer.

The surrealistic vision before him didn't seem possible. Four men and two women inched closer. He could see what they were wearing but couldn't see their faces.

An aimless gust knocked him off his feet. Dan fell on his side.

Pulling himself upright, he searched desperately for the rake.

His grasp empty, they came down on him, blackening his mind.

| 83 |

Howl

They partied hard Saturday night, most sleeping till late afternoon Sunday. Only a few of them witnessed the heavy police presence close to them. James gathered the information from a passing neighbor. The mad neighbor had popped a fuse when her toy boy told her he was leaving, killed him, and ended up doing herself in at the same time.

James liked it. That type of shit would take the heat off their activities.

He'd sent out a few scouts to monitor the vacant house as the situation unfolded at the neighbors. They'd reported no movement at the home, and the police had left the premises at the other property.

He climbed the stairs to the loft in the shed, his eyes approving of the row of rooms they'd sorted out for accommodation. It's good, he thought, but there wouldn't be enough room to house everyone tonight. Until they could build the other shed, they would be squatting in the neighbor's vacant house. After all, they weren't using it. James grinned.

Wiping her eyes and dressed only in an oversized t-shirt, her long caramel hair flowing, Adele greeted her brother.

"Get dressed, sis. You don't want to be walking around like that here." James said sternly, delivering his order and returning to the bar.

They'd trickled in steadily during the day, by sets of two, three, or more, the roar of their engines snuffed out by the wind's tantrum. Hidden in their fortress of pines, the group was invisible. The smell of their barbecue wafted away swiftly; it was impossible to follow the delectable scent to its origins. The constant rumble of music resonated in their bubble within the trees.

They played and talked, and a few others expressed their lust in the glow of the fires held safely within large metal drums affixed with spark suppressors. Standing next to a burning drum, James sipped his beer, his eyes transfixed on the fire's glow.

"Mate, my girlfriend and I need to...umm ...talk," a burly biker said while holding a messed-up-looking redhead. He grinned at James, exposing the few rotten teeth he had left.

"The shed's pretty much spoken for," James responded, his head pointing toward the empty house they could see through the trees. "Make yourself at home there. It's been vacant since we got here," James offered.

It satisfied the dirty biker, and he led his fire-haired companion toward the empty house.

James piped up over the music. "We got an empty house next door for anyone who wants to crash," he said. His announcement was met with cheers, their glasses held high to their leader.

***

He momentarily turned on the hallway lights to give him sight and unlocked all the doors and windows in the house. Once he was done, the biker turned off the lights, the darkness of the house only breached by the intermittent glow of the moon. He entered the darkened bedroom where his plaything for the night was waiting.

She approached him, dropping to her knees. He felt himself become hard as she undid his belt. Within seconds, her warm mouth encompassed him. He stood, his knees shaking as she performed her part of the deal.

A sudden movement outside the bedroom window grabbed his interest. Losing his momentum, he waved his girl off and looked outside.

"I think we have company," he said, whispering. His girl got to her feet to follow him.

They made their way outside, ensuring they hid in the shadows.

"What did you see?" she asked, keeping her voice as silent as possible.

"Five or six of them," the biker responded as he entered the plantation.

***

The Nor'wester transformed the plantation. The vibrations generated by the wind hammering the trees made the forest floor hum. The biker saw them come out from behind the trees, six standing in a straight line in tandem with the row of pines. His girl gasped and grabbed his hand.

As if transported by the gale, all six stood closer to them instantly, magically appearing only a few feet away. The biker tried pulling his girl out of their way but felt her being pulled toward them. Two female figures had a tight grasp on her. She slipped away. He found himself surrounded by four male figures, their faces hidden. His eyes followed his girl. He couldn't believe what he was seeing; they were levitating her.

Her red hair plastered her face, her wide-open mouth the only distinguishable feature. You could barely hear her screams through the chaos. They had her pinned up three meters high on a big pine tree.

One of the female figures threw a big metal object; it flashed before it struck. It made a sickly thud when it made contact.

His girlfriend was pinned to the tree by a giant metal stake.

The biker's mind whirled, his attention on the six before him, terror filling him.

They approached.

His breath came in gasps; he couldn't move, bound by some powerful force they had over him. He felt himself being pushed back until his back was pressed firmly into a pine tree.

Beads of sweat formed on his lined brow, his face forming a scowl. He felt his feet leave the ground. A slight groan escaped his lips as he tried to comprehend what was happening to him. He saw them look up at him, the blackness churning in their eyes, the hum in the air so thick he could taste its metallic flavor. His heart thrashed as he felt the spike enter his chest.

| 84 |

Unhinged

Dan regained consciousness surrounded by darkness, the cool grass under his cheek.

He took a few seconds to realize where he was and how he'd got there.

He swooned as he tried to sit up, realizing he had a splitting headache. Acrid bile rose from his throat, filling his mouth. He spat the vile contents out and carefully made his way to his knees, the abusive air around him swirling, hindering his efforts. The loud hum in his head overwhelmed him.

He crawled to the dining room's glass doors. Recollection of the six people on the back lawn came flooding back. The rake. He looked around. It was nowhere to be seen.

The door handle acted as a support as he pulled himself to his feet and entered the confines of the house.

"Jeffrey! Oh my God, Jeffrey!" he said, terror gushing through his veins. He found the strength to stand up and reach his son's room. In the dim light, he could see Jeffrey sleeping comfortably, his little arm cradling the top of his bedspread.

His eyes moved slowly across the room, straining to see into the depths of the bedroom where only darkness should live.

They were there; the room was filled with them.

There were eight of them now. Dan's heart threatened to explode at the pressure it was under. Dread washed over him, drenching him in a cold sweat. He shuffled slightly before briskly swooping his sleeping son from bed and fled outside the house.

***

"What's wrong, Dad?" Jeffrey rubbed at his sleep-filled eyes.

"It's going to be okay, Jeffrey," Dan blurted out, his attempt to sound rational and calm failing.

"Where are we going?" his little voice asked.

The question remained unanswered by his father. They'd gotten into the cruiser, which made Jeffrey think his dad had been called into work. The speed at which they traveled and his dad's demeanor also cemented his thinking. He probably wasn't wearing his uniform because he'd been called out to something urgent.

They raced down the main road, heading for Rangiora, the car rocking from the howling blasts. He felt the car swerve to avoid a fallen tree.

Darkness and dust filled the windscreen as they barreled down the embankment of the Okuku River.

The car heaved as it ran over bushes. Jeffrey's screams were obliterated by the branches scratching the exterior. The vehicle suddenly stopped, wedged between two large dirt banks the braided river created.

Jeffrey looked over at his father. His head lay on the steering wheel, blood trickling down his forehead.

| 85 |

Reckoning

James was having a blast. He looked over his brothers and beamed at what they'd accomplished in such a short time. Shannon would be proud of what they'd built on her land.

He heard a crack above him.

"That bloody wind," he said. His eyes rolled to look upwards where the treetops allowed the sky to show through.

"How can these people live with this hot mess weather?" he asked Crank.

The big man shook his head. James hadn't expected such poor weather so far inland; he wasn't used to the dry heat and never-ending gales.

Snake parked his bike and approached him. His trust in the man had not wavered in all the years they had ridden together. He trusted him so much that he made him his sister Adele's keeper.

The two became closer throughout the years, Adele making a few apparent advances on Snake. He held fast, not wanting to disappoint his leader, but it was evident he'd fallen in love with James's baby sister.

He was a good man, his brother Snake. James approved of him and knew his loyalty held no bounds. He'd yet to give them his blessing… but felt generous tonight.

"She's a goodie, bro. Everyone is having a great time," Snake smiled, approaching James.

"Damn right. It's good to see everyone made it. I reckon this place is perfect for our new chapter," James replied, grabbing another beer from the ice-filled metal bin.

"Listen, Snake, I'm not stupid. I can see what's happening with you and Adele."

Snake became instantly defensive. "I've never touched her boss." The strong man's eyes glinted with honesty as he stared at James.

"I know, I know, mate," he said, reassuring him, holding his hand up for emphasis.

"I know she wants you, mate. I've seen how she looks at you... and how you look at her." James said, taking another sip from his beer. He paused before he continued.

Snake's expression was blank, waiting for direction from his leader.

"I think it's time you two get a chance together, mate." James looked into his friend's eyes. The seriousness of the situation was not lost on Snake.

"I won't let anything bad happen to her, bro. I swear on my life," Snake declared, sincerity thick in his voice, the glistening in his eyes the only sign of his happiness. He rang his leather gloves nervously, awaiting his leader's orders.

"Listen, take her to the neighboring house. She deserves better than a swag on the loft floor tonight," he finished. Snake nodded, shook hands with James, and left to join Adele.

James smiled. The place was perfect for new beginnings.

***

Holding hands, Snake and Adele exited the headquarters' forest into the neighbor's open yard.

Snake led her to the side of the pond. A small, primarily decorative deck big enough for them to sit on embellished the bank. He bent down and touched the water; it was slightly cool, a welcome reprise from the constant warm wind.

"Wanna go for a swim?" he asked softly.

She wordlessly answered him with action, slowly stripping from her clothes. Snake looked on as her naked body was revealed, her silky mane whipping around, giving her a mystical aura.

He pulled himself upright and removed his clothes, piling them on his boots beside the deck.

"Last one in's a rotten egg," she slurred seductively, the few beers she drank making her words run together. She jumped into the pond.

He followed her, taking her into his arms in the cool, dark liquid.

"I see that big brother's given you his blessings," she said, holding him close.

Their lips met in a long-overdue frolic, hungry for each other. Snake pulled her up from the water, sitting her on the wooden deck, her legs falling naturally on his shoulders.

Longing to taste her, he dived into her warmth, savoring the flavor of her body. He sensed her head fall back as she groaned seductively, enjoying his efforts.

He closed his eyes, thoroughly engulfed in his pleasure. Adele's body spasmed forcefully. He relished bringing her to such a fierce orgasm so quickly, looking up adoringly to meet her eyes.

She had no eyes.

Snake looked up in utter disbelief.

Her head was gone. It was lying on the ground next to her, blood running down her chest from the fresh wound, her body still held upright by his hold.

He immediately let go and pulled back to the depths of the pool.

Something was behind him.

Turning abruptly, he looked at the far end of the pond where it met the forest's perimeter. Five men and two women looked on, standing side by side.

Terror consuming him, he raced to the deck to get out of the water.

As Snake lifted his knee to the deck's rough surface, he felt a delicate touch on his right shoulder.

Shivers ran down his spine as he peeked behind him.

Adele was in the water, black holes replacing her eyes.

What the hell was happening? Had someone slipped him some type of drug as a joke? Panic gripped him.

He tried to mount the deck but felt himself being pulled back into the depths of the dark water.

Adele was pulling him in. Snake screamed; he was staring at her headless body. The wind absorbed his cry.

Powerless from the spell he'd been put under, his eyes washed over the ghostly faces of the beings surrounding the pond as he felt himself descend.

She pushed his head down under the water. He could see her shadow as she held him until darkness came.

| 86 |

Resurgence

Dan opened the door to the cruiser. The wind immediately took hold of it and folded it on itself. He looked to the passenger seat. Jeffrey was gone; only a gumboot and a blanket remained in the car. Panicked, his head humming loudly, he spilled out of the car and crawled to the boot.

The wind forced open the boot after unlatching it, exposing its contents to the sky.

All police cruisers carried an ax in the event of an emergency extraction; he'd never thought he would need it for his protection. Using the tool for support, Dan started hobbling around, scouting the terrain for any clue to Jeffrey's whereabouts.

The wind played tricks on him. He swore he could hear his son's screams throughout the racket rolling through the clearing like a freight train.

The moon allowed for brief enlightenment; Jeffery was on the side of the river, surrounded by a group of people.

He found the strength to reach his son, stopping short at what he saw before him.

They were gathered around him, ten of them spaced equally apart. He could barely make out other figures approaching them from the depths of the Okuku River. They stood like a sentinel. Jeffrey was transfixed, motionless in the middle, holding his hands to his side.

He rushed to grab him, pushing through the ghostly entities and pulling his son into his arms. He looked at him, his face pale in the gloom.

Suddenly, as if shocked by a lightning bolt, Jeffrey's eyes and mouth opened wide. He stared in horror at his son's black swirling eyes, his mouth opening larger than it should allow. He felt more than heard his jaw dislocating. Blackness filled his young body.

He dropped his grip on him, mortified at what had become of his son, and stepped back, aware of the group circling them.

Dan swung the ax wildly, trying to make contact with the unknown assailants.

A hand touched his back. He turned swiftly to face the assailant, the ax following his movements.

The weapon found resistance. The edge was embedded deeply in Jeffrey's stomach.

Dan screamed, the strength of his howl reverberating in the riverbed, washed clean by the wind.

Falling to his knees by his son's body, he absorbed the consequences of his actions.

The figures floated in a circle around them, their movements blurry as they followed the waves of air, unaffected by the uneven ground.

Severely compromised, Dan lifted his head and stood next to Jeffrey. His tear-filled eyes gazed at the blur of specters becoming part of the wind around them. He sobbed as he pulled the ax from his son's abdomen.

Dan looked up at the sky, the entities creating a vortex around him, his head pulsing with the overpowering hum.

Unable to take any more and forever broken, he raised the ax and let it fall hard on his head.

EPILOGUE

Kate waved the kids away as all three of them walked to the bus stop. She looked over to Mike's old shed. He was there, putting the last finishing touches on the building. He'd rebuilt it as a farm shed since they'd moved back into his house. Their big home could provide all their required accommodation.

She returned to the house, now decorated with all her furniture, to put the kettle on. As she waited for the water to boil, her mind ventured to the horrific day that changed all their lives.

It had started with the discovery of Mona and Kevin's death that windy Sunday afternoon. The night held more atrocities, all hidden by the howl of the wind. They would come to discover the devastation when dawn broke.

Mike decided to check on the Paterson place the following day before heading into town to tend to Mona's funeral arrangements. The wind had been especially ferocious that night. He noticed a few fallen trees and entered the forestry to assess the situation.

That's when he saw them. The man and the woman spiked to the trees. He rapidly left and called for police assistance. They found more than the two dead bodies in the trees; a decapitated young woman and a drowned man were found in the pond.

No implement capable of driving the spikes was ever found on the property; the house was unlocked, but nothing was amiss.

The bodies came from the neighbors where the decapitated young woman's brother had recently moved. As quickly as they'd moved in, they returned to the West Coast, claiming the place was evil.

No one was charged with the gruesome murders; the police couldn't find any evidence to convict anyone.

Kate had enough and petitioned for the balance of her rent to be paid out. The murders made the press, and the landlords knew they would face a court battle if they didn't do the right thing and return her money. She was happy to cut ties with the damned place.

The wind wasn't finished unveiling its secrets. They found Officer Dan Talbot's cruiser on the side of the Okuku River that afternoon. Driven mad by the stress of his job, his marriage breakup, and being away from his son, he ended their lives in an apparent murder-suicide. The Nor'wester took no prisoners.

Dan's place was eventually put back on the market. Lorraine refused to set foot in New Zealand. She arranged for her young son's body to be returned to England.

Dan had a quiet, informal funeral. It wasn't a good look for the force to have the supervisor lose the plot. They hid as much as they could to save face.

The wind came in hard and heavy, quickly spending itself and leaving the land after only a few days, but the damage had been atrocious.

***

Kate heard his motorbike, poured his coffee, and met him at the front door. He disembarked wordlessly and made his way to her, pulling her into his arms to kiss her. It had become their morning tradition since they'd moved into Mike's house.

Mike took Kelly and Jake out of boarding school before their mother's funeral and enlisted them in Rangiora High School. They had a hard time coming to grips with their mother's death.

Mona's actions had been so vile and drug-fueled that they wanted nothing to do with her and refused to acknowledge her as their mother. Kate's heart broke for them, knowing it would take a long time for the wrongs their mother did to be forgotten.

***

"I'm taking over for Matt this afternoon, babe. He and Melissa are headed to the clinic to get a final scan," Mike said as he took a bite of his biscuit.

"I'm so happy for them," Kate replied, smiling, thinking back at the strange circumstances under which Melissa had gotten pregnant.

The storm that brought on the horrifying events at the house left Melissa alone. She felt the initial symptoms come on and feared it was imminent, but it dissipated quickly. It was the first time the wind hadn't brought on the dreadful episodes.

She claimed she got pregnant that weekend, although Matt claimed he couldn't be the father. He wasn't up to romance after having found Mona and Kevin.

It was a private joke, but Kate saw something dark lurking in Matt's mind.

He'd told Mike he hadn't made love to his wife that weekend. Mike told him it was probably an error in dates, but Matt was convinced something more was happening.

***

Matt stopped to speak to Mike on their way back from the scan. His friend's body language showed that the examination went well. He was relieved. Her pregnancy, to date, had been a dream. They enjoyed every minute.

"She's doing well. The baby should be here any day now. I am shocked her headaches disappeared. Remember last month when the wind came, she had no symptoms at all," Matt said, shaking his head, confused at the turn of fortune. Melissa, struggling to move in her advanced stage of pregnancy, stayed in the truck.

"Yeah, she suffered for years. Good to see her happy and healthy," Mike answered, smiling at both of them as Matt boarded their Hilux and drove away. He was looking forward to sharing the news with Kate.

***

"I can't wait for Matt to see that baby's face. He's still stuck on the date issue. He'll stop that bullshit when he looks into his own eyes in a few days," Mike said entirely, convinced as they worked together fixing a gate.

Kate giggled. Mike was looking forward to this baby as much as Melissa and Matt.

Something caught their attention, making them look toward the main road.

A black sedan followed by a moving van took a right turn onto Harper's Road, the shadows of the plantation swallowing their presence.

Kate and Mike looked at each other, fear in their eyes.

Another family was moving into Paterson's place.

www.ingramcontent.com/pod-product-compliance
Lightning Source LLC
Chambersburg PA
CBHW060653190726
48289CB00002B/388